The Missing Ink

"Karen E. Olson has launched a delightful new series with *The Missing Ink*, featuring tattooist Brett Kavanaugh. Brett is proud that she makes grown men cry. She also makes grown women laugh. I look forward to more adventures for this Las Vegas needle artist."

—Elaine Viets, author of the Dead-End Jobs Mysteries

"In *The Missing Ink*, Karen E. Olson has penned a winner, full of crisp dialogue, a red-hot setting, and a smart, sassy tattooed protagonist. Viva Las Vegas!"

—Susan McBride, author of the Debutante Dropout Mysteries

"Has it all, with edgy characters and a tight plot."

—*Mystery Scene*

"[A] pleasantly jargon-free themed mystery. . . . Readers need not be conversant with 'street flash' or other industry terms to enjoy the setting and follow Brett down a trail of needles and gloves to the dramatic finale." —*Publishers Weekly*

"Olson uses the fresh setting of an upscale Las Vegas tattoo shop . . . for a fast-moving tale with quirky but affectionately portrayed characters. Although stubborn, Brett never becomes too stupid to live in her determination to solve the mystery. The tension is kept at a high pitch." —*Romantic Times*

The Annie Seymour Mysteries

Shot Girl
Shamus Award Nominee for
Best Paperback Original

"Olson excels at plotting—with liberal doses of humor—and Annie grows more fascinating, and more human, with each novel. This one's a winner from page one."

—*Richmond Times-Dispatch*

"Olson continues a winning streak with her latest Annie Seymour outing. . . . This first-rate mystery will not only keep you guessing; it will provide fun and laughter along the way."

—*Romantic Times* (4 stars)

continued . . .

"Olson . . . step[s] up to a new storytelling level."

—*The Baltimore Sun*

"[*Shot Girl*] features the same clever plotting, great local color, and terrific personal touches that have been a hallmark of the series since it began."

—*Connecticut Post*

Dead of the Day

"Karen E. Olson knows this beat like the back of her hand. I really enjoyed *Dead of the Day*."

—Michael Connelly

"*Dead of the Day* takes the Annie Seymour series to truly impressive territory. Absolutely everything a first-rate crime novel should be."

—Lee Child

"Karen E. Olson draws on her experiences as a journalist to write an excellent series about Annie Seymour, a salty police reporter in New Haven, Connecticut. *Dead of the Day* is a fun mystery with just enough edge to make it sparkle."

—*Chicago Sun-Times*

"Like an alchemist, Karen E. Olson blends together wildly disparate elements into pure gold. *Dead of the Day* is a delightful dance with the devil—dangerous, dark, and romantic."

—Reed Farrel Coleman, Shamus Award–winning author of *The James Deans*

"A reporter and editor for Connecticut newspapers for twenty years, [Olson] brings a journalist's eye for detail and immediacy to this series. You'll want to give yourself an early deadline to read her latest story."

—*Richmond Times-Dispatch*

Secondhand Smoke

"Annie Seymour, a New Haven journalist who's not quite as cynical as she thinks she is, is the real thing, an engaging and memorable character with the kind of complicated loyalties that make a series worth reading. Karen E. Olson is the real thing, too, a natural storyteller with a lucid style and a wonderful sense of place."

—Laura Lippman, *New York Times* bestselling author

"Authentic urban atmosphere, generous wit, and winning characters lift Olson's second outing. . . . Readers are sure to look forward to Annie's further adventures." —*Publishers Weekly*

"Annie is a believable heroine whose sassy exploits and muddled love life should make for more exciting adventures."
—*Kirkus Reviews*

"Humor enlivens this first-person account.... This remains a series with considerable potential." —*Booklist*

"Olson's characters are her own, and her fast-paced plot and great ending make it a perfect read for patrons who like a bit of humor in their mysteries." —*Library Journal*

"Olson knows exactly how to blend an appealing heroine, an intricate plot, and inventive humor. Annie's is a story worth pursuing and a story well worth reading."
—*Richmond Times-Dispatch*

"Humor, plenty of motives, and strong character development make this a fast, fun read." —Monsters and Critics

"Olson's second mystery hits the mark with setting, plot, and character.... Her lovably imperfect heroine charms, and the antics of her coworkers and the residents of 'da neighborhood' will keep you intrigued and amused."
—*Romantic Times* (4 stars)

Sacred Cows

"A sharply written and beautifully plotted story."
—*Chicago Tribune*

"Olson writes with a light touch that is the perfect complement for this charming mystery." —*Chicago Sun-Times*

"In this just-the-facts-ma'am journalism procedural, Karen E. Olson plunges readers into the salty-tongued world of cynical reporter sleuth Annie Seymour.... [The story] spins from sinister to slapstick and back in the breadth of a page. Engaging." —Denise Hamilton, bestselling author of *Savage Garden*

"A boilermaker of a first novel.... Olson writes with great good humor, but *Sacred Cows* is also a roughhouse tale. Her appealing and intrepid protagonist and well-constructed plot make this book one of the best debut novels of the year."
—*The Cleveland Plain Dealer*

Also by Karen E. Olson

Annie Seymour Mysteries

Sacred Cows
Secondhand Smoke
Dead of the Day
Shot Girl

Tattoo Shop Mysteries

The Missing Ink

Pretty in Ink

A TATTOO SHOP MYSTERY

Karen E. Olson

*To Joann—
Wonderful to meet
you!*
Karen

AN OBSIDIAN MYSTERY

OBSIDIAN
Published by New American Library, a division of
Penguin Group (USA) Inc., 375 Hudson Street,
New York, New York 10014, USA
Penguin Group (Canada), 90 Eglinton Avenue East, Suite 700, Toronto,
Ontario M4P 2Y3, Canada (a division of Pearson Penguin Canada Inc.)
Penguin Books Ltd., 80 Strand, London WC2R 0RL, England
Penguin Ireland, 25 St. Stephen's Green, Dublin 2,
Ireland (a division of Penguin Books Ltd.)
Penguin Group (Australia), 250 Camberwell Road, Camberwell, Victoria 3124,
Australia (a division of Pearson Australia Group Pty. Ltd.)
Penguin Books India Pvt. Ltd., 11 Community Centre, Panchsheel Park,
New Delhi - 110 017, India
Penguin Group (NZ), 67 Apollo Drive, Rosedale, North Shore 0632,
New Zealand (a division of Pearson New Zealand Ltd.)
Penguin Books (South Africa) (Pty.) Ltd., 24 Sturdee Avenue,
Rosebank, Johannesburg 2196, South Africa

Penguin Books Ltd., Registered Offices:
80 Strand, London WC2R 0RL, England

First published by Obsidian, an imprint of New American Library,
a division of Penguin Group (USA) Inc.

First Printing, March 2010
10 9 8 7 6 5 4 3 2 1

Copyright © Karen E. Olson, 2010
All rights reserved

OBSIDIAN and logo are trademarks of Penguin Group (USA) Inc.

Printed in the United States of America

To my niece Anna Corr,
who truly is pretty in ink

ACKNOWLEDGMENTS

I would like to thank Alison Gaylin, Cheryl Violante, and Angelo Pompano for their help with the manuscript. Brett Wilson and Kevin Martino were invaluable sources, letting me in on all their secrets. The First Offenders (Alison Gaylin, Lori Armstrong, Jeff Shelby, and Anthony Neil Smith) are incredibly supportive, as is the whole FO community. Abram Katz can always be counted on to come up with the perfect poison. Craig Phillips is a fantastic illustrator, and his cover art is spot on. Jack Scovil is agent extraordinaire. My editor, Becky Vinter, with her cheery enthusiasm and eye for detail, helped me push the envelope and make this a better book. Kristen Weber, who started me on this journey, is missed but left me in good hands. Thanks to all the staff at NAL, every bookseller, every reader. Finally, I wouldn't be able to do any of this without the love and support from my wonderful husband, Chris, and daughter, Julia.

Chapter 1

If your name is Britney Brassieres, being taken down by a tsunami of champagne might seem only fitting.

One minute she was belting out "Oops! ... I Did It Again," the next she was on the floor, her arms flailing as the Moët—not the really expensive kind, but that White Star you can get at a discount if you look hard enough—showered her.

I know it was Moët because I saw the guy with the bottle. He'd come up to the edge of the stage near my table as Britney was singing, shook the bottle, then popped the cork, which was as loud as a gunshot as it went airborne and slammed right into Britney's chest.

Bull's-eye.

It wasn't an accident, either. He'd aimed it at her.

I jumped up on a gut reflex and impulsively shouted at the guy. "Hey!"

After successfully hitting his target, he turned the bottle on me—confirming that he'd actually heard me—and everyone else in my vicinity.

Unfortunately, it still had some oomph left, and liquid splashed across my face, getting into my eyes and dripping down my face onto my chest. I tried to blink, but it hurt, so I kept my eyes closed and listened to the pandemonium around me: chairs scraping as people scrambled to their feet, glass shattering. The vibration moved through my legs as the floor shook with the weight, the hurry to escape. I wanted to shout out that it was just champagne, but that cork explosion freaked everyone out, and when they saw Britney fall, they figured the worst.

Bodies jostled me as they shoved past, and I struggled to keep my balance, holding out my arms like a trapeze walker and hitting someone who grunted but didn't stop.

"Joel?" I shouted above the din. "Joel?"

An arm snaked around my waist. "I'm here, Brett. You okay?" His voice was soothing as his big belly pressed into my side, and for a second I relaxed before tensing up again.

"Yeah, just got some champagne in my eyes. Is Britney okay?" I asked, trying to open my eyes, but they still stung and I shut them again.

"She's moving," Joel said. "I think she's okay. What happened?"

"Guy with a champagne bottle. Where'd he go?" This time I forced my eyes open, blinking quickly a few times, clearing the fog. I scanned the dimly lit nightclub. There had been about a hundred people here for the show; most of them now were pushing one another toward the door; someone was screaming, someone else wailing.

The scene on the stage looked like something from a Shakespearean tragedy: Britney, in her blue and white schoolgirl outfit and long blond tresses, was splayed across the floor as her fellow performers hovered over her, clucking like the mother hens they were. I spotted Charlotte with them, kneeling and stroking Britney's forehead. Britney's lips were moving, and her eyes were open.

MissTique, who ran all the shows here at Chez Tango, flailed her arms as she teetered on six-inch clear plastic stilettos on the edge of the stage, not because she was going to fall, but because she was trying to calm everyone down. She shouted, "All right," "Everything's fine," and "Get me a cocktail." The last was to a young man with a remarkable physique who'd been dancing shirtless behind Britney before the champagne attack.

"Where's Bitsy?" I had to lean in toward Joel so he'd hear me as we took a couple of steps toward the stage.

Bitsy is a little person, and it was easy to lose her in a crowd.

Or bump into her.

"Watch it!" I heard her say and looked down to see her rubbing her arm where I'd collided with her.

I was about to apologize when it grew darker, sort of like a solar eclipse. But instead of the electricity going out, it was merely Miranda Rites blocking the light behind her. She looked like someone had dumped a bottle of Pepto-Bismol on her: a vision in pink sequins and a high bouffant of pink-accented orange hair, the multicolored butterfly tattoo I'd given her just a few weeks ago stretched between her shoulders just above the ample bosom. It was fake, of course. The bosom, I mean, not the ink.

"She's okay, right?" I asked Miranda, shouting, cocking my head toward the stage.

The dark concrete walls didn't swallow the din; it just bounced off them into my ears with a sort of echo effect.

"I think she's in shock." To compensate for the noise, Miranda's voice had reverted back to its husky tenor, giving her that Sybil split-personality thing: Is she a woman? Is she a man? Can she be both? "She hit her head, though. I saw it from backstage."

"Did you call an ambulance?"

"They're on their way. Cops, too."

I thought about my brother, Detective Tim Kavanaugh. I wondered whether he'd show up. He might be a little surprised to find me here at Chez Tango.

It was opening night of MissTique's new Nylons and Tattoos show, featuring Britney, Miranda, Lola LaTuche, and Marva Luss.

Drag queens.

They'd chosen The Painted Lady, my tattoo shop, as the one they'd entrusted with designing their new ink, because Charlotte Sampson, our trainee, knew Britney, who was Trevor McKay when he wasn't dolled up. In Charlotte's other life, as an accountant, she'd done Trevor's taxes the past couple of years. When Trevor found out Charlotte had ditched her former career choice to be a tattoo artist, he said it must be karma.

Because of our contribution to the show, Charlotte; my shop manager, Bitsy Hendricks; my friend and tattooist Joel Sloane; and I had been given the VIP treatment: free drinks, a great table, a backstage tour. The only one in our shop who had chosen not to come was Ace van Nes, who had issues with the idea of a drag show—but he had issues with a lot of things. I'd been a little leery at first, too, for different reasons than Ace, but I easily caved to peer pressure when Charlotte, Bitsy, and Joel said we just *had* to be there.

So that's how we ended up covered in champagne, the music blasting, a strobe light cutting across Britney's body as she lay sprawled on the stage, her five-inch red platform heels pointing toward the ceiling and looking oddly like the Wicked Witch of the West's just after the house fell on her.

My eyes were still smarting from the bubbly, and I closed them again for a second. When I did, my memory kicked back to the guy who'd sprayed me. I hadn't seen his face. The strobe had created a cutout image, his outline flashing light, then dark too fast for me to remember many details, especially with the oversized hooded sweatshirt and baggy jeans that hung precariously low from his hips, with bunched-up boxers protruding from the top as though he was some urban kid.

But he'd had his sleeves pushed up to his elbows. Maybe he didn't want to get any of the Moët on himself. By doing that, however, he'd given me something I could share with my brother the detective. Something that I would never miss.

He had a tattoo on the inside of his right forearm. A rather distinctive one.

It was a queen-of-hearts playing card.

Chapter 2

Someone finally shut off the strobe when the cops showed up, and replaced the dim lights with bright ones that accentuated the weariness of the night: spilled booze, smudged martini glasses, a couple of shoeless heels. Even the hunky background dancers looked a bit worse for the wear. And while the champagne was spilled only halfway through the show, there had been enough cocktails beforehand to get a third world country drunk.

I didn't see my brother with the two uniforms who'd escorted the paramedics onstage to tend to Britney. Then again, it didn't seem logical that a detective would be sent here. While it was clear to me that the guy who shot the cork at Britney was aiming for her, she may have gotten only a bump on the back of the head when she fell.

But I remembered that actress who'd had what everyone initially thought was a minor bump on the head, too. She died just hours later. Maybe I *should* tell those uniformed cops that the cork was shot on purpose. I could at least give them a description of the tattoo, even though I hadn't seen the guy's face.

I felt something tug on my foot as I started toward them. I glanced down. My shoe was stuck to some spirit gum and sporting a curly blond wig that had somehow lost its drag queen.

"You know you're dragging something that looks like a dead cat, don't you?" Joel asked.

I was one step ahead of him. I leaned against his arm and lifted my foot, pulling the wig off my shoe with a yank. I waved it in front of him, accidentally hitting Bitsy with it. I hadn't seen her come around the other side of him.

She made a face at me and brushed at the wig. "Where'd you get that?"

I tossed it on one of the large speakers next to the stage, where male dancers had been performing as Britney lip-synched. "I saw him," I said simply.

Bitsy looked at me as if I had three heads. "What?"

"I saw the guy with the champagne. The cork—it hit her. He aimed it at her."

Joel tugged my arm. "You have to tell them." He indicated the cops. So even Joel thought it was a good idea.

We made our way over to the stage. Joel is good in a crowd. He weighs about three hundred pounds and few people can get past him. Bitsy, however, was again missing.

As we approached, I did see a detective, after all, near the edge of the stage. I could tell he was a detective because of the cheap-looking green sport jacket and gray Dockers frayed at the bottoms. His hair was cropped short and his ears stuck out, giving him the appearance of an impish Santa's elf. And he had that look about him. That cop look. The one my dad had. The one my brother has.

"Excuse me?" I said loudly, trying to get his attention.

He didn't hear me.

"Excuse me!" I said more loudly.

He turned and looked right through me.

"Excuse me!" The third time is said to be a charm, but he hardly looked charmed. He frowned.

"Yes?"

"I saw the guy who hit her with the cork," I said.

He leaned over and whispered something to one of the uniforms before turning back to me, rolling his eyes and sighing. I didn't hear the sigh, but I could see his chest rise and fall. I thought maybe he should think about asking MissTique for a job. He obviously had a flair for the dramatic. I wondered what he'd look like in a dress, then immediately tried to erase the image from my head. It wasn't pretty.

As he jumped down off the stage to join me and Joel—Bitsy had somehow scrambled up onstage and was talking to Charlotte now—I noticed that he was older than I'd originally thought. Or maybe it was the lighting that showed off the wrinkles around his eyes and the sag of his jaw. I wondered what I looked like in this dreadful light.

Sister Mary Eucharista, my teacher at Our Lady of Perpetual Mercy School, would've said I shouldn't be so vain while Britney was being moved onto a gurney.

A gurney?

"Are they taking her to the hospital? I thought she was okay."

The cop shrugged. "Hit her head pretty hard on the floor. Paramedics want to make sure she doesn't have a concussion." He was distracted, checking out my tattoos. His eyes followed the Monet water lily garden up my arm to the dragon poking its head up through the low neckline of my silk blouse, which was sticking to me because it was wet from the champagne. Fortunately, it was black, so he couldn't see the rest of the dragon curling around my torso, meeting up with the tiger lily that slinked down from my breast to my hip. My jeans hid Napoleon riding his horse up the Alps on my right calf, the ink so new it still had a bubblegum pinkish hue, and my blouse also covered the Celtic cross on my upper back.

In a moment of solidarity, the cop moved his sleeve up to show a snake curled around his left arm just above his wrist.

"Nice," I said politely, although it was probably flash, a stock tattoo. At The Painted Lady, we do only custom ink.

He grinned. "So, what happened here? We can't get a real answer out of any of those fags."

My own smile disappeared. "They're drag queens," I said coldly. "Performers."

"Yeah, whatever," he said, not seeming to notice it had gotten frosty in here. "What's your name?"

"Brett Kavanaugh." I watched him write it down in his little cop notebook, an eyebrow rising as he took a better look at me, not my tattoos this time.

"Kavanaugh?"

"You probably know my brother." Tim and I are carbon copies of each other, except he shaves and has freckles. Sort of natural ink as opposed to my self-imposed ink. A lot of people think we're twins, with our red hair and thin frames, although he's got more muscles while I've got more angles. At six feet, he's taller than I am by three inches, but most people don't notice because I don't shy away from wearing heels.

The cop's expression changed slightly, the corners of his mouth tightening, and he nodded in that way people do when they're just being polite. I wondered whether there was bad blood between him and Tim. Which reminded me . . .

"I didn't get your name."

He gave me a smirk. "So, tell me what happened here."

Definitely bad blood.

I stood up a little straighter, forcing myself not to pay attention to my wet blouse. "There was a guy standing next to the stage. He had a champagne bottle, Moët White Star, I think. He pointed it at Trevor and hit him with the cork."

"Trevor?"

"You do know his name is Trevor McKay?" I indicated the gurney, which was now being wheeled across the floor toward the door.

He blinked at me a couple of times, then asked, "What did this guy look like?"

I shook my head. "I didn't see his features. He had a big gray hooded sweatshirt on, and baggy jeans."

"Maybe it wasn't even a guy; maybe it was a woman."

"No, it was a guy. He had his sleeves pushed up. Definitely man's arms."

"But these guys"—the cop waved his hand, indicating

the stage—"all look like women. Maybe it was a woman who looks like a guy."

I stared at him to see whether he was joking. He was dead serious.

"No, it was a guy," I insisted. "He had a tattoo," I added.

The pencil paused over the pad. "What sort of tattoo?"

"A queen-of-hearts playing card. On his inner forearm. His right arm."

"So you can't tell me anything else about this guy, but you're sure about the tattoo?"

"I own a tattoo shop. The Painted Lady."

The eyebrows went back up again, and his arms fell to his sides. "At the Venetian?"

He seemed to know it. "Yeah," I said.

"Pricey place."

I didn't know whether he was referring to the upscale shops that made up the Venetian Grand Canal Shoppes or my custom tattoos.

"You can get cheaper ink on Fremont."

Sure. I should've known. He was determined to take me down a notch. I had to ask Tim about this guy who wouldn't give me his name.

"There's no cork," he said curtly.

I frowned. "What?"

"No one has seen the cork that *you* say hit him. You're sure it was a cork?"

"No, a frog flew out of that bottle." I rolled my eyes at him, irritated that he was questioning everything I was telling him. As if I would lie.

"No frogs, either," he said humorlessly as he stuffed the notebook in his jacket pocket. "Do you have a card or something? In case I need to ask you more questions?"

"Maybe *you* can give me *your* card," I suggested.

I thought it might work. And for a second, he considered it. But then he grinned and said, "I know where to find you," before heading back to the stage.

Chapter 3

"That was smooth," Joel said.

"You could've helped me out here."

"You seemed to have it under control."

I was going to say something snarky, but I was distracted as I glanced around the club. The pandemonium had quieted down with the arrival of the police and paramedics, who were now rolling Trevor out on the gurney. He'd propped himself up on one elbow and was batting his eyes at the guy holding a blood pressure cuff but who seemed interested in what Trevor was saying. Maybe he'd get a date out of this. Seemed only right, since the rest of the night was a bust.

Charlotte was beckoning us to come up onstage. Joel and I weaved around a couple of tables and climbed the steps.

"Trevor asked if I'd bring his stuff to his apartment," she said. "I'm just so relieved he's okay."

Joel caught her in a hug.

I shifted from foot to foot. I'm not a hugger. At least not to the extent Joel is. Joel would hug anyone anytime for anything.

I started across the stage, figuring they'd join me when they were done.

Bitsy came out from behind the curtain. Like a magic trick. It startled me.

"Hey, what are you doing back here?" I asked.

"Helping Charlotte get Trevor's stuff."

Not a surprise. Bitsy might have attitude now and then, but she was always the first to help out.

"There's something here; I'm not sure it's Trevor's. I need Charlotte to tell me."

We went to the dressing room, where all the queens had gotten ready for their performances. Makeup was strewn across a long table in front of a long, wide mirror meant for sharing. The light caught sequins, and they sparkled against the feather boas; fabric draped over chairs and lay on the floor. Backpacks and duffel bags littered the corners of the room; shoes of all shapes and sizes—but all glittering—were scattered.

MissTique stood by the table, holding a box of Uncle Ben's rice.

What in this picture doesn't belong?

Before I could ask about the rice, Bitsy tugged on my arm.

I looked down to see her holding a gray hooded sweatshirt.

"This was lying on Trevor's backpack, but I don't remember him wearing it," she said.

I didn't remember him wearing it, either. But the guy who hit him with the cork had worn one exactly like it.

I'd opened my mouth to say something when an unearthly sound filled the room.

Bitsy and I looked up to see MissTique clutching the rice box to her chest, which was heaving with sobs. We glanced at each other, and Bitsy shrugged as if to say, *What are we supposed to do?* I shrugged back. No clue.

MissTique dramatically fell into a chair next to her, holding on to the box as if it were a life preserver. The tears that rolled down her cheeks left grooves in her makeup like little mountain rivers.

"It was supposed to be wonderful," she choked, her eyes brimming over as they pleaded with us for some sort of sympathy.

This was Charlotte and Joel's territory. Bitsy and I were just here for the ride. And if I wasn't a hugger, Bitsy really wasn't.

"It was good," I tried. "Great, until, well . . ." My voice trailed off, because she knew what I was talking about and it was no use beating a dead horse.

Fortunately, Charlotte just that moment swept into the room, assessed the situation, and went over to MissTique and put her arms around her. Joel stood awkwardly in the doorway. So I'd found his Achilles' heel. Hugging is good, except in the case of a teary drag queen.

Bitsy and I busied ourselves with Trevor's duffel bag, stuffing his Britney Brassieres costumes inside. I found his makeup case on the table and began putting that together, although I wasn't totally sure just what makeup was his as opposed to his fellow queens'.

I picked up a stray stocking and held it up to show Charlotte, my eyebrows raised with the question.

"Could be," Charlotte said, not being much help at all.

MissTique finally relaxed her grip on the rice box and held it out for me. "This is Trevor's."

I took it from her. "What . . ."

She chuckled, a low, rumbling sound that was like thunder.

"He uses it for his boobs."

She must have seen my expression, because her chuckle turned into laughter. "He fills a sock with rice and then puts that in his bra. It's quite ingenious, because while the rest of us just use plain socks or pantyhose, his boobs actually move like they're real."

I contemplated the box for a second. I could sell the idea to middle school girls and make a fortune. I found a plastic bag on the table, wrapped the box up so no rice would fall out, and put it in the duffel bag.

Joel had come into the room now and was shuffling around, looking at the dresses on the floor. I couldn't tell whether he was wondering why men would dress like this and perform, or whether he wanted to try something on. It was difficult sometimes to read Joel.

"I hope the cops find that guy and lock him up," Miss-Tique said, anger tinting her voice.

I opened a case that had more shades of eye shadow than I even knew existed. "You know, he really didn't do anything except disrupt everything. Trevor's okay. So I'm not sure he'll have the book thrown at him or anything," I said.

"What do you know about it?" she asked.

"Her brother's a police detective," Charlotte said.

"The one out there?" MissTique asked.

I cringed. "No. I don't know that guy."

"Good, because I had serious issues with him," Miss-Tique said. She got up and pulled off her wig. Long tresses of sleek black hair landed on the floor, and she didn't bother picking them up. She kicked off her platform heels, reached under her dress, and tugged, pulling down her hose and sliding them off her legs.

Joel looked away.

Bitsy and I couldn't tear our eyes away.

The wide white plastic belt came off next, and then she tugged at the back of the white sequined minidress. Charlotte unzipped her, and the dress slid off.

MissTique stood before us in her bra and panties, the hairy chest proof that we weren't in Kansas anymore.

Socks spilled out of the bra as he unhooked it, and I watched as he pulled off two pairs of incredibly tight Speedos that obviously had been holding his jewels in place.

He didn't seem self-conscious at all that he was standing in the middle of the room naked.

Charlotte handed him a pair of jeans.

"Thanks, sweetheart," he said.

Bitsy and I turned back to our job at hand. I tried to remember MissTique's real name but drew a blank. Joel's pink face was reflected in the mirror. He hadn't watched any of it. Unless he peeked.

He might have. But I wasn't going to ask.

"Kyle, is there anything else here that's Trevor's?" Charlotte asked, kicking my brain into gear and reminding me that MissTique was really Kyle Albrecht.

I was too young to start having senior moments.

Kyle looked around and shrugged. "Honey, if you leave something behind, he can get it tomorrow."

I'd filled the top of the makeup kit, so I slid open a drawer at the bottom of the case. Trevor had more makeup than I'd managed to acquire in a lifetime. The fact that he was a man made this wrong somehow. Although it could be argued that my ink was a substitute for the stuff I'd put on my face.

I grabbed a lipstick off the table, hoping it was Trevor's, and stuffed it in the drawer. But it went in only halfway. Something was blocking the back of the drawer.

I pulled it out as far as I could, then tried to push it back in. Something had gotten stuck behind it, so I took the whole drawer out and set it on the table before taking the case and leaning it on an angle so I could see what was in there.

I reached my hand inside.

And pulled out a large brooch.

It was covered in sparkling clear and red stones. I had no idea whether they were real or not. But it was the design that made me catch my breath.

It was a queen-of-hearts playing card.

Chapter 4

Kyle had been taking his makeup off with a baby wipe when he saw the brooch in my hand. He waved his hand in the air.

"Trevor made such a big deal over that thing."

I turned it over in my hand. "Where did he get it?"

"At a fund-raiser about a year ago."

Bitsy looked over my elbow at the brooch.

"Pretty," she said, but I knew she didn't mean it. It was garish and over the top, not something either of us would like.

Nevertheless, I couldn't stop staring at it.

"It's the queen of hearts," I said softly.

"Like the tattoo you saw." Joel had joined the party, now that Kyle was Kyle and wearing jeans and a white T-shirt.

Kyle put the baby wipe down. His eyes looked a lot smaller without all the shadow and eyeliner and lashes. "What tattoo?"

I told him about the guy who'd shot the cork at Trevor.

"So you think because of this pin that there's some sort of connection?"

His tone indicated his doubts about that. He was probably right. This was Vegas. Over-the-top brooches and playing-card tattoos were part of the fabric of Sin City.

I put the brooch in the makeup-kit drawer, added the lipstick, and shoved it back into the case. "You're right," I said. "It's just a coincidence, I guess."

"I don't believe in coincidences." Wouldn't you know we'd hear from Bitsy the peanut gallery.

Kyle cleared his throat. "The fund-raiser where Trevor got the pin? It was the Queen of Hearts Ball. They were raising money for AIDS research."

So maybe I wasn't completely off base. But I was hard-pressed to see how the tattoo would be a part of that.

"This isn't the first time someone's gotten hit with a champagne cork."

I'd almost forgotten Charlotte was in the room, she was so quiet.

"That's right," Joel piped up.

"What are you talking about?" I asked.

Joel said, "Some guy's been going to clubs all over the city for months now, spraying champagne on people. I can't believe you haven't heard about that."

So sue me for not paying attention to the local news. The story, however, indicated that perhaps Trevor was just another victim, and the queen of hearts thing *was* just a co-incidence, despite Bitsy's belief. It also would explain why the detective was here. A serial champagne-cork shooter could warrant that.

"He got beat up," Charlotte continued when Joel went silent. "The guy who was spraying the champagne. He got some guy soaked, and the guy went nuts and beat the crap out of him. Cops arrested the guy who did the beating, but they let the champagne sprayer go."

"So why would he keep doing it if the cops know who he is? I mean, he must have pressed charges after getting beat up," I said, then wondered again about the detective. Wouldn't he already know who the guy was?

Unless it was a copycat.

This was the problem being brought up in a family of cops. I always think of all the angles.

Kyle finished taking off his makeup. He had been a gorgeous woman, but he was a good-looking guy, too. The makeup had made his face look even longer and thinner, but without it he looked more normal, less anorexic, perhaps. A little stubble had started to sprout on his jawline and chin.

"Where are the rest of the girls?" Charlotte asked him.

Kyle shrugged. "They're probably drinking for free out there." He got up. "I need to make sure they're all going to come back tomorrow night for the next show." He saw me with a piece of shiny fabric in my hand. "That's Miranda's, not Britney's." He picked up the gray hooded sweatshirt and studied it a second. "I'll see if this belongs to anyone. If it doesn't, we can give it to the police." His eyes skirted around the room. "I think you've got everything. Thanks much." And with that, Kyle disappeared out the door.

I tried not to think about the brooch as we lugged Trevor's makeup case and duffel bag back out into the front of the club.

Kyle was right: Everyone was standing around with cocktails in their hands, gossiping about what had happened. The police had gone; I was glad I wouldn't have to interact with that detective again. Miranda Rites came over to us, her sequins blinding me for a second.

She reached out for the makeup case I carried.

"I'll take that."

"Trevor asked me to take his things back to his place," Charlotte said. I could see the strain on her face; dark circles were starting to form under her eyes, which sagged a little under the weight of exhaustion. This had taken a toll on her. She was Trevor's friend and because of that seemed to take responsibility for him.

Miranda smiled at her. "That's nice of you. But I can help."

"We're all set to go," I butted in. "We've packed up all his stuff, and Charlotte's just going to drop it off."

Miranda's face fell slightly. "I want to do *something*."

Couldn't fault her for that. But I still hung on to the case.

"You could go by the hospital and keep him company until I get there," Charlotte suggested.

Bitsy, Joel, and I stared at her.

"You're not thinking of going over there tonight?" Bitsy asked, sounding like Charlotte's mother.

Charlotte's smile was tired. "I promised."

I could feel all my energy dissipating the longer we stood there. I clutched the makeup kit tighter and nodded at Miranda. "Maybe that's a plan. Come on, guys; let's go."

Miranda drained her martini glass. "Fine," she said with an edge in her voice. So she wasn't happy. I was too tired to care.

We stepped outside into the cool desert night. The sky was clear; the stars flickered over the shadows of the distant mountains. I thought about Red Rock Canyon, with its weathered cliffs, banana yuccas, and Joshua trees, and how I could totally use a hike tomorrow if I could find time for it. Now that it was the end of September, the temperatures had moved from blistering in the nineties and hundreds to perfect in the eighties, and I'd switched from my summer swimming schedule back to anything outdoors.

My Mustang Bullitt looked like a thug next to Joel's sleek green Prius and Bitsy's dainty MINI Cooper that she'd outfitted so she could reach the foot pedals. A few spaces away, Charlotte's Honda Fit had a look similar to a mailbox, all squat and square. She opened the hatch in the back and I put the makeup case next to the duffel bag.

"Thanks," she said, then leaned toward me a little and whispered, "You talked to that cop?"

"I told him everything I saw," I said. "I hope they can find the guy."

"Did he say anything?"

"He didn't tell me about the other champagne incidents," I said, not quite sure, though, whether that was what she meant.

"Okay," she said, and I guess it was. She went around to the driver's-side door.

"Don't stay out too late," Bitsy said, although it was already after midnight, so who knew when "late" was.

Charlotte gave a short wave and climbed into her car. We watched her drive off before going over to our respective vehicles.

We were bidding each other good-bye when the door to the club opened and Kyle came out and walked toward us.

"I'm glad you're still here," he said.

"What's up?" I asked.

"I've been thinking about Trevor's pin."

On reflex, I glanced over to where Charlotte's Fit was pulling out onto the main drag.

"You might want to leave it with me."

I frowned. "Why?" The Fit was getting farther and farther away.

"Eduardo, one of the dancing boys—remember him?"

There had been so many. We all shook our heads.

"Well," Kyle continued, "he said some guy came around the club looking for Trevor this afternoon. He told Eduardo that Trevor had pawned something last week and bought it back today. But the guy said there was a mistake."

"What sort of mistake?" I asked.

Kyle shrugged. "Not sure. But it had to be that pin. Trevor's pawned it before, so he probably did again. I can't think of anything else Trevor had that was worth pawning."

"Are they real stones?" I asked, but Bitsy interrupted.

"We can talk to Trevor about it. Charlotte already took it with her. We don't have it anymore." Bitsy was just as tired as I was, and I could see she just wanted to get going.

Something crossed Kyle's face, but I couldn't read it. "Okay, that's okay," he said after a few seconds, but I could tell by his tone that it wasn't.

"What's wrong, Kyle?" I nudged.

He sighed and put his hands on his hips, staring off into the distance before answering.

"Eduardo is feeling guilty."

"About what?" I asked.

"He told the guy he'd give Trevor the message. But the guy said he'd send his own message, one that Trevor wouldn't be able to ignore."

Chapter 5

I could put two and two together.

"So Eduardo thinks that this is the guy who hit Trevor with the cork?" I asked.

Kyle nodded. "He says everything that happened tonight was all his fault, just because he didn't tell Trevor about this before the show. But he said there wasn't time." He sounded like he was trying to convince himself that Eduardo was telling the truth. Had there been time? Maybe, maybe not. It was water under the bridge now. Or, rather, champagne under the bridge.

"Did the guy leave a card or anything?" Bitsy asked, ever practical.

"No," Kyle said. "He didn't even tell Eduardo his name."

"So he could've been lying," Joel piped up. "Maybe he knows about Trevor's pin and for some reason he just wants to get his hands on it."

Kyle sighed. "Maybe. There was a big basket full of those pins at that fund-raiser. Trevor says all the other ones were fake, but this one is real. He says Lester Fine gave it to him." I could tell by his tone that he was doubtful.

Lester Fine was an Academy Award–winning actor who was running for a senate seat. You couldn't look at a newspaper front page in the last month or so that didn't have his picture plastered all over it. Granted, he was a good-looking older man, and he was a shoo-in for the seat because of his celebrity.

"Was Lester Fine at the fund-raiser?" I asked.

"Sure, he was there."

"So could what Trevor says be true?"

Kyle laughed. "Honey, Trevor would lie to his grandmother if it meant a good story."

"So you don't believe him?"

"Let's just say I don't think Trevor runs with Lester Fine's crowd."

He had a point.

"But maybe the story's true. Maybe that's why the other guy wants it. Maybe there was no mistake at all; maybe Joel's right that he was just angling to get his hands on it." I thought a second. "The stones in the brooch must be real. A pawnshop wouldn't give Trevor money for something that wasn't worth anything."

The look on Kyle's face told me that he wasn't convinced.

I did know one thing for sure: If the guy looking for Trevor was the one who hit him with the cork after making a threat, then the police needed to know about it.

"Eduardo should talk to the cops," I suggested. "He could tell them what the guy looked like. Maybe he could look at one of those books with the mug shots." I watched too much TV.

Kyle batted his eyes a few seconds, then said, "Well, you know, there's a problem with that. Eduardo isn't exactly . . . well . . . legal. He's not going to want to talk to the police about anything."

I could see his point. But at the same time, we needed to try to find out who the cork shooter was. Maybe it was the same guy who'd been doing this all over town, or maybe it was this pawnshop guy.

"You could do a sketch," Bitsy said, pulling on my arm.

I looked down at her. "What?"

"You do great portraits. What if Eduardo told you what the guy looks like and you draw the face? Then you can give it to the police."

"What, like a police sketch artist? That's not what I do. I work from photographs."

Despite my misgivings, Kyle was nodding faster than a bobble-head doll.

"That's a great idea," he said.

I looked at Joel for support, but he seemed to be agreeing.

"Oh, go ahead, Brett. I think it's a good idea, too," he said.

I knew when I was beat.

"Okay, sure. I'll come back in the morning," I told Kyle.

But he was shaking his head. "No, no, you have to do it now. I'm not sure Eduardo will be around tomorrow."

"Why not?" I started to get suspicious about the whole thing.

"He's got another gig in Reno tomorrow night and has to get up there."

It sounded like the truth, but who knew?

"I don't have any sketching paper," I tried.

Kyle threw his arm around me and started leading me back to the club. I twisted my neck around to see Bitsy and Joel headed to their cars.

"Where are you going?" I stopped, turned, and glared at them. "This is your idea. You can't leave me here."

Bitsy shrugged. "I've got to get to the shop early tomorrow to open up," she said. "See you then." She waggled her fingers at me, gave me a quick grin, and got into her MINI Cooper.

I'd talk to her tomorrow. I was too tired right now. I raised my eyebrows expectantly at Joel. His shoulders sagged with obedience as he clicked his key fob to relock the doors of his car, and he joined us as we went back into the club.

The same group that had been drinking when we left was refilling their glasses. Someone had cranked up the music, and Miranda Rites and Marva Luss gyrated on the stage to a Donna Summer song as a couple of the young men hooted their enthusiasm while waving huge white

feathered fans, reminiscent of old-time burlesque shows.
The disco ball splashed little bits of light against everyone,
like glitter come alive. I guess Miranda had decided after
all that she wasn't going to go hold Trevor's hand until
Charlotte got to the hospital.

Kyle led me over to one of the young men and whispered in his ear. His face was classic Latino, with olive skin,
dark, piercing eyes, and high, pronounced cheekbones. He
wasn't wearing a shirt, showing off his rippled abs, muscled
biceps, and tiny waist. He had black tribal tattoos running
down both arms and across his back. His jeans weren't buttoned, showing off white shorts beneath.

He was gorgeous.

Eduardo nodded at me and gave me a small smile as he
assessed my ink. Kyle led us backstage. Rather than going
into the dressing room this time, he took us into a small
office that housed a desk, a laptop computer, and a printer.
Kyle grabbed a few sheets of paper out of the printer and
handed them to me. I helped myself to a pencil that lay
next to the laptop. It wasn't very sharp, but it would have
to do.

"Have a seat," Kyle invited, and I sat in the straight-
backed desk chair. He pulled out a folding chair from the
corner for Eduardo. There weren't any other chairs for him
or Joel, who leaned against the doorframe, his hands in his
pockets.

"So, can you tell me what the guy looked like?" I asked
Eduardo, my pencil poised.

"He had a round face," Eduardo started. "A short
nose."

I contemplated the paper. I'd done my share of portrait
tattoos, and when I was at the University of the Arts in
Philadelphia, I'd drawn more faces and figures than I could
remember. But I always had a model to work from. Not
someone's memory, which could be skewed. Especially, as
I could see, a memory that had been influenced by maybe
one too many cocktails.

I sketched out a round face and a short nose.

"No, no," Eduardo said, touching the base of the nose. "It was rounder here and thinner here." He ran his finger along the line I'd drawn.

Maybe this wouldn't be so bad. He seemed to really know. I did what he said, and he nodded. "Yes, yes, that's good. The eyes were large, with short eyelashes."

With his direction, I found myself filling out the sketch. As I thought about it a little more, I guess I shouldn't have been so surprised that he'd take such close notice of a man's looks. That's what Chez Tango was really all about, after all.

I was glad no one could see my right foot pressing hard into the ground, sort of like a backseat driver who wants to put the brakes on. It was an odd habit I'd developed when I drew, as if I were using the tattoo-machine pedal. I'd gotten so used to drawing with the machine in my hand that a pencil sometimes felt funny.

I tried to remember how it felt the first time I drew a tattoo on my skin. I'd used a sewing needle wrapped tightly with black thread and ink from a ballpoint pen. I'd stuck my skin with tiny stabs, drawing blood, all the while creating a black heart that still adorned the inside of my left wrist. It was crude and took hours, but after the initial pricks, I hardly felt it at all. I was sixteen.

For two years I hid the heart from my parents under a bunch of bangle bracelets that jingled almost constantly. When my mother saw the heart for the first time, her heart almost stopped.

"No, no, no," Eduardo said, bringing me out of my memory and pointing to the cheeks. "These are too large."

I took a guess and shaded in some contour, and he nodded. "Yes, that's what I meant."

We were done.

I put my pencil down and surveyed the drawing, Joel and Kyle behind me, looking over my shoulder. Eduardo was nodding as if pleased with himself.

"You could do that for a living," Kyle said.

"I do," I said thoughtfully, wondering who this person was that I'd drawn. "Does he look familiar?" I asked, knowing that even from this I couldn't say for sure whether it was the guy with the champagne or not. I really hadn't seen his face.

Eduardo shook his head.

"But you met him," I said.

"I don't *know* him," he retorted. "We were not properly introduced."

Touché.

Kyle was looking over my shoulder and frowning.

"Do you know this guy?" I asked, standing up. It was getting late, and exhaustion was stretching through my body like a tight elastic band. Bitsy would open tomorrow, but I had a client coming in at noon. I glanced at my watch. At this rate, I wouldn't get home until two.

Kyle picked up the drawing and studied it, leading us out of the office and into the dressing room. He still hadn't said anything; I wondered whether he recognized the man in the picture.

Miranda Rites was in the dressing room. Or at least her alter ego, Stephan Price, was. He was folding up the pink sequined costume and putting it in his own duffel bag. Like Kyle and Trevor, Stephan was just as good-looking a man as Miranda was a woman, although Stephan was skinnier than his friends.

"You're still here?" Stephan asked.

Kyle held up the drawing.

"See what Brett did?"

Stephan took it and studied it a second, then looked at me with questioning eyes. "Why did you draw a picture of Wesley?"

"Wesley?" I asked.

Stephan looked at Kyle. "It's Wesley, isn't it?"

Kyle took the drawing back and nodded. "Yes. It's not exact—that's why I wanted a second opinion—but it's pretty close."

"Who's Wesley?" I asked again.

Kyle handed me back the sketch. "Wesley Lambert used to be in one of my shows. His drag name was Shanda Leer. But he dropped out of the circuit about a year ago, and no one's seen him since."

Chapter 6

Obviously, someone *had* seen him since, and it was Eduardo.

"You said he was from a pawnshop," I said to Eduardo, who was frowning. Eduardo, Kyle, Joel, and I had left Stephan in the dressing room and went back out into the front of the club.

"I thought that's what he said." He sighed. "But maybe he didn't, come to think of it. He said Trevor had pawned something, and there was a mistake. But that was all."

"Why did he stop doing your shows?" I asked Kyle.

Kyle sighed. "He fell in with the wrong crowd. Bunch of rednecks. He said something once about a lab or something out in the desert, and it sounded like they were making drugs. And then his new friends started hanging around the club. They creeped everyone out. But I couldn't throw them out based on that, until they started harassing some of the girls. I told Wesley if he couldn't keep them out, he needed to find another gig. So he left. It's too bad, because he was great for the club. He'd wear a gigantic chandelier on his head while singing 'Diamonds Are a Girl's Best Friend.' Everyone loved it."

I would've paid to see that.

"But you don't know where he went after that?"

"As far as I know, nowhere. He just disappeared. His friends, too."

"Do you remember where Wesley lived?" I asked Kyle. "I could tell the police when I give them the drawing." This was getting a little complicated, and I wondered whether I shouldn't just give it to Tim instead of that nameless detective, who would undoubtedly have the same number of questions as Tim, but I could handle Tim more easily. Then again, if there was bad blood between Tim and that detective, as I suspected, that might not be a good idea.

I felt like I was between that rock and a hard place everyone talks about.

"I don't remember," Kyle said. "And I paid him in cash whenever he did a show."

"What about a queen-of-hearts tattoo? Did he have one? On his inner forearm?" I looked first to Eduardo.

"He wore a long-sleeved T-shirt when I saw him."

Kyle was shaking his head. "I don't remember a tattoo."

More rocks. More hard places.

I folded the paper up and stuck it in my bag, taking Joel's arm. "We've got to go," I said. "Thanks," I said to Eduardo. "I won't tell the police about you, and hopefully the drawing will be enough."

Kyle and Eduardo hung back as Joel and I went back out into the night for the second time.

"Will you give that to Tim?" Joel asked.

"Yeah, probably. He can pass it along to whoever."

When we got to our cars, Joel leaned over and gave me a peck on the cheek. "You did good," he praised, like I was a puppy, but I knew he didn't mean it like that.

"Thanks. You could've done it, too."

"I don't have your formal training, remember?"

"Yeah, but you've done this long enough so you could."

He opened his mouth to argue again, and I shook my head. "We could go around and around on this."

The door to Chez Tango opened behind us, and the stragglers began spilling out. Definitely time to go.

We said our good-byes and got into our cars. I sped out of the parking lot before Joel, eager to get home. I took the Strip rather than the back roads, because I knew the lights would keep me alert. The reflections of the neon flashed across my windshield, and I was reminded how someone once said that every movie and TV show filmed in Vegas had at least one scene with a car driving down the Strip, the lights cutting across the windows.

I was such a cliché.

The Bellagio fountains were dancing as I sat at a light. Every time I pass them I think about *Ocean's Eleven* and wonder if George Clooney's back in town. I've never seen him—or any other celebrity, except for Howie Mandel. I bumped into him—literally—and spilled gelato all over his Hawaiian shirt at the Palazzo. He totally freaked-out, being the germophobe that he is. Why couldn't I have spilled something on Mark Wahlberg or Leonardo di Caprio? My sister, Cathleen, who lives in Southern California, always seems to be running into Keanu Reeves or Nicole Kidman or even Miley Cyrus at all of her charity events. You'd think that because the Vegas Strip is a lot smaller than Los Angeles, I'd be rubbing elbows with celebrities all the time. Instead, I'm inking tourists next to a fake Venetian canal in a fake St. Mark's Square.

Somebody's got to do it.

I pulled into the driveway at the house I share with Tim in Henderson, the headlights illuminating the banana yuccas by the front door. I've been here two years now, having moved from Jersey when Tim broke up with Shawna, his almost-fiancée, and needed a roommate. I needed an escape from a relationship gone bad, and I'd been getting too comfortable in my job at the Ink Spot. It was time to move on and run my own shop. I'd also still been living with my parents, who'd announced out of the blue that they were selling the house and moving to Florida. Personally, I think it was their way of saying, "You're thirty years old, and you can't live with us anymore," although I would've been happier if they'd just come out and said that rather than plan to move fifteen hundred miles away to a town that rolled up its sidewalks at six p.m. and had a grocery store with its parking lot divided into sections named after the states.

My parents always parked in New Jersey. It was easy to remember.

I knew I wouldn't live with Tim forever, but it was a nice place to hang my hat for a while.

It was dark inside. I parked in the garage next to Tim's Jeep and let myself in quietly, so I wouldn't wake him. I pulled off my jeans and black blouse, which might survive a washing, might not, and put on a pair of cotton pajama bottoms and an oversized T-shirt. The bedside lamp let off a golden glow, casting shadows on the paintings on the walls. I'd indulged myself with works by college friends, splashes of color in oil and acrylic. My own work was in my parents' house in Port St. Lucie, Florida.

My mother still hadn't gotten over my being a tattooist. She told all her new friends in the retirement community that her daughter was an artist but neglected to tell them what kind.

Sister Mary Eucharista would give her a pass. I had a harder time forgiving her for not accepting who I was.

Tim said I should get over it. But who was he to talk? He'd followed in Dad's footsteps and had always been the favorite.

I shut the light off, as if it would shut out my thoughts, too.

It worked after a little while, and I fell into a deep sleep.

Tim was scrambling eggs when I emerged the next morning, rubbing sleep from my eyes. He grinned and took another plate down from the cupboard.

"Hey there, night owl."

I groaned and slid onto one of the kitchen chairs. My bag was still slung over the back.

"So how was the show?"

"Fine," I said on reflex, then, "Well, there was a little excitement."

He dished the eggs out and put a plate and fork in front of me as he sat down with his own. "What happened?"

I told him everything: how I witnessed the cork shooter

and the mysterious nameless detective and Trevor going to the hospital and the queen-of-hearts tattoo and Trevor's pin and Eduardo telling me what to draw. I managed to eat all my eggs while I talked and pulled the sketch from my bag, handing it to him as I chugged a glass of orange juice.

He studied it for a second, taking a drink of his own juice, then put it on the table between us.

"You did that?"

"Yeah, what of it?"

"Nothing, except it's good. Great if it looks like the guy it's supposed to be. You could have a second career if you want to give up the shop."

I chuckled. "Mom would love that, wouldn't she?"

"No kidding." Tim shoveled more eggs in his mouth before asking, "So who is he?"

"Some ex–drag queen named Shanda Leer." I couldn't remember his real name—I knew Kyle had told me—but I remembered his stage name because now I got it. "Chandelier, you know," I said. "Shanda Leer."

Tim chuckled. "How do they come up with those names?" he asked.

I shrugged. "Beats me. Kyle kicked him out of the club because he started hanging with drug dealers or something."

Tim frowned. "Huh?"

I told him how Kyle said there was some sort of lab in the desert.

"Probably not just speculation," Tim said, but then he grew quiet.

I wanted to push it, find out just what was going on out in the desert, but I could tell he'd closed down on that subject. So I tried a new one. "Who's the detective who wouldn't give me his name?"

Tim drank some more juice, buying time. I could tell he didn't want to tell me.

"Come on, big brother. What is it with you two? Did you get into a fight on the playground or something?"

"He's Shawna's fiancé."

Shawna, as in Tim's old flame, the one who wanted a diamond but got a house instead, so she moved on. Guess she finally got her wish.

"So, why would that matter to me? Why not tell me his name?" I asked.

Tim sighed. "He thinks I'm an ass. Even though I've reminded him that if Shawna and I had gotten married, he wouldn't be with her now."

Good point, although Tim *had* been an ass. I didn't understand, either, why he'd go in on a house with the woman and then drag his feet on getting married. I'd never asked him outright, though. It was his business, and if he wanted to tell me about it someday, fine. If not, well, that would have to be fine, too.

"How'd he meet her?" I asked.

Tim made a face. "We had a barbecue here, right before Shawna moved out. They met then. Maybe it was love at first sight."

He didn't sound bitter. Maybe the reason he didn't marry her was because he just didn't want to. Maybe it was that simple.

"She's a pit boss now," he volunteered during my silence.

"Really?" Shawna had been a blackjack dealer, like Tim had been when he met her. He'd had more fun trying to catch people cheating at the table than he did dealing, and finally figured he would go to the police academy so he could go after real bad guys.

"She got promoted a few months ago."

I didn't really care, and I could tell he was just making conversation.

"What's the guy's name?" I asked.

"Frank. Frank DeBurra." He paused. "I'm surprised he was there. Must be putting in some overtime."

"Why surprised?"

"He's with Metro Homeland Security."

"Huh?"

Tim chuckled. "Yeah, LVPD's got its own homeland security force. All those threats, you know."

I didn't know, but he didn't elaborate.

Before I could ask, he tapped at the sketch. "You know, come to think of it, if DeBurra was the responding officer and he talked to you last night, he won't be happy if he knew you gave this to me."

I nodded. "Yeah, I thought of that. But I didn't know his name. How was I supposed to get it to him if I didn't ask you?"

"Okay, we'll go with that story. But you could've just called the department and asked for the detective on the scene last night."

"That would be too much trouble."

"On second thought, I don't want to deal with the fallout." He pushed the sketch back toward me. "Call the department. Tell him you've got this. Leave me out of it. Believe me, it'll make my life a lot easier."

He had a point.

"What's the best way to explain how I did the drawing without mentioning Eduardo?" I needed a little guidance on this.

"Just tell him . . . I don't know." Tim ran his hand through his hair and sighed. "I know you want to protect the guy, Brett, but . . ."

"I'm not ratting him out, Tim. I promised."

"Okay, chill. You'll think of something." He got up and started clearing up the dishes.

The doorbell rang.

We looked at each other, both of us frowning. Tim went into the front foyer and looked through the peephole. He gave me a funny look as he opened the door.

Speak of the devil.

Detective Frank DeBurra walked in.

Chapter 7

"Hello, Tim," DeBurra said, although I noted he didn't offer to shake Tim's hand. He spotted me at the table. "Just the person I was looking for."

I was acutely aware that I was still wearing my pink and red plaid pajama bottoms and the T-shirt that hung low, showing more of the dragon than usual. My short hair was spiked up in cowlicks from sleep. I hadn't bothered taking off my mascara before I went to bed, and it was smudged around my eyes in a sort of raccoon look.

But my mother always taught me to go with the flow, so I stood and stuck my hand out. He did shake mine as he walked past Tim, obviously dismissing him.

"I'll get in the shower," Tim said to me, then turned to DeBurra. "Nice to see you, Frank."

The detective grunted, wouldn't even look at him. Made me dislike him even more than I did last night. He could at least be polite in our home.

Tim disappeared into the back of the house, and I motioned that the detective should sit.

"Coffee?" I asked. I hadn't had my first cup yet, but Tim had left it brewing on the counter.

"No, thanks," he said, and his eyes moved over the sketch that sat on the table. "What's this?"

I busied myself with pouring a cup of coffee, then getting the milk out of the fridge. "What?" I feigned ignorance.

When I turned with my coffee, he was holding it, studying it. "What is this?" he asked again, looking at me this time.

I took my cup to the table and sat. "It's a guy who was poking around Chez Tango yesterday afternoon, asking questions about Trevor. I didn't know if you would want it." I'd conveniently insinuated that perhaps I had actually seen Shanda Leer and did the drawing from memory.

"You drew this?" His incredulity was worse than Tim's.

"I studied as an artist," I said flatly, taking a sip of my coffee. "And I do portraits now."

DeBurra didn't say anything for a few seconds, then, "Do you know who this is?"

"Someone at the club told me it looked like a former drag queen named Shanda Leer."

"So you've never seen him before?"

I shrugged. "No. Should I have?"

"You don't recognize him as the person with the champagne?"

"I really didn't see that guy, like I told you last night."

"But you saw this man backstage?"

He was firing questions at me so fast, I didn't have time to think. So because Sister Mary Eucharista had ingrained it in me not to lie, I said, "Someone else saw him and described him. I drew it for him."

"Who?"

Now I was in a pickle.

"One of the dancing boys. I don't know which one," I said, hoping I didn't blush to reveal my lie.

"It'll be easier if you just tell me," DeBurra said impatiently.

So much for hoping I didn't blush. Now I felt my face grow hot.

"Isn't this enough?" I asked. "This guy was asking about something Trevor had pawned, said there was some mistake, and then just hours later, Trevor gets shot with a champagne cork. Seems a little suspicious to me."

"Why?"

"He told the dancing boy that he'd give Trevor a message he couldn't ignore."

His eyes narrowed and he studied my face for a second, like his next question was going to be about whether I wanted world peace or something.

Finally, he asked, "But if Trevor pawned something, then why would this guy ask him about it? Trevor wouldn't still have it, would he?"

"He bought it back, apparently." This guy should know how it worked. Run out of money at the tables, find the most valuable belonging you have, take it to a pawnshop, sell it for a few hundred or more, and buy yourself a little more time at the tables. If you won, you could buy your valuable back.

"Which pawnshop?"

"I don't know."

"There's a lot you don't know," he said accusingly.

"Detective, you're in my house. You insult my brother by not shaking his hand, and you're calling me a liar. Why don't you just take the picture and see what you can find out and leave us alone?" I stood, gripping my cup so my hands wouldn't shake. I had planned to tell him about the drugs, but his attitude got my back up and I just wanted him to leave now. If he was as smart as he obviously thought he was, then he could find out for himself. I didn't want to help.

He was trying for a smile, I think, but it came off more as a sneer, and he got up. "Thank you for your time, Miss Kavanaugh."

As I walked him to the front door, I saw him glancing around the house.

I couldn't help myself.

"Say hi to Shawna."

For a second, I saw his surprise; then he caught himself and masked it. "I will," he said as he went out the door.

I shut it behind him and leaned against it, relieved he was gone. Tim came out wearing a pair of Dockers, his hair wet. He clapped his hands together. "That was pretty good, little sis," he said. "Thanks."

"You won't get into trouble, will you?"

"He got to see the house, see if anything's changed since Shawna moved out, and he can report back to her. He got what he came for."

"You think he just came here for that? Not to talk to me?"

Tim laughed. "He could've just called and asked you to come to the department." But his expression grew serious again. "You should've told him about the drag queen's friends."

"I don't know if that has anything to do with this."

"True, but you didn't tell him everything you found out, and it could come back and bite you on the ass."

I slugged him on the shoulder. "You mean it might come back and bite *you* on the ass."

"Yeah, okay, maybe I meant that," he said sheepishly.

I walked back into the kitchen and put my cup on the table, noticing now that DeBurra hadn't taken the sketch with him. I picked it up and raised my eyebrows. "Do you think he just forgot this?"

Tim looked genuinely puzzled. "That's a clue. He wouldn't want to leave that behind."

I grabbed it and went toward the door. DeBurra's car was backing out. I ran down the driveway, waving the sketch. He rolled the window down as I approached.

"What is it?" he asked, irritation lacing his words.

I shoved the drawing at him. "You forgot this."

"Why would I need that?"

"It's a clue."

He snorted. "I know what Wesley Lambert looks like. I certainly don't need any amateur drawing of yours."

He gunned the accelerator, the car skidded into the street, and he took off with a cloud of exhaust following him.

Chapter 8

It was clear DeBurra was already on to Wesley Lambert for some reason, but Tim had no idea what sort of game he was playing. Tim promised to look Lambert up in the database when he got to work to see whether he had a rap sheet or some sort of alert out about him. He took the drawing with him.

I looked longingly at the mountains in the distance as I drove toward the Strip. Red Rock was beckoning. I hadn't been up there in a couple of weeks, and after the previous night I could have used some time chilling out. I wanted to fill my daypack with sandwiches and water and a sketchpad, and put on my too-expensive-but-I-couldn't-resist hiking boots.

Sometimes I sketched when I went up there, using pastels; their soft, pliable texture lent an Impressionistic look to my drawings. But most times, I just hiked, the desert hard beneath my boots, the air still enough so you could hear a coyote from miles away. The pale browns and pinks of the mountains were interrupted by bright red stripes, as if Christo had decided to wrap them, like he'd wrapped those islands off Miami years ago.

During my first visit there, the ranger told me Red Rock was where the West Coast had ended once upon a time, which was why the mountains looked the way they did. I tried to imagine the ocean licking the same rocks that I gripped, the brown desert floor once the sea floor.

I was deep enough in thought that I missed my turn onto Koval Lane, which ran behind the MGM, Planet Hollywood, Paris, Bally's, the Flamingo, Harrah's, and finally the Venetian. I had to take the Strip now, which was annoying because of all the traffic and the lights. I was stopped at the one just before the turn off Tropicana. The MGM golden lion loomed large over me, a replica of the Statue of Liberty at New York New York across the way. Through the power of suggestion, I had a sudden hankering for bagels. Real bagels, like I could get at Il Fornaio Panetteria.

Parking was usually an issue, but for some reason the parking gods were with me today, and I managed to easily slide into a free self-parking slot in New York New York's parking garage.

Il Fornaio Panetteria was near the casino, which was enclosed in what the developers had hoped would look like Central Park. Fake trees hung over craps and blackjack and roulette tables, brownstone and other building facades on either side. Somehow it seemed wrong. The casino shouldn't be immersed in the illusion; it should just be what it is: a casino without all the bells and whistles. Not like the gamblers really cared.

I walked up the fake sidewalk to Il Fornaio Panetteria, a small shop that sold real New York bagels, fresh fruit cups, muffins, pastries, and coffee. I bought a dozen bagels to bring back with me to the shop and added some cream cheese to the tab. Despite the eggs Tim had served me that morning, I was still hungry, my mouth salivating as I watched the girl behind the counter fill the bag.

On impulse, I decided to play hooky for a few minutes and sit and enjoy one of the bagels there. I took out one with poppy seeds, slathered some cream cheese on it, and savored it. Since I'd have to wait to go to Red Rock, this was going to have to be my Mecca for the moment.

Until my cell phone rang.

I dug it out of my messenger bag and looked at the caller ID. Bitsy.

"Hey, there. Picking up some bagels," I said, hoping that would appease her if she was upset I wasn't there yet.

"Good idea," she said. "Just wanted to let you know your noon appointment canceled."

I sighed, but I'd been doubtful that she'd show. Emily Sokol was just eighteen and had been at the shop the day before with a gaggle of friends egging her on to get a tattoo. I told her that a tattoo is private—and permanent. If she had any second thoughts about it, she shouldn't do it. Emily insisted that she wanted to go through with it, told me she wanted a butterfly in pinks and golds. I said I'd do a sketch and we'd look at it when she came back, to make sure it was what she envisioned.

Guess not.

Now I had a little more time to spare. I was only halfway done with my bagel.

"Joel's here. He told me about the sketch you did last night," Bitsy said. "Like a police artist or something."

"Yeah. And that detective who I talked to last night came to the house this morning." I quickly told her about Tim and Shawna and how DeBurra knew who the mystery guy was all along but didn't let on. "His drag name is Shanda Leer." I chuckled. "Get it? Chandelier?" I had no idea why this amused me so much. "Bits?" I asked, wondering whether the call was dropped, it got so quiet.

"Well, that police detective was here already. About ten minutes ago. I told him you'd be here soon, and he said he'd be back."

I sat up straighter, the anger moving through me. Was DeBurra going to start stalking me? First he comes to my house, and now to my shop? He was the one who wouldn't take the sketch. That wasn't my fault.

I tried to calm myself down by thinking that maybe he'd changed his mind about the sketch and he figured he'd catch me at the shop.

That must be it. Although something was still nagging at me about him.

I stared at the last bit of my bagel. Well, he was just going to have to wait for me. "When did he say he'd come back?" I asked.

"He didn't." Bitsy paused. "What's going on, Brett?"

"I have no idea. I'll be there as soon as I can." I stuffed the last of the bagel in my mouth as I closed the phone.

While the gods had been on my side today as far as parking, it seemed that's all they were going to be good for.

I put the bag with the bagels in it in my messenger bag. Times like this, I needed a real backpack. Instead of slinging the bag across my chest, like I usually did, I just put it over my shoulder and let it bounce against my side.

I wandered past the gaming tables in the faux Central Park on the way out to my car. There were a few early-bird diehards eager to make their fortunes. I passed a couple of blackjack tables, ignored the craps, and stopped at the roulette table. The dealer was spinning the wheel.

But I wasn't watching the wheel. I stared at one of the players, a young guy, maybe late twenties, slight build, wearing a white, almost see-through T-shirt that clung to his frame. His arms were bare.

Except for the queen-of-hearts playing-card tattoo on his inside right forearm.

"Care to place a bet?"

The dealer's voice shook me out of my trance. He was staring at me expectantly, as was the young man with the tattoo and an elderly gentleman wearing a straw hat.

"Um, just watching," I said.

"Need a chip?" The young man tossed a chip toward me, and instinctively I reached out and caught it. Nice to know something stuck from those couple years playing softball in middle school.

"Thanks, I guess," I said, moving closer to the table, noticing that he wasn't looking at me like I could identify him in a lineup. That was a good thing. The bad thing was, I had no idea just how to play this game. I turned the chip over in my hand and saw it was worth fifty bucks. Startled, I looked at the young man and held it out toward him. "I can't take this."

He grinned and with a little wave of his hand indicated that the huge pile of chips on the table was his. "I'm on a streak. Have at it," he said.

"Place your bet," the dealer said.

I studied the table, covered with red and black squares and numbers. "Why not," I muttered, and put the chip on 18 red. It was a shot.

The wheel spun and then slowed. It stopped. The little ball fell into a slot.

Eighteen red.

My mouth hung open as the dealer added some chips to the one I'd had. The young man still won—he had put his chips on red—but I wasn't exactly sure how all this worked.

"Where'd you get your ink?" I asked as we both moved our chips to other spots.

"Sssh," the older gentleman said.

But the young man obviously didn't have any respect for his elders. "Murder Ink. Know it?"

Murder Ink was owned by Jeff Coleman. We had a complicated relationship in that while we were competitors and started out hating each other, we were growing on each other. His mother had done the Napoleon ink on my calf.

I nodded, and the wheel spun.

Go figure, but I won again. My head told me that I should quit while I was ahead, but my adrenaline was racing and I couldn't help myself.

"Why don't you go for a split?" the young man asked, and when he saw my confusion explained I could place chips on two adjoining numbers.

Why not?

I won again. The chips were piling up. The young man had started betting with me. I'd forgotten about the bagels in my bag, how I had to get to my shop, why Frank DeBurra was stalking me. All I could think about was the game. I kept moving my chips around the table, and each square I put them on won. Well, not all of them, but because I'd done the split I was doing better than if I was going for broke on just one square each time. My heart was pounding with each spin of the wheel, every time the dealer said, "Place your bet."

The young man with the ink and I kept winning. The elderly gentleman disappeared at some point, and a few other people wandered over. And then the spell broke. Not because I lost. But because the young man spoke.

"We're doing great, aren't we, Brett?"

I hadn't told him my name.

Chapter 9

It was like the volume had been pushed up to eleven. While my blood pressure had been racing with the adrenaline of the game, my heart began to pound even harder as I tried to catch my breath.

He realized his mistake. His eyes grew wide, and he swept up his chips faster than I could get mine.

Sure, I could've just left them. I'd been playing with his chip initially, after all, but he'd *given* it to me. I grabbed my chips, too, shoving them into my bag around the bagel bag, and rushed off after him.

He wasn't heading to the cashier, but up the escalator, taking two steps at a time.

I had longer legs than he did and gained ground, noticing that he didn't have a bag like I did, and he was trying to put the chips in his pockets. He had a lot of chips—a lot more than I did—and he wasn't completely successful, leaving a trail of them sort of like Hansel and Gretel in the forest.

He pushed open the glass doors and went outside.

I followed him out, but the sun was blinding, so I blinked a few times to focus, glanced around, and saw him running across the concrete footbridge that connected New York New York with the MGM Grand. A huge video display ahead of me advertised Journey's next concert in Vegas. So they were still performing. Who knew?

I sprinted off the concrete as I followed the mysterious guy.

He took a quick right, and as I got closer I saw him running down the escalator steps.

I went after him.

At the bottom, he was crossing the street, going back toward New York New York, making a circle. It was harder this way, though, since dodging traffic was part of the equation.

He crossed between cars, and I got lucky because the light had turned and the traffic was stopped.

I kept my eye on him and turned right toward the Brooklyn Bridge.

Of course it's not the real one, but a smaller, accurate replica.

It was the first time I was going across it, but I didn't have time to stop to admire the workmanship, which was pretty remarkable. Just as I reached the end of the bridge and was about to hit the sidewalk, a family of six, including a baby stroller, stepped into my path. I tried to sidestep them, but I'd been going too fast and found myself spinning like that roulette wheel toward the ground.

The bagels broke my fall.

The father leaned down. "Are you all right?" he asked, although I could see his wife frowning, wishing that he hadn't bothered to try to be a Good Samaritan in Sin City. Her eyes traveled over my tattoos disapprovingly.

"Yes, I'm fine, thank you," I said, and the wife looked surprised, as if she didn't think someone like me would be able to speak such good English and be so polite.

I brushed off my cotton skirt, noticing now that I'd skinned my knee and blood was trickling down the front of my leg. The family walked past me as I rummaged in my bag for a napkin from the bagel place.

I didn't even want to look at the bagels. It wouldn't be pretty.

I dabbed at the wound and looked up, trying to see whether the guy was anywhere in sight, but no. I'd lost him—and any chance of finding out how he knew my name. I thought about his ink and wondered if he was the guy from last night, the guy who shot Trevor with the cork.

I shook the thought away. Was I going to think that every guy with a queen-of-hearts tattoo had been the one who attacked Trevor last night? Odds were that Wesley Lambert was the true culprit, since he'd been poking around Chez Tango and had sent Trevor a warning through Eduardo. That would make the most sense. Kyle said he didn't remember Lambert having a tattoo, but he could've easily gotten one in the time since he'd last been at the club.

Something bugged me, though, about this roulette guy. The ink was in the right place; it was the same design I'd seen. And he knew my name.

I had to get back to my car, which was in the self-parking garage. The sun was blasting, and even though late September isn't as steamy as, say, July, the asphalt absorbed the heat and sent ribbons of it into the air.

The chips made little clicking noises in my bag. I wondered how much they were worth. I pushed the glass doors to the casino open, and as I passed the escalator I noticed a couple of stray chips on the up side, the ones the guy had dropped. For a second, I had a crazy thought that I could go back and collect them, adding to my winnings.

I knew I shouldn't be so greedy. Technically, the chips I won might not even be mine because I wasn't playing with my own money. And considering what had just happened with that guy, I was uncomfortable with the whole situation.

Still, I found myself at the cashier window, pushing the chips through the little slot. While I waited for the cashier to count them, I looked around at the fake trees, the fake brownstones, the fake New York City. I missed the city. The real one. There was something vibrant about it that no other city could match.

I was distracted by my thoughts enough so when the cashier pushed the wads of money through the slot, it surprised me. I glanced at the receipt.

I'd won more than sixty thousand dollars.

I stopped breathing for a second.

The cashier grinned. "Congratulations," he said.

"Thanks," I said, carefully putting the bills in my bag next to the smashed bagels. I needed to get to a bank before I got mugged.

"Where have you been?" Bitsy demanded when I walked into the shop about an hour later.

I didn't answer right away. I wasn't quite sure how to explain everything so it wouldn't sound like I was nuts.

My eyes skirted around the shop, my home away from home, checking everything out, sort of like when a cat goes on the prowl to make sure everything's still where it was an hour ago. The blond laminate flooring was sleek; the mahogany desk near the door was shining. A spray of light pink orchids from Bitsy's greenhouse gave the place elegance, as did Ace's new paintings we'd just hung: comic-book versions of Caravaggio's *Lute Player*, Dürer's *Adoration of the Magi*, Holbein's *Henry VIII*, and Corot's *View of Venice*—which offset the canal and gondolas and St. Mark's Square just outside our shop at the Venetian Grand Canal Shoppes.

Four private rooms were closed off in the middle of the shop, and a waiting area fitted with a black leather sofa and glass-topped coffee table was behind the rooms to the left. A staff room was to the right, and an office off that. It was classy, no flash—stock tattoos—lining the walls like in a street shop. We prided ourselves on the custom designs we created. And since Charlotte had arrived, we'd bought a new Apple computer for even more design options. I didn't have a background in computer graphics—I was a painter—but Charlotte had been teaching herself and had begun to show us some of her tricks. Joel was getting into it more than anyone; he'd started in street shops and didn't have formal art training like Ace and me, but he somehow managed to take his raw talent and transfer it to the computer.

"So?" Bitsy asked, following me into the staff room, bringing her small stool with her. She needed the stool to compensate for her height, but her habit of dragging it along the floor caused it to squeak in that fingernails-on-the-blackboard kind of way that made me cringe.

"I had to go to the bank," I said, trying not to meet her eyes as I pulled the bag of bagels out of my messenger bag and set it on the small table we used for eating. We also had a light table, but that was for work.

"What happened to that?" Bitsy asked, staring at the bag, which had ripped and now bled portions of onion, poppy seed, and sesame seed bagels on the table.

Ripping the bag even further, I saw that the container of cream cheese was also a victim of my fall: It had exploded all over the bagels and the bag, leaving a white, creamy mess.

"I fell." I lifted my knee to show her my wound.

"You better start at the beginning," she said, shoving the stool to the side and plopping herself down on one of the chairs as I tried to clean up the bagel mess.

"Well, I stopped for bagels—you know that—and then I got a little distracted by the roulette table." Her eyebrows went up, but before she could say anything, I continued. "There was a guy there, a guy with a queen-of-hearts playing card on his arm, and I stopped, and he gave me a fifty-dollar chip, and I put it on a square, and it won, and then I played again and again and again, and I won over sixty thousand dollars." I sank into the chair opposite Bitsy as I took a deep breath.

"No, really, Brett, what happened?"

She thought I was kidding.

So I told her about the guy knowing my name and about running and falling because of the stroller and the woman who looked at me like I was from Mars.

"Sixty thousand?"

I nodded, unable to believe it, either.

"Remind me to go with you the next time you're playing the tables."

She wasn't kidding.

"So how did he know your name?"

"I have no idea. He ran before I could ask him."

"So he knows that he shouldn't have known your name."

"He might be the guy with the cork last night."

"The guy in the picture you drew?"

"No, a different one."

She snorted. "So there are two?"

"Maybe."

It all sounded so far-fetched.

Bitsy got up. "Joel's finishing up with a client, Ace has gone who knows where, probably that oxygen bar to get his fix, Charlotte called in, said she was going to spend the day with Trevor. Guess she brought him home from the hospital this morning; everything's fine."

But everything wasn't fine. At least not in my world. I was sixty thousand dollars richer because of a stranger who knew my name.

And then I thought of something.

He said he'd gotten his tattoo at Murder Ink. I could call Jeff Coleman and see whether he knew the guy.

Could it be that easy?

Bitsy was picking at one of the bagels, sweeping it across some of the loose cream cheese. She stuck it in her mouth and nodded. "Good," she said through the poppy seeds.

Nice to know they still tasted okay, even though they looked like a cement roller had run over them.

We heard the front door buzzer, and Bitsy went out to see who'd come in. I took the wad of cream cheese–covered paper towels and threw it in the trash.

"Brett?" Bitsy had returned, sticking her head in the staff room door. "Someone's here to see you."

I didn't have a client scheduled for another hour, but Bitsy didn't hang around for me to ask who it was. I followed her out.

Detective Frank DeBurra was standing by the door.

Chapter 10

He was becoming my new best friend.

I didn't like it.

But I admittedly was curious as to why he would show up both at my house and now here, at The Painted Lady.

"Yes?" I asked. "I thought I answered all your questions."

His ears were more pronounced now, since his hair was slicked back, like he'd just taken a shower, making him look even more elfin. But a tall elf.

"Is there somewhere we can talk privately?" he asked, shooting a look at Bitsy that I didn't much like.

Bitsy noticed it, too, and she rolled her eyes at me behind his back. Being a little person, she's got to deal with that sort of thing a lot more than I do and she's pretty comfortable in her own skin.

I led Frank DeBurra to the back of the shop, to the office rather than the staff room, as if he'd suck all the creativity out of it and leave us with nothing.

When I settled myself in the leather chair behind the desk, indicating that he should sit on the folding chair across from me, I said, "Okay. What do you want?"

He gave a little snort accompanied by something he probably thought passed for a smile. "I'd like that sketch back."

Uh-oh. Tim had it. I had a feeling that DeBurra might not like that.

"It's home," I said.

"Then can you go home later and get it for me?"

It was the way he asked that made me begin to wonder whether he didn't already know that Tim had it. That he was testing me, in some sick way.

"I can't get away today. I've got clients coming in."

"Where's your brother?"

"Not my turn to watch him." Okay, so it was a little flip, but this guy brought out the worst in me.

He really did smile this time, but it wasn't a warm smile; it didn't spread to his eyes. "Funny."

"I thought you said you didn't need the sketch." I couldn't help myself. Really.

"Maybe I want to frame it and put it on my wall."

So we were both baiting each other. This wouldn't get us anywhere. I got up. "Detective, unless you're here for some practical purpose, I have work to do."

He stood up. He was wearing the same frayed sport jacket from last night. I wondered about Shawna. She'd been into material things. This guy didn't look like he could buy a loaf of bread. Maybe he was good in bed.

Yuck. Definitely did not want to go there.

I went over to the door and opened it. "Thank you for stopping by."

"I need to ask a couple of questions about your employee, Charlotte Sampson." Frank DeBurra leaned over past me and shut the door again, indicating that I should sit down.

I did because I was too surprised not to.

"What about her?" I asked.

"What do you know of her background?"

I thought about Charlotte, the first time she'd come in for ink. She'd asked me to fix a heart she'd tattooed herself on her wrist, sort of like the one I'd done on my own. She was studying to be an accountant at the University of Nevada, Las Vegas. She graduated but admitted she didn't want to work with numbers; she wanted to work here. I hired her as a trainee.

I didn't know what this detective wanted with Charlotte, so all I said was, "She was going to be an accountant but decided to become a tattooist." I had another thought. "Why don't you talk to her yourself?"

"Is she here?"

His tone was so casual, my antennae went up. Something wasn't right. I hesitated for a second before saying, "She's spending the day with her friend Trevor McKay, you know, the guy who got hit with the cork last night."

"He got released from the hospital this morning," De-Burra said.

I nodded, not sure where this was going.

"He left alone."

"Maybe she's meeting him at his place." Although that's not what she told Bitsy on the phone.

Frank DeBurra leaned forward in his chair, his elbows on his knees, his hands clasped together in front of him. His eyes met mine.

I had a bad feeling.

"Charlotte Sampson is wanted for questioning in an incident at a pawnshop this morning."

Chapter 11

I couldn't catch my breath. Finally, I sputtered, "Excuse me?"

"You heard me," he said flatly.

"An incident? What type of incident?"

"She hasn't been here at all this morning?" He was being dodgy.

"No."

"You haven't seen her?"

"Not since last night. What's this all about?" I was going to keep asking until he answered me.

"I'm not at liberty to say."

"Are you sure it's Charlotte you're looking for?" I couldn't wrap my head around this.

"Those derringer tattoos on her arms are very distinct."

I'd inked those derringers myself.

My brain was skipping so fast over a million thoughts, like a stone in a rocky riverbed. I was thinking about pawn-shops and how Wesley Lambert had been poking around the club yesterday, saying something about a mistake with something Trevor had pawned. Charlotte had spent quite a bit of time with Trevor in the last twenty-four hours.

"Wesley Lambert," I said.

"Hmm?" He acted like he didn't know what I was in-sinuating, but a flicker of his eye told me we were on the same page.

"Do you think this has something to do with Wesley Lambert? He was at Chez Tango talking about pawnshops."

"Does she have a locker or anything here? Any personal items?"

His change of subject threw me for a second. I thought about her room, which was just next to this office. But I couldn't have him poking around in there. "No," I lied, hoping he wouldn't see through me. "She's just a trainee. She works wherever we have room at the moment."

He pursed his mouth, like he knew. But instead of calling me on it, he stood. "Okay, well, if she contacts you or comes in here, I expect you to call me." Then he handed me a business card, the one I'd wanted last night but he hadn't given me. Guess I was more important to him today. "You're close enough to the law to know what the punishment is for obstruction."

A direct reference to Tim.

But obstruction? How serious was this?

I didn't get a chance to ask, however, because Frank De-Burra strode across my blond laminate flooring and went out the front glass door so quickly, he didn't even say goodbye. Bitsy watched after him, her mouth forming a perfect "O."

"What was that all about?" she asked.

I frowned. "I wish I knew. You were eavesdropping."

"And wouldn't you? He comes in here like gangbusters and I'm not supposed to make sure he's not beating the crap out of you back there?"

"Isn't that a little extreme?"

"Seems like it's serious, whatever it is," Bitsy said.

"I guess. He wanted to see her stuff. I don't get that. What's he fishing for? It doesn't make any sense. But if she calls or comes in, we're supposed to call him. I don't think so." I waved his card. "He wouldn't give it to me last night."

Bitsy took it and stuck it under the phone. "We'll leave it here," she said matter-of-factly. "So we all know where it is and we can call when we hear from Charlotte."

I knew that was her out. The card could get lost, easily.

Even though I didn't trust DeBurra, he had planted some doubts about Charlotte. Why had she lied about picking up Trevor and bringing him home this morning?

It was exactly those doubts that made me push open the door to her room and stand on the threshold as I took everything in.

She'd taken a fancy to a couple of Ace's smaller works. They weren't his comic-book versions of classic paintings; instead, they were his own cartoon creations: a superhero rat and a rooster playing baseball. I'm not one to judge someone's artwork, but I was glad they were in here and not out where the public could see them.

Charlotte's own artwork hung on the walls, too. She created geometric and tribal designs in acrylics and then re-created them as tattoos.

The chair almost glistened, it was so clean; Charlotte's inkpots and tattoo machine were lined up along the waist-high counter. On a shelf below that, she had a supply of disposable needles, some stencils were scattered, and a cup held some fine-point markers.

It was clean, thanks most likely to Bitsy's efforts, and organized, again Bitsy's doing. Other than the paintings, there were no personal items.

I had a client in half an hour, so I went into the staff room and sat at the light table to finish up a stencil of palm trees, dice, and Hello Kitty. About twenty minutes later, Joel wandered in with a box of doughnuts, unaware that I'd brought in smashed bagels. He took one of each.

Joel had started Weight Watchers, but we hadn't seen any difference.

I raised my eyebrows when he took a bite of bagel.

"Oh, don't get on my case," he chided. "I count my points."

"And you probably round down, too," I said.

He made a face at me.

I didn't want to get into it any further, so I told him about Frank DeBurra and Charlotte.

Joel actually stopped eating as I told him.

Bitsy stuck her head in the door and nodded at me. "She's here." She meant my client.

I glanced at the clock. Hello Kitty was just about done. "Tell her I'll be a few. She can hang in the waiting area."

Bitsy disappeared.

"Looking good," Joel said, leaning over my shoulder, getting a little doughnut dust on the light table.

I brushed it off. "I don't want the stencil messed up. Stay over there if you're eating."

"So this is the gambling Hello Kitty? I've never seen that one before." Joel spoke as he moved over to the staff table and sat down.

"Hello Kitty likes Vegas," I said. "She's one hot cat." As I said it, I thought about Rebecca Sinclair, my client. Nice girl, first tattoo. As I surveyed my work, I didn't think this would have to be one she'd regret. Hello Kitty was always in style.

I finished up the stencil and carefully cut around it before bringing it out to Rebecca, whom I beckoned into my room.

"Here it is," I said, showing her. "And you want it just below your shoulder on your back on the left side?"

Rebecca nodded. She was smiling, but her mouth was tight. First time was always a little nerve-wracking.

With a baby wipe, I washed down the area where I'd do the ink and shaved it with a disposable razor so it would be completely hair free. I then rolled a little glycerin-based deodorant over the same area before placing the stencil down, rubbing it so it would transfer onto her skin. I pulled it off carefully, then surveyed it. Perfect.

I handed Rebecca a hand mirror and told her to go out and look at it in the full-length mirror in the waiting area. While she was gone, I organized my inks, took a new needle out of a package, and slid it into my tattoo machine.

"It looks good," she said softly when she returned.

"It'll be fine," I said as soothingly as I could as I put the chair flat so she could lie down on her stomach. "You'll feel it sting at first—I won't lie about that—but then your endorphins will kick in and it won't hurt as much." I couldn't tell her it wouldn't hurt at all. In fact, tattoos over bone hurt more than when they were inked on more fleshy areas. But she'd been insistent about placement.

When she was as comfortable as she would be, I pulled on my latex gloves, dipped the needle in black ink, pressed the foot pedal, and the machine whirred to life. I pressed the needle to her skin and felt her jump slightly.

"Try to stay as still as possible," I advised as I began outlining Hello Kitty.

By the time I started filling in the palm trees, Rebecca was chatting up a storm, telling me about the classes she was taking at the university.

It didn't take too long before I was taping plastic wrap over the tattoo and handing Rebecca a typewritten sheet of paper that explained how to take care of it for the next few days. She shouldn't keep the plastic wrap on long, just until she got home. Washing it with unscented antibacterial soap and an antibacterial gel would be the next step, but it would still peel like a sunburn.

"It'll look a little faded for a while, but don't worry. The color will come back once it's healed."

I followed her out to the front desk, where Bitsy would take her credit card.

But Bitsy wasn't there.

Trevor McKay was.

Chapter 12

"Where's Bitsy?" I asked as I took the credit card machine out of the drawer in the mahogany desk.

"Joel needed her for something. I said I'd wait," Trevor, aka Britney Brassieres, said. Without his Britney costume, he looked like any normal guy: close-cropped bleached blond hair, brown eyes, long nose, short chin. He was slightly shorter than me, and I stand about five-nine. He wore his clothes—a pair of faded jeans and loose T-shirt—with casual style.

I'd asked him why he decided to do drag, and he said it was a lark at first, a Halloween costume. But something had clicked; MissTique saw him and convinced him to try performing. He loved it, the acting, the dancing, the lip-synching.

"Not that I want to be a woman," he'd said. "Believe me, I like being a boy."

He looked all boy today. I gave him a look that I hoped would convey that he was to stay put while I took care of Rebecca. It was just a few minutes; Rebecca signed her receipt and left with a smile.

I took a breath when the door closed, turned to Trevor, and asked, "Are you okay?" His shirt didn't conceal the outline of a bandage in the center of his chest.

He saw me looking at it, and he touched it gently. "Broke skin. Can you believe it? Got blood on my dress. I'm not sure I'll be able to get it out."

I murmured my sympathy, then asked, "Where's Charlotte?"

"That's what I was going to ask you," he said. "I'm worried about her. She said she'd stay at the hospital with me, but they wouldn't let her. She called early this morning, said she'd come get me, but she never did. I've tried her cell, but there's no answer, just voice mail. That's not like her."

None of this was like her.

I shook the thoughts away. "The police were here looking for her."

Trevor's eyes skittered across the wall behind me. "What for?"

Hmmm. Did he know something? "Said they wanted to question her about some sort of incident at a pawnshop this morning." I mentally kicked myself for not getting the name of the place out of DeBurra.

Trevor still didn't meet my eye. "Really?" He didn't sound too surprised, but he was trying. I could tell.

I played along. I told him the little that Frank DeBurra had said, how he wanted to see her things. I studied his facial expressions as I spoke, and now I noticed that his eyes were a little too bright and his skin was flushed.

"A guy was looking for you yesterday at the club. Wesley Lambert."

"Wes? Looking for me?"

"You know him?"

Again he looked a little uncomfortable. "Sure. But I haven't seen him in ages."

"He was talking about how you'd pawned something, but he seemed to think it was a mistake. Do you think Charlotte went to the pawnshop about that and something happened while she was there?"

Trevor wiped some sweat off his forehead. "I'm not feeling very good."

I didn't want to let him off that easy, but he really wasn't looking well.

"Are you okay?"

He took a deep breath. "Maybe if I sit down. Last night took a lot out of me."

I motioned that he should sit in the leather chair behind the desk, and he plopped down like a rock, his head in his hands.

Bitsy and Joel came out of the staff room. "You're still here," Bitsy said to Trevor, adding, "Are you sick?"

Trevor looked up, his eyes now twice as bright. "I think so."

"You should've stayed home. You could've just called to ask about Charlotte," I said.

"Charlotte? What about Charlotte?" Bitsy and Joel asked the same thing just seconds apart, giving it sort of an echo effect.

"Charlotte was supposed to pick Trevor up this morning but didn't show," I said, then turned back to Trevor. "What pawnshop did you take the pin to?" I couldn't be a hundred percent sure that it would be the same pawnshop Charlotte had been to this morning, but it was a place to start, anyway, even if it wasn't.

"Pin?"

I didn't know whether it was because he was ill or because he was just being cagey, but he was certainly not answering my questions.

"Oh, come on, I know about the queen-of-hearts pin from the fund-raiser. I just need to know which pawnshop. Maybe this is all just a huge misunderstanding. I'm sure there's some explanation." Even as I said it, I knew that if Charlotte had gone there to straighten out Trevor's "mistake," it had gone wrong somehow.

"It's up on Las Vegas Boulevard, just up from the Sahara." Trevor had turned green. "I think I'm going to be sick."

Joel was one step ahead of him. He'd slung his arm under Trevor's armpits and was carrying him to the bathroom.

I'd wanted to ask Trevor whether he knew anyone with a tattoo of a queen-of-hearts playing card, but the sounds that were coming from the bathroom indicated that he wasn't in a state to have a chat at the moment.

Joel emerged from the back of the shop. He was moving faster than I'd ever seen him move, and his expression showed his worry. "I think we should call for an ambulance," he said.

"It's that bad?" I asked, but Bitsy was one step ahead of me.

She had the phone in her hand and was giving our location.

The paramedics showed up in less than ten minutes. Trevor was still in the bathroom. I hoped our next client would be late, because Trevor being sick wouldn't be good for business.

Two paramedics guided a gurney toward the back of the shop, and after several minutes they wheeled Trevor out quickly. Mall shoppers stopped and watched the gurney rolling off into the distance. One paramedic stuck around and asked questions: When did Trevor become ill? What had he been like when he arrived? How long had he been in the bathroom?

We answered as well as we could. I wanted to tell him I still had questions of my own, but they would have to wait until Trevor was feeling better.

"He was in the hospital overnight," I offered and found myself telling the paramedic about the incident at Chez Tango last night. "But that wouldn't make him sick like this, would it?" I asked.

The paramedic shook his head. "You never know. Or it could be flu." He added that maybe we should disinfect everything, just in case Trevor was contagious. Great.

He left Bitsy and Joel and me staring at one another, looking at our hands—had we touched anything Trevor had touched? Contagious was never good.

The phone startled us. Bitsy answered, "The Painted Lady," then listened a few seconds, said, "Okay," and hung up.

She turned back to us.

"Client?" Joel asked.

She shook her head.

"That was Ace. He's with Charlotte."

Chapter 13

Ace didn't tell Bitsy where they were, just that Charlotte was okay and knew the police were looking for her. He said he'd call back later.

Talk about obstruction of justice.

I tried his cell, but it was turned off. I left a message.

I needed to know more about what happened at that pawnshop this morning. I wouldn't get anything out of De-Burra. But I might get something out of my brother.

Unfortunately, I got his voice mail. I left a cryptic message and hung up.

"What's my schedule like this afternoon?" I asked Bitsy.

She leafed through the appointment book. "You've got a client at seven." Bitsy tossed her head back at Joel. "You've got someone coming in any moment."

Shoot. I'd wanted to ask Joel to come with me when I hunted down that pawnshop, but I'd have to go alone.

He knew what I was up to.

"Don't go playing detective, Brett," Joel said, putting his arm around my shoulders.

"I have to do something," I said. "And when I see Ace, I'm going to wring his neck for not telling us where he and Charlotte are." I gave Bitsy a glare. "I don't know what you were thinking, letting him just hang up without getting any information out of him."

"He said to trust him. I do, so there." She stuck her tongue out at me.

It looked so ridiculous, I couldn't help but chuckle. "I guess I'm just on edge," I said, and Red Rock Canyon flashed through my thoughts again.

Bitsy went off to try to disinfect the bathroom and get the stench out of the air that we now noticed was hanging like an invisible cloud.

I went into the staff room to get my bag, and the tracing paper on the light table caught my eye. I didn't have the sketch of Wesley Lambert, but I had a name. I could ask about him. But the guy this morning at the roulette table was still nameless. I couldn't help but think that his ink was a clue; he was possibly the champagne shooter from last night. I wondered whether I could make a sketch of his face, too, and get an ID on him.

I put my bag down and sat at the table, grabbing a piece of paper and a pencil. I closed my eyes and willed myself to see the guy's face. I began to sketch.

I'd had to do a similar exercise in school. It wasn't easy, and the face I'd drawn was all over the place.

Like this one. I peeked.

I erased a few lines, drew new ones; the guy's face was etched in my memory, and an image slowly began to emerge. I couldn't remember some of his features—the cheekbones might be too wide—but others, like the length of his nose and his eyes, were clear.

Bitsy walked through the room spraying Lysol. I coughed.

"I thought you left," she said, standing behind me.

"Just trying something," I said.

She looked over my shoulder. "Who is he?"

"The guy at the roulette wheel this morning."

"He looks like a girl."

A closer look indicated that she was right. If I drew long locks of hair, he definitely would be mistaken for a girl.

He was that pretty.

Why hadn't I noticed that this morning? Oh, yeah, I

was possessed by the gambling devil and distracted by that spinning wheel.

I drew the spikes of hair, and he began to look a little like Annie Lennox.

"He looked more like a boy in person," I said to Bitsy. This could all be a skewed image in my head; memory was a slippery thing.

I didn't have time for more than this, though. It would have to do. I folded the drawing up and stuck it in my bag. "I'm off," I said.

"You'll be back for your appointment?"

"Yeah. Thanks for holding down the fort," I said as I swept past her and went out of the shop.

I heard music—a harpsichord maybe, definitely violins—and I looked over at St. Mark's Square—not the real one, but the Vegas imitation—to see a group of costumed dancers bowing and curtsying to one another. A gondola glided by on the canal, the gondolier expertly guiding it. The ceiling was a bright blue, with fluffy white clouds that seemed to move. Sometimes when I stopped for a moment and took it all in, rather than just as a backdrop, I could see why the tourists would fall for it. Even though it seemed so wrong on so many levels.

There was a small strip mall on the far side of the Sahara. It housed a convenience store, a nail salon, and a pawnshop. Cash & Carry. According to the signs in the window, they'd take my gold and silver jewelry off my hands for a good price.

I had rows of silver hoops lining each ear, but I didn't think any of them were worth anything. I didn't wear rings because I'd found early on that they get caught in the latex gloves. My watch was a simple Timex. It kept on ticking.

At home, in my jewelry box, was the engagement ring Paul had given me. He hadn't wanted it back. I tried to give it to him when I broke it off. Maybe Cash & Carry could give me a good price for it. Although with all that money I'd won at roulette, I certainly didn't need to pawn it.

I parked next to a beat-up old blue pickup truck, my Mustang looking out of place here and way too classy. I made sure my CDs were out of sight before I locked all the doors.

The pawnshop door and front windows were lined with bars. I pushed the door open and stepped inside.

A long glass display case stretched from my right all the way around the perimeter of the room. Inside, stones sparkled, timepieces ticked, delicate china pieces leaned easily against velveteen holders, old toys in mint condition were positioned just so.

On the walls, electric guitars, light fixtures, paintings, and sports team jerseys hung suspended from hooks. Mountain bikes were stacked three deep behind the display case at the back of the shop. Televisions and VCRs and DVD players were stacked on shelves.

It was neat and orderly. Not what I was expecting.

A big man—not fat, just muscular—came out from behind a door I hadn't noticed and walked toward me, behind the case. His bald head shone in the glow of the bright lights; he had tattoo sleeves and wore a Yankees T-shirt.

"Can I help you?" he asked.

"I'm looking for Wesley Lambert," I said.

He frowned. "Who?"

Okay, so maybe this wasn't the place. But I had another idea. "Trevor McKay sent me over here."

At the mention of Trevor's name, the man's face grew dark, his eyes narrowing at me. "What does he want?"

"He's pawned a pin here; it's got stones, and it looks like a queen-of-hearts playing card."

"He hasn't been in with that in a while."

"Are you sure?"

"Listen, lady, I've helped him out. I know he needs the cash, and for some reason he always comes back for it, so if I give him a hundred bucks I know he'll end up paying me more than I paid him because of interest."

Interest?

He must have seen the question on my face, because

he sighed and said, "Say you want to pawn something. I give you a percentage of what I think it's worth. You've got thirty days to come buy it back, for the same price I gave you plus interest."

So that's how it worked.

"Do a lot of people buy their own stuff back?"

He waved his hand to indicate everything in the shop. "Sometimes they do; sometimes they don't." He reached inside the glass display case and pulled out a pair of diamond studs that shone in the light. "These are a steal."

I studied them a second, then shook my head. "I'm not here to buy anything. I'm just trying to find Wesley Lambert."

"And I told you I don't know who that is."

As he said it, his eyes skirted over toward where he'd appeared from. Made me wonder whether he was lying, if Wesley wasn't back there somewhere. But I wasn't exactly sure how to find out unless this guy played along.

I figured I'd try to throw him off again, so I pulled the sketch I'd just made out of my bag. "Do you know this man?" I asked, showing it to him.

He glanced at it, and his face froze for a second; then he said, "What are you, police?"

I shook my head. "No. I own The Painted Lady, a tattoo shop."

He looked like he didn't believe me, but then his eyes ran up my arm and over the dragon head that stuck out of my tank top on my chest. He nodded. "You're Brett Kavanaugh."

I didn't like it that strangers knew my name.

Before I could say anything, he added, "Jeff Coleman talks about you."

Of course. Jeff. He hung with nefarious people; this didn't surprise me. Then I realized: The roulette guy had said Jeff did his ink. Maybe Jeff had mentioned me to him as well, and he just recognized me from a description. Maybe that's how he knew my name.

I began to feel a little silly.

Until I had another thought.

Why did the guy run, then? Why not just stick around and continue on our winning streak?

The pawnshop guy was looking at me expectantly.

Oh, right.

"You didn't by chance have some sort of . . . well . . . disturbance or something here this morning?" I asked.

"No. Should I have?"

"Guess not."

This guy wasn't any help. I stuffed the sketch back in my bag, said, "Thanks for your time," and walked toward the door.

As I stepped outside, a man was walking quickly to the pickup truck parked next to my Mustang. I took another step, and he spotted me. We weren't that far away from each other, and I recognized him.

It was the guy from the roulette table.

Chapter 14

My first thought was that I did a lousy job on that drawing. His eyes weren't nearly as close together as I'd remembered, and his nose was longer. But he *was* pretty.

And he was getting into the truck, a panicked look on his face.

I stepped up my speed and almost ran to the truck, which started to back away. I hit the hood and he honked the horn, startling me and rendering me momentarily deaf. I looked up into the cab and saw him grinning at me as the truck screeched out of the lot, heading north.

I got into the Mustang as quickly as I could, trying to keep the truck in sight. But by the time I got to the street, the pickup was gone.

I hung my head in defeat, my hands on the steering wheel. What to do now?

I could go back into Cash & Carry and try to lean on that big guy about the guy in the truck. I had a feeling he knew him. But I doubted he'd be willing to help me out.

I could drive around checking out all the city's pawnshops. That might take a while.

Or I could go up to Murder Ink and pump Jeff Coleman for information. We'd never been friends, but I'd helped him out over the summer and we now had a grudging respect for each other. He just might be able to ID that guy, if he'd done the ink.

I chose door number three.

Goodfellas Bail Bonds was next door to Murder Ink, and across the street was the Bright Lights Motel, whose name seemed an oxymoron. There was nothing bright about the dingy concrete building, and there were no lights. Just a bland sign that advertised HBO and hourly rates.

I shuddered as I parked in the motel's lot and crossed the street.

Jeff Coleman looked up when I came in. "Hey, Kavanaugh, what are you doing on the dark side?"

He was inking a guy's back—a basic skull and crossbones; couldn't he be more creative? Oh, yeah, Jeff only did flash, the stock tattoos that lined the walls of his shop.

"Got some questions."

The machine stopped whirring for a second as he frowned at me; then it started up again as he resumed what he'd been doing. "Pull up a chair."

While The Painted Lady has separate rooms for each tattooist and client for privacy, Jeff's shop let it all hang out in the open. There were three stations divided only by short cabinets and shelves, on which I noted the baby wipes, inkpots, piles of sterilized needles in their packages, and boxes of black latex gloves.

I have blue gloves—a little more cheery.

Jeff inherited his business from his mother, Sylvia, who was one of the women pioneers in the tattoo business. He was maybe ten years older than me, with a salt-and-pepper buzz cut and tattoos covering his arms and chest. He was a couple inches shorter than me and skinny, but looking at him now, I thought maybe he'd put on a little weight—or at least had been working out a bit.

A quick glance around told me that this was the only client at the moment, and Jeff was the only tattooist in the place. I grabbed a chair on wheels from one of the other stations and rolled it near Jeff.

He grinned at me. "Now you can see a master at work."

"Yeah, right," I said, although for someone who did only flash, Jeff did have a certain style, a way of shading and coloring that stood out. I would never tell him that, though. For sure he'd use it against me at some point.

I pulled the sketch of the pretty boy out of my bag and stretched my arm out so he could see it. "Do you know this guy?"

The machine stopped again. The client lying facedown on the flattened chair mumbled, "Are you done?"

"No," Jeff said, then saw my expression. "Not you." He turned back to his client. "No, we're not done yet. Give me a second, okay?" He peered more closely at the drawing. "Guy's eyes are too close together."

I felt my heart take a leap. "So you know him?"

"Did his ink. Queen of hearts. Maybe last year sometime?"

Sounded good to me, but . . .

"How do you remember?" Sometimes I couldn't remember what I had for lunch two days before.

He tapped the side of his head and smirked. "Bionic brain."

I made a face at him, and he chuckled.

"I remember because I did three of them at the same time."

"Huh?"

"There were three guys. All came in late, maybe two in the morning or so. I remember because two of them were dolled up, like women. Weird."

My heart jumped again.

"There were three?"

"Yeah. Hey, Kavanuagh, what's up? What do you want with a bunch of trannies?"

"They're not transvestites," I said patiently. "They're drag queens." At least I thought so. "There's a difference."

Jeff rolled his eyes. "Could've fooled me."

"This guy wasn't dressed up, though," I said.

"How do you know that?"

"If he was, then you wouldn't recognize him as a guy, only as a girl, right?"

He shrugged. "Okay, Kavanaugh, you're right. This guy wasn't in drag."

"Do you know this guy's name? Do you have a file?"

His expression grew concerned. "Why are you looking for him? What did he do?"

I figured I should keep it simple. "I met him this morning in New York New York. We were playing roulette."

Jeff's eyebrows shot up into his forehead. "You? Really?"

"So what's wrong with that? Can't I gamble?"

He shrugged. "You just don't seem to like it."

"And you're the big expert on what I like and don't like?"

"Don't get your panties in a bunch, Kavanaugh." He chuckled. "Your face turns red when you get mad."

I hadn't noticed before, but now I did: My face was hot, and I knew it must be almost as red as my hair. Jeff Coleman brought out the worst in me. I struggled to get back to the matter at hand.

"So the picture, the guy, what's his name?"

But he wasn't going to let it go.

"Did you win?"

"What?"

"Did you win? At roulette?"

I felt myself blush even deeper.

He let out a large chortle. "You did, didn't you? Kavanaugh, no one wins at roulette. At least not to live to tell about it."

Okay, I got it, the reference to Russian roulette. I wasn't born yesterday.

"How much did you win?"

"None of your business."

"You were playing with this guy?"

The conversation veered so fast back on track that I got dizzy for a second. I found myself telling him the whole story, how we kept winning, and then how he said my name and took off trailing chips when he realized his mistake.

"You inked those tran—I mean, drag queens—for that show, didn't you?" Jeff asked.

I nodded. "Yeah."

"And this guy was with drag queens when I inked him."

"Okay." And then I got it. "You think that he knew me because of Trevor and Stephan and Kyle?"

"If the dress fits."

I snorted. "Ha-ha, funny." I had another thought. "Did you tell him about me? I was talking to a guy in a pawnshop this morning who knew me because you'd told him about me and my ink."

"What are you doing in pawnshops?"

I shrugged, indicating I wasn't going to elaborate. He made a face at me.

"Okay, be that way. Maybe I'm just trying to help you out, get you some business."

"Don't do me any favors."

"Oh, I forgot, you're above all this." He cocked his head to indicate the flash on the walls. "So maybe I told a couple people about you."

"This guy, too?"

"Could be I mentioned you; I don't remember."

"But then why did he run away from me?"

"I'm not a freaking psychic, Kavanaugh." Jeff turned back to his client. "Ready?" he asked him, picking up his machine.

"Hey, you didn't tell me his name," I said. "Can you show me his file?"

"Client confidentiality," Jeff said, touching the needle to the guy's back again.

I couldn't fault him for not telling me. I probably wouldn't tell me, either. As tattoo artists, we do have an obligation to our clients to keep their information confidential, sort of like psychiatrists and doctors. Getting a tattoo is deeply personal, and I've had clients tell me stuff they'd probably never told anyone else. Still, I got up off the chair and shoved it away with maybe a little too much force. It rolled back toward the cabinet and slammed into it with a loud crash.

Jeff didn't even look up.

I slung my messenger bag across my chest and started to walk out. "Thanks for nothing," I tossed behind me.

"Rusty Abbott."

I stopped and turned. Jeff was grinning at me, and he was waving the tattoo machine around like a cowboy with a six-shooter.

"His name is Rusty Abbott. He's Lester Fine's personal assistant."

Lester Fine, the actor running for a senate seat.

Chapter 15

I headed back to the Venetian, my thoughts all mixed up like scrambled eggs. Now that I knew his name and whom he worked for, I could track Rusty Abbott down. I could ask him why he ran at the casino this morning, and why he took off on me this afternoon in that truck. But I had an uneasy feeling that he wouldn't want to talk to me and might keep ducking me. He *did* run away from me. Twice.

What if he was the guy with the champagne last night? Jeff said he inked two other guys at the same time. Why didn't I push for their names, too, while I was at it? That was stupid of me. Jeff had caved more easily than I thought he would when I asked about Rusty, surprising me into forgetting about the other two guys. Now he might just give me those names, although I was sure he'd try to make me beg. It would be out of character if he didn't. I'd just have to suck it up and call him later about it. Granted, playing-card tattoos weren't exactly a rarity, especially in Vegas. I had no reason to think Rusty Abbott or the other two he was with that night had anything to do with what happened at Chez Tango.

Except a nagging feeling.

Why had he run?

I kept coming back to that.

I was stopped at a light when I looked over at a strip mall and saw another pawnshop. It was a block up from

Cash & Carry, just past the Sahara, like Trevor had said. Why not check this place out, too? I was here.

I inched over into the left-hand-turn lane, hearing the horns behind me. Too bad. The light turned green, and I pulled into the parking lot. The name of the shop was Pawned—clever. There were some wordsmiths at work here. It wore the same ubiquitous bars over its windows as Cash & Carry, and again neon signs advertised I'd get a good price for my gold jewelry.

Maybe if nothing else, this was a sign that I *should* get rid of that engagement ring. I really had no idea why I was holding on to it. It wasn't as if I was waiting for Paul to come find me. It had been two years. I'd moved on; he'd moved on.

Pawned was not as tidy as Cash & Carry. It looked like the local landfill. Piles of discarded bicycles, kids' toys, skateboards, Rollerblades, televisions, computers, and various sporting equipment were scattered throughout the small space. It, too, had a long glass case, but instead of the neat displays, jewelry and watches were clumped together in spots, with large empty spaces between them.

A short, emaciated guy with a couple of teeth missing and tattoos crawling up his arms and across his neck leered at me.

"Can I help you?" he asked, his voice unnaturally high.

"Was there some sort of incident here this morning?" I asked, noting now the cameras in the corners of the room.

"Incident?"

"Were the police here for any reason?" I wished that Joel were with me. Guys tended to talk to other guys in a way they'd never talk to me.

"Where'd you get your ink?" he asked, ignoring my question.

"Most of it in Jersey," I said. "You?" I added, to be polite.

"Murder Ink."

I nodded. "I know Jeff Coleman." Maybe that would give me an in with this guy.

"Nice guy."

Well, I wouldn't go that far, but I nodded again.

"You a cop?" he asked.

Same question as in Cash & Carry. I didn't think I looked like a cop, but maybe some of Tim and my dad had rubbed off on me.

I shook my head.

"Private dick?"

Now, that would be an interesting career choice. But I shook my head again.

He was looking suspicious. I had to give him something.

"A cop came to my shop looking for one of my workers. He said she was involved in an incident at a pawnshop; he wanted to talk to her." I paused, then added, "She's got derringer tattoos." I pointed to my inner upper arms. "Here."

He licked his lips. "Hot chick. Came in here this morning."

"What happened?"

"Cop didn't tell you?"

I shook my head.

"She came in asking about a pin I had. Fancy thing, rubies and diamonds. Like a queen-of-hearts card. I told her I didn't have it anymore. Guy who pawned it bought it back."

Charlotte already knew that. What was going on?

The guy wasn't done yet, though.

"Funny about that pin."

I frowned. "What?"

"Every week I get a list from the cops of things that are stolen. You know, like in robberies or stuff like that." He paused. "Two days ago, I got the list. That pin was on it."

I frowned. "Stolen?"

He nodded. "Guy who owns it comes in regular. But he hadn't been in in a long time."

"When did he buy the pin back?"

He grinned. "Great minds think alike." He tapped the side of his head. I don't think so. "It was reported stolen after he bought it back. Someone must have stolen it from him. I haven't seen it since."

But I had seen it. In Trevor's makeup case last night. It certainly hadn't been stolen. What was up with this?

"Did you tell the girl it was on your list?"

He nodded. "Yeah. Said if she saw it somewhere else she should call the cops. And then that guy came in."

"What guy?"

He shrugged. "Some guy. Pushed her around a little, said he knew what she was up to. I told the guy to lay off her. Got the impression it was domestic."

Charlotte wasn't married. I didn't even know whether she was dating anyone. "Did you call the cops?"

"I pushed the alarm button, but she ran out, and then he went after her. By the time the cops showed up, they were long gone."

"What did he look like?"

He shook his head. "He kept his back to me, wore a big gray sweatshirt with a hood."

Sounded like the guy who shot the cork at Trevor. But the sweatshirt had been found in the dressing room *after* the incident. So it couldn't be the same one. I was making connections that couldn't possibly be there.

I pulled the drawing of Rusty Abbott out of my bag and put it on the counter. "Was it him?"

He pushed the picture of Abbott right back at me and gave me a squirrelly look.

"I don't know," he said, looking away.

Now I knew how Tim probably felt when he was questioning reluctant witnesses. I decided not to push it.

"Do you know Wesley Lambert?" I asked.

He frowned and shook his head. "Should I?"

His reaction seemed genuine.

I'd been wondering how Frank DeBurra knew the woman who was in here was Charlotte, so I asked, "The girl who was in here this morning. Did you tell the police about her derringer tattoos?"

He nodded. "And the cool ivy and flower chain ink around her neck."

The description fit. But still, how did DeBurra get her name?

"She never told you her name?" I asked.

"I asked her about the tats. Asked where she got them. Told me she worked at The Painted Lady." He paused a second; then a wide grin spread across his face. "I know who you are now. I recognize you. Jeff told me about you."

Of course he did.

"He said I should try your shop next time I want a tat," he continued.

I was going to have to tell Jeff to stop talking up my shop. I didn't need his help. I tried to smile as graciously as I could, considering I never wanted to see this guy in my shop. Ever. I gathered up my sketch and stuffed it back in my bag. I had to get out of here. "My rates start at five hundred," I said.

I think the rest of his teeth almost fell out as I gave him a little wave and left the store.

My phone warbled "Born to Run" when I got back into the car. I flipped it open after seeing Ace's number on the screen.

"Tell me you're still with Charlotte," I said without saying hello.

"I am."

"This idiot detective is looking for her. I need to talk to her."

I heard muffled talking, then, "Hello? Brett?"

"A cop came to the shop looking for you, something about an incident at this pawnshop."

A long silence, then, "What of it?"

"I was just in the pawnshop. I talked to that creepy guy with no teeth. He said some guy came in and harassed you. He thought it was a domestic. What's going on?"

"It's nothing, really."

"Then why are you hiding?"

Silence.

"It's not like you did anything wrong," I said after a few seconds. Although I was starting to think that there might be a bit more to this than what Mr. Pawned had described. "Why did you go there asking about Trevor's pin? Did you know it had been reported stolen?"

"Trevor can explain."

Trevor? "I talked to Trevor. He came by the shop looking for you. He didn't know anything about you going to a pawnshop or that the cops want to question you. At least that's what he said." I paused. "Anyway, Trevor's back in the hospital. He got really sick at the shop. We had to call the paramedics."

"He's sick?"

"Yeah, he was looking for you."

"Is he going to be okay?"

"I don't really know."

"You have to go see him, find out. Tell him I'm okay. He can tell you about the pin, why I went there."

And then the phone went dead.

I didn't like visiting hospitals, but it didn't seem like I had much of a choice. I had no idea where Charlotte was, so I decided to take her up on her advice and try to get some answers out of Trevor. Problem was, I didn't know where they'd taken him. We'd just let the paramedics leave the shop with him and not asked. I called Bitsy and asked her whether she could call around, see if he had been admitted anywhere.

"What's up?" she asked.

"Charlotte tells me Trevor can explain what went down this morning at that pawnshop."

"But he says he wasn't with Charlotte. And why can't she tell you?"

"She just won't. I don't know why. So I figure I'll see if Trevor will be a little more forthcoming. Can you make some calls?"

Bitsy knew Las Vegas a lot better than I did. She'd lived here for most of her life, could remember when the Strip was just a shadow of what it was today.

I waited only about five minutes before my phone rang. I looked at the caller ID. Bitsy.

"That was fast."

"UMC on West Charleston. University Medical Center."

She told me how to get there from where I was, and I headed north.

"They said he's still in emergency, so go there."

I felt like I'd been running all over the planet today. Back and forth like a yo-yo. I found the medical center and the parking garage, going around and around until I was on the roof. Must be a busy day. I didn't want to know how much they were going to charge me for parking.

The emergency room was packed. All sorts of people, some moaning, some wailing, some bloody. I went over to the information desk.

"Yes?" The woman's voice was sharp, as if she'd spent the whole day shouting at a bunch of preschoolers who'd gotten out of hand.

"I'm looking for Trevor McKay. The paramedics brought him over here from the Venetian earlier. I understood he was still in emergency."

She was one step ahead of me, her long nails clicking against her keyboard. She stared at the screen, pursed her lips, and looked up at me. "Just a second, please, miss. Are you family?"

I decided to lie. A little white lie.

"Yes."

The woman picked up the phone and indicated I was to go sit and wait.

There were no seats. Not that I'd want to sit anywhere. Not that I wanted to even have my feet on the floor in this room. There were smells in here, booze and vomit and body odor mixed together. Some blood splattered the floor near a young man holding a dark cloth over his arm. A closer look showed that the cloth had blood on it.

No, thank you. I think I'll stand.

About five minutes passed, and I heard the woman saying, "Miss? Miss?"

I turned to see a man in a white lab coat standing next to her, a smile on his face. Sister Mary Eucharista would say that a smile in this place was nothing short of a miracle.

A second look at him told me he was good-looking, *very* good-looking, in that George-Clooney-in-*ER* kind of way. He was taller than me, thin, with spiky dark hair, green eyes, a long nose, and a nice jawline. My heart did a little jump, as did other parts of me.

"Miss McKay?" he asked.

I shook myself out of my reverie and shook my head. "Kavanaugh. Brett Kavanaugh."

Confusion clouded his eyes. "I was told you were Mr. McKay's family."

I couldn't lie to this guy. "I'm a friend. He became ill in my shop."

He frowned, obviously uncertain whether he should continue talking to me, but then made a decision.

"Please follow me."

We walked through sliding frosted doors into the actual emergency room. Beds were lined up in a semicircle around a big nurses' station. We didn't stop, just kept walking until we reached a door to a small office. He indicated I was to go in, and he came in behind me, shutting the door.

"I'm Dr. Bixby."

He held out his hand, and I took it, a shock running through my arm. I let out a nervous giggle, pulling my hand away too quickly. A glance at his face told me he felt it, too. He was blushing. Really blushing.

I saw now that his name tag read, DR. C. BIXBY.

"What's the 'C' for?" I asked, indicating his tag.

He put his hand up and fingered it. "Colin."

"Nice to meet you," I said.

He pointed to a chair. "Have a seat, please, Miss Kavanaugh."

I did as he asked. I might have done mostly anything he asked.

I'd dated a guy a few months back who was rich, good-looking, and a playboy. We'd had some laughs, but I knew I had to pull out of it before I got sucked in even further. He was the kind of guy who'd break my heart if I let him.

Since Simon, things had been a little slow on the dating front.

Maybe that's why I found myself admiring Dr. Colin Bixby's obvious attractive physical attributes.

Not to mention his nice smile.

Which had disappeared. His eyebrows were furrowed slightly, his lips pursed in a grim line.

"I'm deeply sorry to have to tell you that Trevor McKay passed away about half an hour ago."

Chapter 16

I felt like I'd swallowed a bag of marbles.

"Excuse me?" I managed to sputter.

His expression conveyed his compassion. "He didn't indicate a next of kin on his paperwork. I'm glad you came in."

Next of kin? I barely knew anything about the guy except he could lip-synch to Britney songs while dancing on six-inch heels and look like he was having the time of his life. I also knew he had a pinup girl who looked remarkably like Britney Brassieres on his upper left arm. Ace had done the ink.

I didn't even know where the guy lived.

Charlotte did. As I thought of her, I took a deep breath. This would devastate her.

"How?" I asked softly.

"He was incredibly dehydrated when he came in. He lost a lot of fluids. We couldn't keep anything down him."

"He didn't look good when he came to my shop earlier."

Colin Bixby frowned. "Yes, I meant to ask. What shop is that?"

"The Painted Lady."

His eyes traveled over the garden on my arm, the dragon poking up over my tank top. "You're the painted lady," he said softly.

I nodded. "That's right." His gaze was a little disconcerting, but not in a bad way. I had to keep talking or I'd get too distracted. "He was at my shop when he became ill. Although, come to think of it, I think he was sick when he arrived. You know he was in the hospital overnight?"

"Yes." Colin Bixby leafed through a file folder that he picked up off the desk. "He had a concussion and a small chest wound. According to the report, he was perfectly fine when he was released this morning. All tests showed normal."

Covering his tracks in case I wanted to file a malpractice suit or something.

"It doesn't say how he got the concussion," he added.

"He got knocked over."

The doctor's eyebrows rose.

I nodded. "Some guy shot a champagne cork at him. Hit him square in the chest. The shock knocked him off balance, so he cracked his head against the floor. He was wearing six-inch heels, so he didn't have too much traction."

"I hate to ask . . ."

"Trevor McKay is a drag queen," I said matter-of-factly. "He was performing at Chez Tango last night."

"MissTique's show?"

Now I was the one who was surprised. "That's right. Do you know her?"

He nodded, and by the way his jaw was set, I knew that was all I was going to get. Interesting. But a little troublesome. Here I was, feeling all warm and fuzzy and other things about this guy, and this admission meant quite possibly that he was gay. I hated to think my radar was that off center. I totally had felt that little spark.

"I'd like to get some information from you," Colin Bixby was saying.

It took me a second to realize that he didn't want to hear about *me*; he was talking about information about Trevor. Information I didn't have.

"I really don't know him very well," I said.

"But you came to see him. He was in your shop." His

green eyes were mesmerizing, teasing me a little, like he knew I was a fraud but didn't care.

He couldn't be gay. He couldn't.

"I wanted to see how he was, and I wanted to ask him about something." Right. Charlotte said Trevor was the one who could explain everything. Now Charlotte was going to have to come out of hiding. I pulled out my cell phone. "A friend of mine knew him better. She can tell you what you need to know."

Colin Bixby put his hand over mine, the one that was holding the phone, and I felt it again. The spark, the warmth—and the firm way he closed my phone.

"You can't use that in here," he said softly, leaning toward me.

I usually don't like to share my personal space, but I didn't have a problem with that right now. He smelled nice, like fresh Ivory soap with a splash of Purell thrown in for good luck.

"You can use this one." He lifted his hand off mine and waved it over a landline on the desk.

"Thanks." I picked up the phone and dialed Charlotte's cell.

The voice mail kicked in, and I said she needed to call me right away. I hung up and dialed Ace's number. It rang a few times before I got his voice mail. I left the same message. I turned to Colin Bixby and shrugged. "I can have her call you."

He was looking at me sideways in a way that made me sure he'd aced chemistry class. "How many tattoos do you have?"

I couldn't help myself. "That's for me to know and you to find out." I sounded like I was in sixth grade. Yikes.

But it didn't seem to turn him off.

"That sounds like a challenge."

Okay, so he knew MissTique, but the way he was looking at me now definitely clinched it: He was so not gay.

He slipped a card out of his breast pocket and pressed it into my hand. "Call me."

Just try and stop me.

I stuck the card in my bag and stood up. He shook my hand, holding it a second longer than he should have. But I wasn't complaining.

All right, so I knew nothing about Colin Bixby except he was a doctor and he worked in the emergency room at UMC. But to a single woman of thirty-two who hadn't had a date in a while, it was nice to know the man at least had a job. I just hoped he didn't live with his mother.

I took one of my own cards out and handed it to him. "In case you don't want to wait," I flirted shamelessly.

He gave me a sort of half smile and blushed again, and I had to leave before I said something even more stupid. I almost sprinted out the door but stopped when I heard him calling me back.

"Miss Kavanaugh, you might want to know that Mr. McKay was delirious when he arrived here because of his dehydration. We did not find any ID on him. All we found was this."

Colin Bixby held out a stone-studded pin with the queen of hearts on it.

Chapter 17

He didn't let me take it. Instead, he just asked me if I could identify the pin as belonging to Trevor. I felt like I was living an episode of *CSI*.

I told him yes, the brooch was Trevor's.

"Since Mr. McKay became ill in your shop, did you notice whether he had a wallet or any other identification on him there?" Bixby asked.

I thought about how quickly Trevor had gotten sick and shook my head. "No. We told the paramedics his name, but they moved really fast to get him out of there."

"So you don't know where he lives?"

I felt like an idiot. But then I had a thought: "MissTique probably has his address, because he works for her."

"Thank you, Miss Kavanaugh. I'll give Kyle a call."

So he knew MissTique's name was really Kyle. Uh-oh. Those doubts again started to bubble up.

But then he winked at me. "And I'll call you, too, if you don't mind."

I was bouncing back and forth like a pinball.

"You can call me Brett," I said, giving him a short wave as I turned and practically skipped away.

I picked up takeout from Noodles in the Palazzo shops. When I first came to Vegas, I could never figure out whether I was in the Venetian or the Palazzo, since they're connected and there isn't a real definitive line on the border between them. I count the waterfall that spills down to the first floor as the start of the Palazzo shops, but I think they start before that, possibly at the end of the canal.

It's easy to get lost, with all the walkways between the fancy, expensive shops. Sometimes I end up at Double Helix, an open-air bar that sits in the middle of a star-shaped area with paths going in all different directions. I found the box office for Blue Man Group downstairs one day when I was looking for a ladies' room. I've never seen the Blue Man Group, but it's nice to know it's there if I ever want to.

Noodles is a large, bright restaurant with massive tables so you can meet your neighbor. I'm not one to embrace eating with strangers, so I always get takeout. The food is fabulous, and today I picked up a variety of duck, shrimp, and chicken entrees. It was the least I could do for my staff—well, Bitsy and Joel—who'd held down the fort all day while Charlotte and Ace were in hiding and I was out playing Nancy Drew.

Joel met me at the front desk when I came in.

"You went to Noodles," he said, unable to keep the glee out of his voice as he took the bag from me. "Bitsy, look, Brett went to Noodles."

He didn't wait for her to answer, just went immediately into the staff room.

Bitsy, who was sitting at the front desk doing paperwork, didn't look as happy.

"Thanks for letting me play hooky a little," I said, uncertain how to approach this. Bitsy liked being in charge whenever she could be, which is why I sometimes made her think she was in charge. But when she really was, like today, she could get a chip on her shoulder about it.

And since her shoulders were little, like her, those chips could be a bit large.

But she didn't look mad. Her eyes, which were a bright, clear blue and offset by her blond hair, which she recently cut short in a really attractive bob, were clouded by worry.

"I haven't heard from Ace or Charlotte," she started.

I put up a hand. "I have. I also have bad news. Let's go in the staff room."

Bitsy followed me as we joined Joel, who was already dishing noodles into his mouth. He stopped when he saw my expression.

"What, do you want to say grace or something?"

I sighed and sat down.

Joel finished chewing and followed suit. Bitsy kept standing. We were all at the same eye level that way.

"Trevor died this afternoon." I told them about going to the emergency room after Charlotte said I should find Trevor, and how I met Colin Bixby and he told me the news.

Bitsy was the first to speak.

"Have you talked to Charlotte?"

"She's not answering her phone, and neither is Ace."

"This is going to devastate her."

I agreed. I didn't know Trevor very well, but I felt awful. I couldn't even imagine how Charlotte would feel.

"So if Charlotte told you that Trevor was supposed to tell you what was going on, what happens now?" Joel asked. "Should you just talk to Tim about all this?"

I wanted to. It was better than the alternative, which was talking to Frank DeBurra. He was too hostile.

At the same time, though, I was seesawing about how I felt about Charlotte's reaction when I asked her just what went down this morning. Why not just tell me? Why tell me to talk to Trevor? What was she hiding?

I told Bitsy and Joel about my visits to the pawnshops, what the pawnshop guy told me about the guy who'd been angry with Charlotte, and how he wouldn't say whether he recognized Rusty Abbott from the sketch.

"There's so much; you're making me dizzy," Bitsy said.

Joel didn't have that problem. He'd resumed eating the noodles with the duck, his chopsticks flying. It did smell good. I'd missed lunch while I was on my travels. I picked up the container of noodles with shrimp, grabbed a pair of chopsticks, and started eating, too. Bitsy decided to join us.

The three of us sat, chewing our noodles, not talking, not looking at one another, just eating.

Considering the circumstances, I suppose I should say I didn't taste the food.

But I did. And it was delicious.

From the slurping sounds next to me, I could tell Joel and Bitsy were enjoying it just as much as I was.

The buzzer indicating that someone had come into the shop startled us. Bitsy got her bearings first, put her container down, and went out to the front. I glanced at the clock on the wall and realized it was probably my seven o'clock. I saw a few file folders on the light table, found the one I needed, and followed Bitsy.

I was right. It was my client Hunter Ross. I wouldn't have time to muse over the day's events for the next two hours.

After I cleaned, shaved, and placed the stencil of the tiger on Hunter's back, I set out my inkpots, slipped a new needle into my tattoo machine, and pulled on a pair of gloves. Hunter was facedown on the chair, and I pressed my foot to the pedal. The machine began to whirr. I dipped the needle into a pot and began to draw, washing away extra ink and blood with a soft cloth as I worked. Everything that had happened in the last twenty-four hours slipped away as I lost myself in the ink, the tiger's stripes mesmerizing as I filled them in, shading the face, outlining the eyes.

I heard voices out in the front of the shop as I stopped the machine and looked at my handiwork. There was something about working on skin, knowing it was alive, that I was creating art on a living being. Beat the heck out of working on that hard canvas.

I didn't have time to finish the tiger today. Hunter knew we'd have at least two or three sessions before it was done, but I gave Hunter a hand mirror so he could go see the partial tiger for himself in the big, full-length mirror out in the back of the shop. I started cleaning up my inks, taking the needles I'd used and disposing of them in the hazardous waste container under the table. The needle bar would be put in the autoclave for sterilization.

Joel was with a client when Hunter finally left after making his second appointment and paying for today's session. Bitsy closed the drawer that hid the credit card machine and looked up at me expectantly.

"What?" I asked a little too sharply. She frowned, so I immediately said, "I'm sorry. It's just been a really long day. Has Charlotte or Ace called?"

"Ace is in with a client."

"Did you talk to him?"

"His client was already here. We couldn't exactly have a heart-to-heart." She paused. "I did ask him about Charlotte. He said she was in a safe place."

What on earth did that mean?

But my brain was shutting down. I was exhausted. All I wanted to do was go home and crawl into bed, forget that this day ever happened. Well, except maybe for Dr. Colin Bixby. Since I hadn't talked to Charlotte, I had no excuse to call him. I wondered whether he really would call *me*.

As I was thinking that, the phone rang. Like karma or something.

"The Painted Lady," Bitsy said when she picked it up. She listened for a minute, nodding, then turned to me, holding the receiver out. "It's Jeff Coleman."

So much for karma. I took the phone. "Hey."

"Hey, yourself, Kavanaugh. You know, you've got yourself in a bit of a pickle."

"Huh?"

"Rusty Abbott was just in here. Asking all sorts of questions about you."

I felt my chest constrict, and I stopped breathing for a second. "What sorts of questions?"

"Personal stuff. How long have you had your shop, are you dating anyone, where do you live. That sort of thing. It was weird, almost like he was sweet on you. But in a stalker kind of way."

"Oh, that makes me feel better," I said sarcastically. "Why doesn't he just get in touch with me himself?"

"I'm not sure you want to have a cup of coffee with the

guy, Kavanaugh. He was a little skittish. I didn't tell him anything, but I did ask him about the roulette game, and he said he'd just happened to be there when you wandered over. You know, your reputation precedes you. He recognized you by your tats."

Like I'd recognized him.

"So why would he run away, then?"

"I think you make him nervous."

Great. A nervous stalker.

"I didn't realize you were such great friends with the guy."

"I'm not. First time I've seen him since I did his ink."

"But you did tell him about me, didn't you? When you inked him."

"I must have. Otherwise how would he have known about us?"

Us. Like we were some sort of couple. I totally did not want to go there.

"He asked me to give you a message."

I waited, could hear him take a breath.

"He said you might want to be careful, because you never know. Accidents happen."

Chapter 18

My heart jumped into my throat. "Accidents happen? What's that supposed to mean?"

"I've seen my share of crazy, Kavanaugh, and I think you better be on the lookout. I don't think he's playing with a full deck."

Considering the tattoo on Rusty Abbott's arm, Jeff Coleman was taking liberties with his puns.

"You really didn't tell him anything?"

Bitsy was openly listening to my conversation, and I waved my hand in front of her face and turned my back to her. She walked around me to go to the staff room and stuck her tongue out at me. I stuck mine out in return. We were like a couple of third graders.

Jeff was talking. "All I said was if he wanted to talk to you, he could find you at your shop—that was public information—but he said that wasn't the plan."

"What does that mean?"

"That's what I asked. He wouldn't say any more than that, but I'd watch your back, Kavanaugh."

I was quiet a second, digesting this information.

"Do you want me to come over there, follow you to your house, make sure you get there okay?" Jeff's voice was unnaturally soft, and the fact that he was offering made me take this a lot more seriously. He must really think the guy was a nut and could cause me some sort of trouble.

Accidents happen.

I heard Joel's and Ace's tattoo machines whirring in harmony in their rooms.

"No, Jeff. Thanks, I really appreciate it, but I can have Joel or Ace do that. You don't have to leave your shop and come down here."

"Wouldn't be a problem, Kavanaugh."

I thought about Jeff Coleman, how he called me only by my last name, like he was some sort of tough guy, and how he always made cracks about my "upscale" shop.

"Thanks, Jeff, really," I said, hoping he could hear the gratitude in my voice.

I could hear a smile in his. "You know, Kavanaugh, I think I'm growing on you."

He didn't give me a chance to respond. I heard the dial tone and hung up the phone, pondering what he'd said. Not about him growing on me—the jury was still out on that one—but about Rusty Abbott. What was his game? Even though he told Jeff that meeting up with me was just a coincidence, in a completely paranoid moment, I wondered whether he'd actually set me up. If he were the champagne shooter from last night, maybe he was following me around to make sure that I couldn't identify him.

I was being totally irrational.

Or was I?

I was so deep in thought that when Ace's client came up behind me, I jumped.

"You scared me," I said, holding my hand to my chest to see if I could make it stop thumping so hard.

"Yeah, sorry," he said with a lopsided grin.

Bitsy had come back and was taking his credit card. I wandered over to Ace's room, where he was cleaning up his inks. He looked up when I came in and sat on his client chair.

"Hey, Brett," he said casually, as if it were like any other day.

"Where's Charlotte?"

He stopped fiddling with the inkpots and shrugged.

"She called some friend who came and picked her up at my place. I don't know who he was—he stayed in the car—but she said she'd be okay."

"You're sure about that?"

"She's a big girl, Brett."

"Did she get my message about Trevor?"

"That's why I made her call someone. I had to be back here, and I didn't want her to be alone. She was pretty broken up about it."

"But not enough to come out of hiding."

He didn't say anything.

"What's going on? Why is she in hiding? Was it that guy at the pawnshop? Has he threatened her? Is it an old boyfriend? Is that who she's hiding from?" I couldn't stop the questions once they started coming out.

He bit his lip and shrugged. "She hasn't really told me anything, except that it's not what it seems. Said I just have to trust her. So that's what I'm doing."

"Not what it seems? That's pretty evasive. She has to talk to the police."

Ace shook his head. "No cops. She's pretty adamant about that. Says it'll all come out eventually, and she wants it on her terms."

"What does that mean?"

He sighed. "I'm not totally sure, Brett. Believe me, I tried to get her to go to the cops. Tell them what really happened this morning at that pawnshop. But she won't. I can't force her."

"What about Tim?"

He gave a short snort. "He's the cops, Brett. No cops."

"Should I talk to him for her?"

He went back to putting away the inks. "Whatever you want."

"When did you and Charlotte get so chummy?" I asked.

I could see only the side of his face, but the smile was obvious. It was as if someone hit me over the head; otherwise, I would never have figured it out.

"You're dating her, aren't you? Why are you keeping it secret?"

He shrugged and looked back at me. "We didn't want anyone to know. The whole 'office romance' thing is so clichéd." He made little quote marks with his fingers as he spoke.

I could understand that. "Listen, then, you really do need to convince her that going to the cops is the best thing. If she needs some sort of protection, then it's for her own good."

"I think she knows what she's doing."

"Does she?" I asked. "Do you? You could be charged with obstruction for hiding her." I was repeating what DeBurra had said to me, and I didn't catch myself in time to stop.

"Don't pull that cop talk on me, Brett. I know what I'm doing, too. And not for nothing, but when she's ready to tell me what's going on, she'll tell me. I'm being patient with her. I'm not going to bug her about it." He really turned his back on me now, dismissing me.

It felt like I had a hundred-pound weight on my chest. I was just trying to do the right thing and help the girl. Sister Mary Eucharista had taught me well. But she didn't tell me how to do the right thing when no one else was cooperating.

Joel agreed to follow me home to make sure I got there okay. Ace and I didn't talk for the rest of the night, and I let Bitsy go early because she had a date.

I had a million things swirling around in my head: Rusty Abbott warning me about accidents, the toothless guy at Pawned, Charlotte and Ace and their discreet romance, Trevor's untimely demise, Dr. Colin Bixby. The latter was the most pleasant place for my thoughts to hang their hat, but even he got pushed aside when I flashed back on that sketch of Wesley Lambert. What role did he have?

My cell phone rang. I had it hooked up to my hands-free device.

"Want to stop for a bite?" Joel's voice came through loudly.

"I just want to get home."

"You wouldn't know that by the way you're driving."

So I went the speed limit. Sue me.

"You know, if anyone wanted to follow you, it would be so easy," Joel continued.

"You must be hungry. You're grumpy."

"Come on, stop for something. There's a little Mexican place not far off the exit."

I knew it. And the power of suggestion had my stomach growling. The noodles were a few hours ago. "Sure, fine."

"Nachos," he said, drawing the word out.

I was also thinking margaritas. That would be a nice way to top off the day. So I mentioned it.

"Way too many calories," Joel said. "I'll go through a week's worth of points."

"And nachos are fat free? Give me a break."

I pulled off the highway and turned off the exit.

"It's just up there," Joel said when the strip mall came into view.

"I see it."

I ended the call and threw the hands-free unit on the passenger seat as I pulled into the parking lot. The lights were still on, the neon advertising Corona beer.

But as I was about to get out, a glance in the sideview mirror made me freeze.

Detective Frank DeBurra was walking up to my door.

I lowered the window, waiting for DeBurra like he was going to ask for my license and registration. Joel had already gone inside, not noticing I wasn't behind him.

Some bodyguard he turned out to be.

"Miss Kavanaugh, can you get out of the car?" DeBurra's voice was low, measured.

"What, was I speeding or something? Am I under arrest?" I should know better than to question a cop. It wasn't as if I didn't know how to behave with one. But DeBurra got my hackles up.

"Just get out of the car, please." His tone was laced with exasperation.

I had that effect on some people.

I opened the door and climbed out, smoothing my skirt, pulling down on my tank top, which had started to ride up over my abdomen.

"Are you following me?" I asked. If I'd known that, I wouldn't have asked Joel to come along. DeBurra would've been my shield against Rusty Abbott.

"Have you heard from Miss Sampson?"

That old song and dance. Should've known.

"I'm going in for some nachos now. I haven't seen Charlotte all day. I have no idea where she is." None of what I said was a lie.

"Her friend Trevor McKay is dead." It sounded even more final the way he said it.

"I know," I said.

"I know you know. You were at the hospital. You spoke to Dr. Bixby."

I shifted a little. "Yeah. I wanted to see how Trevor was. But he was dead before I got there." I added that last part in case he thought I had something to do with Trevor's demise.

"And you went to two pawnshops."

I tried to keep my anger out of my voice. "Have you been following me all day?"

"What's your relationship with Jeff Coleman?"

This had gone on far enough.

"I'd love to stand here and play *This Is Your Life*, Detective, but my friend is in the restaurant and I really want a margarita right now. Unless you're going to charge me with something, then I'm going inside." I started walking even as I spoke.

DeBurra fell into step beside me. "I can arrest you—for obstruction. But I won't."

"Don't do me any favors," I said, the attitude slipping out because I was unable to stop it.

"I think you've had contact with Charlotte Sampson today. And I think you're keeping it from me."

I stopped short and whirled around to face him. "You

know, Charlotte's the one who was threatened. It's not as if she committed a crime or anything. You should be trying to find the guy who threatened her, not acting as if an innocent girl was guilty of something."

As I spoke, an expression crossed his face that I couldn't read. I began to wonder whether she *was* guilty of something, regardless of what that pawnshop guy said. That would explain why she was hiding, why DeBurra was going after her like a dog after a bone.

DeBurra gave a short snort. "So you don't know where she is, do you?"

I sighed. "No, I really don't. I'm telling the truth. I did talk to her, but she won't say where she is. I'm doing my best."

"Miss Kavanaugh, if you were doing your best, Charlotte Sampson would be turning herself in."

I rolled my eyes. "Fine. But there's just so much I can do."

"It's for her own good," DeBurra said.

"Like I don't know that."

"No, really," he said, his voice lower now, like he was going to tell me a secret.

I leaned forward slightly to hear him better.

"Charlotte Sampson got mixed up with the wrong people. Wesley Lambert, for one. And her life may be in danger."

Chapter 19

First Wesley Lambert gets involved with the wrong people, and now Charlotte. What was Lambert involved in? If it was drugs, like Kyle suggested, how did Trevor's brooch come into play? And then warning Eduardo that he'd send a message to Trevor. Sort of like how Rusty Abbott was warning me through Jeff.

"I haven't seen her," I said again and pushed my way past DeBurra.

I'd taken about three steps when I heard his voice behind me.

"I'm going to be your shadow. She has to show up eventually."

That was going to be a royal pain. But I didn't turn around, didn't acknowledge that I'd even heard him. Instead I went inside and found Joel already chewing on chips and salsa at a table near the back. A margarita sat on the table.

I slid into the chair across from Joel and took a sip. Smooth, tart, perfect. I smiled. "Thanks."

"Where'd you go?"

I told him about my close encounter of the irritating kind with Frank DeBurra. He murmured appropriately throughout.

"What's up with this guy Lambert? Is he a drug dealer or does he just deal in gaudy jewelry?" he asked.

"I don't know, but I think he's the guy in the pawnshop who threatened Charlotte."

"What does he want?"

I had no idea.

A waitress came over and set down a gigantic plate of nachos slathered in cheese and chili. Joel thanked her politely before taking a handful onto his plate. I suddenly wasn't very hungry anymore, but I needed something in my stomach to soak up all that tequila; otherwise, the good detective who'd vowed to keep following me would have a legitimate excuse to pull me over on my way home.

We ate in comfortable silence, my thoughts all over the place. I wondered whether I'd be able to get any sleep tonight with the activity going on in my brain.

When the nachos were gone and the margarita glass drained, I opened my mouth to start up again, but Joel shook his head and put his fingers to his lips.

"I'm worried about Charlotte, too, Brett, but I think Ace is taking care of her and you should just go home and get some sleep."

"What, does everyone know about Ace and Charlotte but me?"

He chuckled. "Brett, they've been dating practically since Charlotte started working for us. You haven't noticed how they moon at each other?"

I thought about it. "No."

"You should pay more attention. They make a pretty couple."

That they did: Ace with his handsome, movie-star looks and Charlotte with her long, sleek dark hair, bright eyes, and pixie face. Each of them, too, had symmetrical tattoos—Ace had sleeves that ended in perfect matching fleur-de-lis, and Charlotte had those derringers.

I just hoped that when all this was over I wasn't going to lose one or even two of my employees.

Joel gave me a kiss on the cheek before I got into my car to head home. I told him not to bother following me anymore, since I was sure DeBurra was out there somewhere.

I arrived at my house in one piece; I hadn't noticed anyone behind me. Maybe he was full of hot air.

Tim was already asleep. I put on my cotton pajama bottoms and a big T-shirt, crawled into bed, and, despite my worries, fell into a deep, dreamless sleep.

I got up about nine. I missed Tim again; he had gone to work while I slept. We didn't see each other very much, even though we were roommates. His job had odd hours, and mine kept me at the shop until midnight most nights. Every once in a while, like yesterday, our paths crossed.

I'd hoped to talk to him again about DeBurra and tell him what had happened last night. I'd have to try to call him later. I wanted to know, too, whether he'd poked around about Wesley Lambert and if he'd found out anything about him.

I brought my laptop into the kitchen—wireless Internet is a beautiful thing—and drank my coffee while I booted it up. I wanted to check out that Queen of Hearts Ball Kyle had told me about—the one where Trevor got that pin.

The Queen of Hearts Ball was a fund-raiser held about a year ago to benefit an AIDS organization. Lester Fine had been there, as well as other celebrities and political luminaries. The organization had raised more than five million dollars at the event, which took place at the MGM, which happened to be right across the street from New York New York, where I'd had my gambling windfall. Not that that had anything to do with anything.

The MGM used to have a *Wizard of Oz* theme going, with statues of Dorothy and her friends in the lobby. It also had an amusement park in the back, to try to lure families to Sin City.

It didn't work.

Now the resort was sans roller coasters but boasted five pools, Joël Robuchon's restaurant, Studio 54, and one of the ubiquitous Vegas Cirque du Soleil shows. The lobby was spacious, with a gilded lion standing sentry in a fountain of flowers under a gold-lit inverted dome that distorted its reflections like a funhouse mirror.

Could be a cool place for a fund-raiser.

I read through a couple of newspaper articles announcing the event, and a couple more that reported on it. Small, jeweled pins with the image of a queen-of-hearts playing card were handed out as giveaways.

Since about five hundred people had attended, there were hundreds of those little suckers floating around.

But Trevor had one that was real. A gift from Lester Fine, according to him. What was up with that?

I clicked on images and found plenty of pictures from the ball. A lot of sparkly evening gowns and tuxedos. Ah, there was Lester Fine, dashing in his tails. His acting career had started thirty years ago, when he was twenty. He starred in a political thriller that grossed more than anyone expected. Fine had played the bad guy.

Another picture showed Fine with his arm around his wife, Alice. I knew their story. He'd married her before his first big hit; they were high school sweethearts. Hollywood praised their ability to keep it together when so many celebrity couples broke up.

A closer look at Alice showed a fairly attractive middle-aged woman who'd had a little too much Botox. She had that perpetual look of surprise in each picture; it couldn't be the flash every time. She was used to the limelight, hanging on Lester's arm. She wore a bright blue babydoll dress that was about twenty years too young for her, and her obviously dyed blond hair was too long. Women her age shouldn't try to hang on to their youth; it made them look older.

I made a mental note to follow my own advice.

A close-up of the couple showed each wearing a queen-of-hearts pin.

I clicked on the next picture.

MissTique was posing with Lester Fine, who looked decidedly uncomfortable. A little homophobic, perhaps?

The next pictures were all of drag queens who'd performed at the ball. Britney Brassieres, Miranda Rites, Lola LaTuche, and Marva Luss had been together before Miss-

Tique brought them into Chez Tango. I had a small pang of sadness looking at Britney, aka Trevor McKay. He, or she, I suppose, looked like she was having the time of her life.

And here was Britney with her arm around none other than Rusty Abbott.

I still thought Rusty was pretty enough to do drag himself, but he was wearing a tuxedo and looking rather dashing. It was a lot better than the jeans and T-shirt he'd been wearing at the roulette table.

Thinking about Rusty Abbott prompted me to remember Jeff Coleman's call about how Rusty warned that accidents happen. I jumped up and went to the front door to make sure Tim had locked it.

I should have known better than to doubt Tim. The door was locked, as was the one that led out to the garage.

I settled back in with my laptop and a fresh cup of coffee.

I clicked through to the next page. There were a lot of pictures from the ball, mixed in with images of queen-of-hearts playing cards.

Another one caught my eye, and I double clicked.

A drag queen I didn't recognize. This one looked like she was Donna Summer's twin, only white: a big bouffant of black hair, thick, bright blue eye makeup, a slinky white sequined dress, and high boots straight from the seventies. I clicked on the picture. It was the images page from the Queen of Hearts Ball Web site. I read the caption and held my breath.

Shanda Leer.

Otherwise known as Wesley Lambert.

And he was standing with his arm around Charlotte.

Chapter 20

I sat back and sipped my coffee, staring at the picture. So DeBurra was right: Charlotte knew Lambert, and they had both been at the ball with Trevor and Rusty Abbott. I asked myself just how well I knew Charlotte Sampson.

I hated that I was doubting her, but the police were looking for her and she refused to come out of hiding. Instinct, or maybe it was growing up with a dad who was a cop, told me that hiding meant guilt. Or maybe she was just truly afraid of something or someone.

I sighed and took another sip of my coffee, which had grown cold.

I clicked on the next picture, just to get this one off my screen.

I sat up a little straighter in my chair as I looked at the image. It was Rusty Abbott and Lester Fine. Obviously later in the evening. Rusty wasn't wearing his tuxedo jacket; his shirtsleeves were pushed up to his elbows.

He didn't have a tattoo.

I tried to remember when Jeff said Rusty had come in with the two drag queens. I didn't think he'd said specifically, just maybe sometime last year. From the looks of this picture, it could have been after the Queen of Hearts Ball.

I thought about the other two tattoos Jeff had done. Who were those drag queens? I had to find out.

I was willing to bet one of the three was the champagne

shooter, though. It just seemed like it should be connected. It had to be.

I put Rusty Abbott's name into Google. I wanted to see whether I could find *his* address before he could find mine. I'd at least feel like I had the upper hand that way, and I could tell Tim. Maybe he could check Abbott out for me.

There was nothing on the guy. I found a couple of Rusty Abbotts, but they were obviously not the one I was looking for. One was a contractor in Texas and the other a park ranger in Alaska.

I did find a phone number through Lester Fine's campaign Web site. I jotted it down on a pad we kept next to the phone in the kitchen.

Just as I was about to call the guy—might as well nip this in the bud—the phone rang, startling me. I picked up the receiver, absently going back to the laptop as I said, "Hello?"

"Brett?"

"Charlotte?"

"Brett, I'm in trouble."

"No kidding." I couldn't keep the sarcasm out of my voice. I mentally slapped myself. I shouldn't kick someone while they're down. "Sorry," I said when she didn't respond. "What's wrong?"

"I need you to help me."

"Sure," I said, thinking that maybe now I could talk her into talking to the police, especially since DeBurra said her life might be in danger.

"I need you to meet me."

"Charlotte, before you go any further, why don't I bring Tim along?" Tim would be more friendly than DeBurra.

"You can't bring Tim. Just yourself. I need your help."

This was the second time she'd said that, and I grew concerned. "What have you got yourself involved with, Charlotte?"

I heard a sob. "Don't tell Ace, either, okay? I didn't call him. He wouldn't understand."

This was getting more and more mysterious. But I was

willing to give her a chance to explain herself. Before I called Tim.

"Calm down, okay? Where are you?"

She gave me an address. It was just off the Strip, one of the high-rise condominiums. "It's number twelve thirty-two," she said. "Just go into the lobby, and take the elevator to the twelfth floor. Can you come now?"

She sounded so desperate, I couldn't say no. "I'll be there in about fifteen minutes, okay? Can you hang tight?"

But she'd already hung up.

I put on a pair of jeans and a stretchy black T-shirt with a pink peace sign on it. The outfit covered up most of my ink, except the garden sleeve. Usually I liked to be a walking billboard for my shop, but I wasn't sure I should bring that much attention to myself on this mission to help Charlotte.

What could she have gotten into?

As I climbed into the Mustang, I debated calling Tim anyway, then chided myself for being a tattletale. I'd talk her into letting me call him later. She was going to have to listen to reason.

It was nine o'clock, and I knew I had an eleven o'clock client, so I hoped this wasn't going to take too long. Fortunately, I'd already done the stencil so I just needed to go in and do the ink.

The Windsor Palms condominium was one of myriad condo buildings that had gone up around the Strip a couple years back, sold mainly as second homes. The condos were not for the poor and hopeful. They were for the rich who had enough money socked away that they didn't need to worry about the foundering economy. But still, because of the real estate bust and the high rate of foreclosure in Vegas, a lot of developers had scrapped plans to build even more condos. I couldn't help but think that Vegas would survive and those plans would be revived at some point. Sin City was too popular a destination and the climate too desirable.

I turned down the private road that led to the Windsor

Palms and noted the palm trees that lined the sidewalks, allowing it to live up to its name. When I reached the circular drive with a fountain in the center, a small, discreet sign pointed me in the direction of the parking garage.

I found a spot on the second level and continued to follow signs to the elevator and then out toward the building lobby. I pushed open a glass door and stepped into a spacious atrium with a waterfall and all sorts of lush greenery. It was sort of like those science museums where you can walk through different ecosystems. Humidity hung in the air, the kind that I hadn't felt since leaving Jersey, the kind that clung to your skin in a clammy sort of way.

I liked it.

A security guard sat at a tall desk with a monitor in front of him. He was a big, heavyset black guy with an Afro from the seventies. His smile was warm.

"May I help you?" he asked.

I told him the condo number Charlotte had rattled off.

"You have to sign in." He pushed a clipboard with a sign-in sheet on it toward me.

I noted that Charlotte's name wasn't on the sheet, but the time of the first visitor was eight a.m. Maybe she'd been here earlier, or even all night.

I printed my name neatly as the instructions indicated, wrote down the condo number and the time, and handed the clipboard back to the guard.

"Elevators are around the waterfall and to your right," he said.

I thanked him and found them easily. As I went up in the mirrored elevator, I thought about how I might want to move out of Tim's house at some point and get my own place. I made pretty good money, and housing prices had come down considerably. And if that sixty grand I'd just won at roulette was legit—I wasn't too certain, since Rusty Abbott had given me that chip—it would make a nice down payment. I liked the idea of a security guard, although the waterfall was a colossal waste of water in a city where waterfalls were not a natural phenomenon, especially during a drought.

The elevator doors opened and I stepped into the hall. I found number twelve thirty-two with no problem and pressed the buzzer.

I pressed it a second time when about a minute passed and no one responded.

When I didn't get an answer that time, I figured knocking on the door might be a good idea. Where was Charlotte?

The second I knocked, the door swung open by itself. It hadn't been closed shut.

A funny smell hit my nose: a mixture of vomit and smoke.

I hesitated. I'd been in situations like this before, and I had a bad feeling. I should go right back downstairs and get that security guard.

First, though, I called out, "Charlotte? Charlotte, are you here?"

Silence.

I thought about how paranoid she'd been acting.

I was still in the hallway, and I made an executive decision. I stepped inside.

The room laid out before me must have been about sixteen hundred square feet by itself; floor-to-ceiling windows overlooked the Strip. The space was split in two: a living room area and a kitchen. In the former, elegant furniture was scattered around the room; each wall was a different shade of blue and held gigantic oil abstracts that complemented the décor. The floor was a laminate, but plush throw rugs gave the room some warmth. A long, dark granite countertop separated the two areas. Top-end stainless-steel, state-of-the-art kitchen appliances, and cherry cupboards told me that no price was too high.

I took another couple of steps, calling for Charlotte as I went. I hoped I had the right condo.

A slider to a balcony that stretched along the other side of the windows was just around the kitchen. I walked toward it, not sure what I was looking for, but as I turned the corner, I saw something I couldn't see from the front door.

A bedroom the size of the living room, with the same view.

And a man's body on the floor.

Chapter 21

The smell was stronger in here. I suspected that whoever this guy was, he was no longer among the living. His arms and legs were splayed at angles that weren't normal. This room also was where the vomit odor came from. It looked like he'd been sick for days in here, so sick he couldn't clean up after himself. I covered my mouth and nose with my hand, but it didn't help much.

I scanned the room: a round king-sized bed, a dark walnut wardrobe, and, at the far side of the room where there were no windows, a workbench of sorts, with a couple of Bunsen burners and a tray of test tubes, like a do-it-yourself chemistry kit.

I couldn't linger here anymore; the stench was too much. I didn't see Charlotte anywhere. A door to the back of the bedroom probably led to a bathroom, but I wasn't going to walk through this room to see whether she was in there. Instead I called, "Charlotte?" one more time before heading back out into the living room.

Who was that guy, and what had Charlotte gotten me into?

All I knew for sure was that I had to call the police, or, rather, Tim.

I hesitated, glancing back toward the bedroom. I wanted to go in and see who it was, but I couldn't stand the smell any longer. He'd still be dead in ten minutes, so I went out into the hall, closing the door a little behind me. It didn't do much good. The smell was wafting out here now.

I flipped open my phone and punched in Tim's number.

"Busy, Brett."

"I know, but I'm in a bit of a situation."

Silence, then, "What is it now?" he asked, like I was always in trouble. It was only some of the time.

"I found a dead body."

A quick intake of breath, then, "You making a habit of that?" He was referring to an incident a few months back.

"It's not on purpose," I said. "Do you want to hear about it or not?"

"Where?"

I told him.

"Do you know who this dead body is?"

"No."

"Then how did you happen upon it?"

"Just get here, okay?" I said, ending the call because I really didn't quite know how I was going to approach answering that question. I knew there would be another chance later, but later rather than sooner appealed to me at the moment.

I needed to let the security guard downstairs know that Tim and the cavalry were on their way.

I was just making excuses not to go back inside that condo, regardless of my curiosity about who that man was. But my gag reflex had kicked into full gear and I couldn't stand the thought of it.

I punched the button for the elevator a few times, like it didn't register the first time. Finally, I heard the whirring, and the doors opened a few seconds later. Within a minute, I was back among the plant life and humidity that was the lobby of the Windsor Palms.

The security guard was playing a game on an iPod.

"The police are coming," I said.

His eyes grew wide. "Why?"

"That condo? The one I went up to? The guy in there is dead. Looks like he was pretty sick before he died, too."

Alarm flooded his face. "Dead?"

As he said it, I heard the sirens getting closer. Tim didn't waste any time.

The guard started toward the elevators, but my little knowledge of police procedure made me say, "You might want to hold off going up there until the cops arrive."

He didn't have to wait too long.

Four uniforms arrived with paramedics. I didn't want to burst their bubble as they crowded into an elevator, guided by the security guard. I figured I'd wait down here for Tim, who arrived only about five minutes later.

He ran a hand through his short red hair, looking exasperated as I told him what I had found.

"Lots of vomit," I said, trying not to remember too vividly, but it was impossible not to.

"Charlotte called me. That's why I'm here," I volunteered.

Tim's eyes grew wide. "Charlotte Sampson?"

I told him how she'd said she needed my help. "She's sort of been in hiding. Frank DeBurra told me last night that she might be in danger. And when I showed up here, there was this dead guy, so maybe he's not off base."

"So where is she? Obviously she must have known about this guy, knew what you'd find when you got here."

"And she knew I'd call the police." I nodded at Tim as I realized this. "She didn't want to call you herself. She couldn't risk it."

Tim frowned. "I think you better explain."

"DeBurra came to my shop yesterday to tell me she's wanted for questioning in an incident at a pawnshop."

"What kind of incident?" Tim asked.

"She was in there asking about a brooch, and some guy came in and they had some sort of argument. Bad enough so the pawnshop guy called the cops." I paused. "DeBurra's been on my case about where she might be."

Tim had a puzzled look on his face. "I hadn't heard DeBurra was looking for her. And I don't know anything about the pawnshop, so I really don't know what the deal is. I can find out when I get back."

"You mean they don't tell you everything, Mr. Detective?" I teased.

He smirked. "It's more like DeBurra doesn't want to let me in on things."

I told him how DeBurra had shown up outside the Mexican place last night. "I think he's stalking me," I ended.

"Obviously not; otherwise, he'd be here now, wouldn't he?" Tim said flippantly, although I could see that perhaps he was a little pleased that DeBurra was falling down on the job.

I thought about that a minute, how DeBurra *wasn't* following me today. Why not? Charlotte's call this morning had come so out of the blue that I'd completely forgotten about DeBurra.

Maybe he'd slept in.

Or maybe something else was going on.

By now we'd gotten up to the twelfth floor. The doors slid open and we heard the pandemonium down the hall. Tim started walking toward the condo now, and I followed.

"It's pretty gross in there," I said, although my adjective didn't even come close to what we were smelling. I plugged my nose and tried to breathe out of my mouth, but it didn't help.

"Wait here," Tim said at the door, putting up his hand to indicate I shouldn't go inside. I wasn't exactly upset about being excluded. "You've already contaminated the scene. I don't want you to add to that."

I started to say I hadn't touched anything except the outside of the door, but he didn't wait around to listen.

I hovered in the hall, listening to the voices murmuring in the back of the condo. I tried to hear what was being said, but everything was muffled. A couple of uniforms were checking out the living room, neither of them speaking. One of them picked something up off the floor, and when he showed it to his colleague, I could see what it was: a pink Hollister hoodie.

I caught my breath. That was Charlotte's.

It seemed like just seconds since he'd been gone, but

suddenly Tim rounded the corner and shouted, "Everyone out!"

The paramedics were on his heels, and the uniforms almost plowed me down. I jumped to the side of the door, waiting for Tim.

"So who is it?" I asked when he emerged.

"You didn't see his face?" Tim asked. He'd come outside now and pulled the door so it was almost closed, but not all the way. The uniforms were already down the hall, banging on doors.

I was distracted, but Tim asked again, "You didn't see his face?"

I stopped watching the hallway and turned back to Tim. "No. He was looking the other way. And I didn't spend a lot of time in there because the smell was so bad." I paused. "What's going on?"

"I thought you would've recognized him," he said, his voice barely above a whisper.

"Why?" I asked.

"Because you sketched him the other night. It's Wesley Lambert."

Chapter 22

Wesley Lambert?

Frank DeBurra had said Charlotte was involved with him, with the "wrong people." What had she gotten herself into?

Tim interrupted my thoughts.

"How far into the bedroom did you go?" There was an urgency in his voice that I hadn't heard in a long time. Not since my own trip to the emergency room ten years ago. My boyfriend at the time rode a Harley; I was twenty-two and felt invincible. I did wear a helmet. But it didn't keep my leg from getting broken in three places when the bike fell on top of me after we got sideswiped by a car on the highway. My boyfriend? He wasn't so lucky.

"I didn't go in," I said, concern in my voice now in response to his. "What, is there a problem?"

The uniforms had managed to rouse a few residents, who were being herded toward the elevators. A busty woman wearing a tight shirt and jeans carried a small white dog that started yapping. A middle-aged couple was still in their pajamas, but the uniforms were telling them they couldn't go back in; they had to evacuate.

Evacuate?

I caught Tim's eye, but he was distracted. There was another condo on the other side of the hall, and he strode over to the door and banged on it like there was no tomorrow.

"Police. Ma'am? You have to leave the building," he shouted after a muffled reply on the other side of the door.

The door opened a crack, and I could see Tim leaning in, talking to someone. Finally, she stepped outside. She was short, dark—Mexican from the look of it. She held a dust rag. Cleaning woman, most likely. Her eyes were wide as Tim hustled her past me.

I didn't quite know what to do or where to go, but since everyone was leaving, I didn't want to stick around to see why. Something in that condo wasn't safe.

I went over to the elevator and tugged on Tim's sleeve. "I think I'll go downstairs now," I said.

Before Tim could answer, we heard the *ding* of the elevator and Frank DeBurra stepped into the hall. I didn't have a chance to react, though, because two men and a woman came out behind him. They were all wearing big white hazmat-type suits with booties and gloves. They held face shields and goggles.

"Who's still in there?" DeBurra asked Tim, ignoring me.

"No one."

DeBurra looked at his companions. "Go on in," he growled.

They stuck on their face shields, making them look remarkably like those guys at the end of *E.T.*, and went into the condo. The residents were all on the other elevator now, going down. I wished I were with them, because DeBurra was staring at me. "Why am I not surprised to see you here?" he asked.

I had no idea what he was talking about.

"She came here because Charlotte Sampson called and said she wanted to meet her," Tim volunteered.

I shot him a look, but it was too late now.

"I told you to call me when she contacted you," he scolded.

I didn't take well to his tone. "I figured you'd be following me anyway," I snapped back.

He looked from me to Tim. "She didn't get anything on herself, did she?"

"I don't know."

"What about the Sampson woman?"

"Brett says she wasn't here."

"Yes, she was," I said. "Just not when I got here."

"How do you know?" Tim asked.

"One of the cops in there found a pink hoodie. Exactly like the one Charlotte has. It can't be a coincidence. She wanted me to meet her here. She knew what I'd find."

"Maybe she's okay," Tim said hesitantly.

"We'd better hope so," DeBurra said.

"What's going on?" I asked. "What's in there?"

"Why is the air-conditioning still on?" DeBurra growled, but not to me or Tim. He was talking to one of his team, who had just come out to join us.

"The guard is going to get it shut off now. It's on some sort of main circuit."

"Now. It needs to be turned off now." I thought DeBurra was going to have a heart attack; the veins in his neck were bulging, and his face was bright red. He turned back to me. "You have to tell me everything you know."

"Everything about what?" I asked.

"Did Charlotte Sampson tell you what was going on? What is the extent of her role?" Before I could answer either question, however, he turned back to Tim. "You know, this puts that queen's death into question now."

"Trevor?" I asked. "What does this have to do with Trevor's death?"

DeBurra looked sorry that he'd said anything.

I couldn't pursue it, though, because the woman who'd come in with DeBurra was coming toward us. She'd pulled off her hood.

DeBurra nodded at Tim. "Leslie's going down with you. She'll show you what you have to do." He turned to me. "This is Detective Holcomb. Do what she tells you." As if I wouldn't. DeBurra went into the condo, and Leslie Holcomb indicated that we were to follow her.

More white-clad aliens got off the elevator and headed to the condo. I hesitated, but Tim took my arm and said in my ear, "We need to go outside. DeBurra's going to need to ask you more questions."

"I've got some questions of my own," I started, but Tim shook his head.

"This isn't the time. You'll know what's up soon enough. You need to try to think of where Charlotte might have gone; you need to get in touch with her."

"Is she in danger?" I asked.

"She could get very sick."

I thought about Trevor getting sick in my shop. And then Wesley Lambert. "Is some sort of swine flu thing?" I asked. "Who are those guys in there in those suits?"

Tim didn't answer. We went down in the elevator with Leslie and stepped out into the lobby behind the waterfall. It was pandemonium, condo residents filing outside like it was a school fire drill. Three ambulances had joined the one that had arrived first, their lights joining those of the cop cars that crowded the circular drive. Leslie waved us past the residents and brought us outside, around the side of the building to the delivery entrance, where a large box truck stood. A sort of round contraption had been set up next to it.

She looked at both of us and said, "You're going to have to disrobe."

My heart jumped into my throat. "What?" I sputtered, turning to Tim. But he was nodding.

"We have to wash," he said. "Homeland security regulations."

Homeland security? What was going on?

"I'm not taking my clothes off here," I said defiantly.

Leslie did not look pleased with me. "It's regulation," she said firmly. "We'll make sure you have privacy." She turned to Tim. "Over there." She pointed to another white-suited person on the other side of the truck. The four uniforms and two paramedics who had gone up to the condo were there, too.

Tim squeezed my arm. "It's going to be okay. Just do what she says, please?"

From just the tone of his voice, I could tell that this was serious—more serious than anything I'd experienced before. Tears sprang into my eyes as I nodded. "Okay," I agreed.

I followed Leslie around the other side of the truck, where there was another setup. Looking more closely, I saw it was a sort of shower.

She brought me behind a curtain and surveyed me. I was used to being studied, but she wasn't looking at my ink.

"Take off your earrings," she instructed. "And your watch. Do you have any other piercings, any other jewelry on your person?"

I shook my head, my hand shaking even more as I struggled with the posts and the hoops that ran along the length of my ears. She disappeared for a few seconds and came back wielding a pair of scissors. She approached me, and I instinctively stepped back.

"You can't take your shirt off over your head," she said, her voice soft and her eyes kind. "I'm sorry about this." And with one movement, she slipped the scissors under the back of my shirt and slid them up to the neck, expertly cutting so I could take it off over my arms.

"Why did you do that?" I asked, handing her all my earrings and my watch.

"You have to take off everything." Again her tone was kind, almost apologetic. "You have to take a shower. You might have gotten some on you, and you have to be decontaminated."

Decontaminated? Now I truly felt like that kid in *E.T.*

It was as if a weight was sitting on my chest; my arms and legs felt leaden. I stripped off my clothes, and Leslie's eyes took in my tattoos this time.

"Nice," she managed to say just as she led me into the shower. She handed me a container of liquid soap. "You have to wash thoroughly."

Instead of a showerhead, though, I saw she held out a sort of wand. It was a hose.

It was not an experience I would ever choose to repeat.

I did what I was told and used the soap. Fortunately, the water was lukewarm, but the stream was so strong that it bounced off me almost as soon as it hit my skin, spraying every which way.

Leslie appeared at one point, and I was too exhausted to even feel like I had to cover up. She took the wand and aimed it at my back.

Finally, it was over. I felt like Rocky Balboa must have after the fight with Apollo Creed. Every muscle, every bone hurt. I almost expected my skin to be wiped clean of all my ink.

Leslie disappeared for a second, leaving me naked and shivering despite the warm desert air. When she reappeared, she handed me a white towel. "Dry up and change into this," she instructed, holding out a suit like hers in her other hand.

I took both towel and suit and contemplated the severity of this situation as I dried off and put on the suit. I hoped it wasn't see-through, since there was no underwear. I stepped outside the shower and saw her waiting for me.

"What about my clothes?" I asked.

"Confiscated." She was a woman of few words.

"Can you tell me what exactly I came in contact with up there?"

Leslie shook her head.

"I just went through complete humiliation and let you sandblast me with water. I think I'm owed an explanation."

Tim was coming around the side of the truck, also dressed in a white suit. We looked more like twins than ever. He'd overheard my comment. "She'll find out soon enough," he said apologetically to Leslie.

To me, he said, "Brett, Wesley Lambert was making ricin up there. And there was enough to kill all of us."

Chapter 23

Ricin, it turns out, is a poison that's made from castor beans. Just a little bit can kill.

"It's a hot zone up there," Leslie said. "He had about ten vials of the stuff, and some had spilled. We can't take any chances that you or anyone else who came in contact with that condo will get sick."

"What are the symptoms?" I asked.

"Difficulty breathing, fever, cough, nausea, sweating." She paused. "Or severe vomiting and dehydration."

Which is what seemed to have happened with Wesley Lambert.

I didn't have any of the symptoms she listed, except maybe the difficulty breathing. But I think that had more to do with stress.

"We're sending you to the hospital to be checked out," Leslie continued, leading Tim and me to an ambulance. I saw the other responding police officers and the paramedics, all wearing suits like ours, being led into ambulances as well.

The driveway was crowded with city police vehicles, SWAT teams, and something called Metro Homeland Security. That's right. Frank DeBurra worked with Metro Homeland Security. I remembered Tim telling me. I raised my eyebrows at my brother.

"Ricin is used by terrorists," he explained.

Was Wesley Lambert a terrorist?

I didn't have time to think about it as Tim and I climbed into the ambulance. The doors closed behind us; we sat on little benches across from each other. The vehicle moved forward. I hadn't even noticed there was a driver up there. They probably didn't want to have anyone back here with us just in case we were contaminated.

"I've got a client," I said, remembering now. "I have to call the shop." Leslie had taken my messenger bag when she took my clothes. "Can I get my phone? The other things in my bag?"

"I'll talk to DeBurra. We'll have someone call the shop for you when we get to the hospital," Tim said, his mouth tight.

I didn't remember the last time I saw him scared, but he was. It made me even more tense. My big brother was supposed to be the calm one. But I found myself telling him it would be okay.

"Yeah, I know, but I'm worried about you. How did you get yourself involved with something like this?"

"Charlotte," I said softly, thinking about her somewhere out there, not knowing whether she was contaminated, not knowing if she was going to get sick. I really needed a phone, not only to call the shop, but also to call Ace. She'd run to him before; why not now?

I gave Tim the whole rundown on what had happened yesterday: going to the pawnshops, the hospital, trying to track down Charlotte. It was the short, abridged version, so when we pulled up outside the emergency room, he had most of it.

The back doors opened and a doctor in a white coat stood waiting. We stepped outside before I realized who it was.

"Dr. Bixby," I said. "Long time no see."

He seemed surprised to see me. But I couldn't figure out whether it was because I was the one involved with the ricin or because it was just me.

"Oh, yes, Miss Kavanaugh," he said, and Tim's eyebrows rose higher in his forehead.

"Dr. Bixby told me about Trevor yesterday." I felt an urge to explain, like someone would get the wrong idea.

Tim nodded, a small smile of amusement tugging at his lips.

"This must be your brother," Bixby said, looking from me to Tim, my carbon copy.

"She's adopted," Tim said with a straight face.

Bixby frowned. He didn't get it. Okay, something worse than living with his mother would be not having a sense of humor.

Not that he'd be interested in me now. I was contaminated.

Ugh.

Bixby led us through the emergency room waiting room, stopping at a small office just before the doors that led into where all the activity was. A short woman in a bright yellow sweater smiled at us from behind a desk. Before Bixby could say anything, she said, "We need your insurance information."

Tim and I looked at each other, and we both started laughing at the same time.

"What's so funny?" The woman got up and walked around the desk toward us.

Bixby looked confused.

Tim and I couldn't stop laughing. I think it was the stress.

Finally, I managed to sputter, "They took everything."

"Who?" The woman looked concerned, like we'd been mugged.

"They stripped us, took all our clothes, everything. We've got nothing but our birthday suits under these." Tim indicated the white suits.

The woman's eyes widened, as if she would rather think of anything else than Tim naked. I'd have to give him some grief about that later. She had her hand on the phone, her eyes asking Bixby whom she should call.

He put his hand up, and Tim and I started to calm down. "That's right, June, I didn't think."

"But we can't admit them without their insurance information," she argued.

This could be a long day. I pointed at the phone. "Can I use that?"

June looked at me as if I'd asked her if she was starring in the newest strip show downtown.

"You have to use the pay phone."

"That would mean that I need to have loose change," I said. "June, I've been exposed to some sort of poison, the police took all my clothes and my other worldly belongings, including my phone and my insurance card. I need to call my business and tell them I'm delayed."

Tim was nodding. "I'm a detective with the LVPD. I can vouch for her."

"This is highly unusual," June said, but she was wavering because Bixby was giving her that smile that he'd given me yesterday that made me all weak in the knees. "All right. As long as it's local."

"I'll take your brother back," Bixby said to me, then turned back to June. "Send her back when she's finished with her call."

June sat back down behind her desk and pushed the phone toward me. So much for any privacy. I dialed the shop number.

"The Painted Lady."

I was never so happy to hear Bitsy's voice as I was right that minute. While I'd just been laughing hysterically moments before, now I wanted to burst into tears.

"Bits, it's Brett," I said.

"Where are you? Your client will be here in a few minutes."

"I'm in the emergency room."

"Are you okay? What's wrong?" Panic rose in her voice.

"I had a little exposure to some sort of poison this morning, and they brought me here," I said.

She was quiet for a moment before asking, "What's going on, Brett? Poison? Exposure? What, did you drink some Drano or something?"

I found myself telling her what had happened; June's eyes grew wider with each word. She didn't even try to pretend she wasn't eavesdropping. I tried to ignore her. "And you have to call Ace, tell him to tell Charlotte to come to the emergency room. She needs to be decontaminated."

More silence, then, "Ace is here. He's worried about Charlotte. He says he hasn't seen her since last night and she won't answer her phone."

"Have him try everything he can think of. She needs to be looked at."

"Okay, will do. What about your client?"

"Do Ace and Joel have any clients now?"

"Joel's free for the next couple of hours."

"Can I talk to him?"

"Hold on."

A few seconds passed and I tried not to look at June, who was overtly staring at me. Finally, "Hey, sweetie, Bitsy says you got poisoned?"

At the sound of his voice, I lost it. Tears dripped down my cheeks, and I couldn't stop them. "I think I'll be okay," I sniffled.

"You want me to come over there?"

I wanted him to come in the worst way. Even though Tim was here, I felt like I needed a band of friends around me now. But I wiped my cheek with the back of my hand and said, "No, not now. But you have to take my client, okay?"

"No problem."

"The stencil's in his folder. It's a dagger wrapped with thorns. He wants it on his outside thigh; you'll see the space. There's not much, but it's there. It'll fit." As I gave the instructions, I felt myself calming down. The tears had stopped.

June, however, was frowning, trying to make sense of my conversation. With the suit on, she couldn't see my ink. Too bad. I bet she would've loved that story to tell her husband when she got home.

I asked to speak to Bitsy again. "Listen, Bits," I said. "Tim and I are going to need some clothes. They took ours.

They're probably going to burn them or something. Can you get to the house and bring something over for us? Underwear and all."

Bitsy has a key to our house. I lost mine at one point and couldn't get in touch with Tim for hours because he was on some sort of police stakeout thing, so I knew I needed a backup. Bitsy was one of the most responsible people I knew. She also had the code to our security alarm.

"No problem. When Joel's done with your client, he's got an hour or so. I'll get over to your house then."

"Thanks a lot, Bitsy. I really appreciate it."

Bitsy signed off, and I handed the phone back to June. She pointed out the door and down the hall. "Dr. Bixby is in there."

As I left the office, a frosted glass door slid open for me. Dr. Bixby was talking to Tim in a curtained area kitty-corner to where I was. Tim was on the bed, and a nurse was taking his blood.

I averted my eyes as I approached. Sure, I drew blood every day myself when I gave someone a tattoo, but seeing large amounts of it in vials didn't do much for me.

Dr. Bixby met me just beyond Tim's curtain. Tim smiled at me, and I smiled back, then met Dr. Bixby's eyes.

"We need a urine sample," he said, handing me a little cup with a screw-on lid.

How romantic.

He led me to the bathroom, and I felt like an over-achiever. It had been a long time since I'd been to the bathroom.

A nurse was hovering outside the door when I emerged with my cup, and she took it, handing me a johnny coat. "Can you put this on?"

I was more than happy to shed the white suit, but the johnny coat had an open back. There were a few snaps, and I did what I could to fasten them. When I emerged for the second time from the bathroom, Dr. Bixby was at my side again.

"We want to keep you here for the day," he said, "just in case you start exhibiting symptoms."

Great. But then he flashed me that George Clooney smile again and suddenly I didn't mind quite so much. It was obviously very one-sided, but it kept my mind off what had happened this morning.

Until those sliding doors opened, and Frank DeBurra walked in.

Chapter 24

DeBurra was sans white suit, and he wore the same frayed sport jacket he'd been wearing at Chez Tango and the other two times I'd seen him. Maybe he owned only one.

I thought again about Shawna. This guy was the polar opposite of Tim.

But then, that was probably the point.

DeBurra pointed at me. "I need to talk to you," he said.

Dr. Bixby shifted around and stood between us. "We need to get her a bed first. Then you can talk to her. I need to monitor her vitals."

I was ready to have him monitor my vitals all right.

Bixby's hand was under my elbow, and he was leading me toward the curtained area next to Tim, who was watching the whole thing like it was the Super Bowl on TV. Bixby pulled the curtain around the bed and motioned that I should get in.

"Thanks," I said. "He's been stalking me for two days." Again, however, I remembered that he hadn't been following me this morning. Why not? Maybe *I* had some questions for *him*. Suddenly it seemed really important to find out why he'd abandoned his mission to irritate me.

Bixby slapped a blood pressure cuff on my arm.

"Don't nurses usually do that?" I asked.

He gave me a long look, one I couldn't read. "Yes."

"Did you ever get in touch with Kyle about Trevor?" I asked.

He pumped up the cuff so much, I thought I'd lose circulation. Slowly he let it out, his stethoscope against the inside of my elbow. It was cold.

He noted my blood pressure on a piece of paper in a file, then cracked the folder shut. "We've been in touch, yes," he said. His tone was curt and professional.

"Did he come get Trevor's stuff?" I had nothing better to do than badger the good doctor.

But instead of looking annoyed, he let a smile tug at the corner of his mouth. He turned his head to try to hide it from me.

"Not yet."

"Are you done yet in there?" came a voice from beyond the curtain. Frank DeBurra. Bane of my existence.

"No," Bixby barked back.

I was liking this guy more and more.

"So do you hike?" I asked.

Bixby cocked his head to one side and studied me for a second before grinning and nodding. "Yes. What is this, twenty questions?"

"How long have you worked here?"

He chuckled. "Okay, I'll play. I've been here about five years."

"Where did you come from?"

His left eyebrow rose higher than the right one. I had no idea anyone could really do that. "Where most people come from," he said.

I snorted. "No, I know that. But where? What part of the country?"

"I grew up right here. In Vegas."

"Ha. No one actually grows up here."

"I did."

I started to get worried that he really did still live with his mother.

"Where did you go to medical school?" Figured I should stay on safer ground.

"Johns Hopkins."

Not too shabby.

"Did you always want to work in emergency medicine?"

"Did you always want to own a tattoo shop?"

I nodded. "Okay, turning things around, I see. No. I wanted to have an easel by the Seine in Paris and sell my paintings and live in a garret, a poor, starving artist."

"You studied art?"

"University of the Arts in Philadelphia. Concentrated in painting, yes."

"How did you get into the art of tattoo?" He seemed really interested. Go figure.

I held out my arm and turned it around so he could see the heart on the inside of my left wrist. "Gave myself that tattoo when I was sixteen. I liked the way it felt."

He didn't laugh. Instead he asked, "The way it felt when you drew it?"

I nodded. "Yeah. And then I went to a shop. The Ink Spot. My friend Mickey, he owns the place. He took me in as a trainee. Then I moved here a few years later." My life in a nutshell. Somehow it seemed like I should've done more in my thirty-two years, but I was happy, so I guess that was all that mattered.

"Do you have any ink?" I asked, turning the tables on him now.

He turned his head, wrote something down. "Chicken, I guess. I don't like needles." Then he put a tourniquet around my upper arm, told me to make a fist, and slid a needle into my vein.

"For you, not other people," I said, turning my head so I couldn't see the blood filling the vial.

He noticed.

"Does blood make you queasy?" he teased.

"Only in large quantities," I said.

I felt the needle slide out of the crook of my arm, then a pressure. When I looked, Bixby was holding a small piece of gauze to the spot where he'd stuck me.

"Are you doing anything tonight?" he asked.

"I might be contaminated," I said.

He peered into my face. I noticed his eyes were a clear green with a tint of brown. His hair was spiky, like it was yesterday. All he needed was an eyebrow piercing and he'd be totally punk.

The thought of it made me all hot and bothered.

"You're okay," he said after a few seconds.

"How can you be sure?"

"You're not exhibiting any signs. And if you got that close, you would be having difficulty breathing now."

I could argue that I *was* having difficulty breathing, but it was only because his face was just inches from mine and I was having impure thoughts.

"What about my brother?" I managed to ask.

It was as if I'd popped a balloon. He stepped away and turned his back to me as he put the vial into a holder on a tray.

"How about tomorrow night?" he asked.

"All right, so you're hedging your bets now that I might be okay tomorrow, if not today."

I could see the side of his face and the grin.

"Tomorrow?" he asked again.

I thought about the shop. Bitsy did all the scheduling, and since my love life was a tad dry these days, I just let her make my appointments without any thought to actual dating. "I have to check my schedule," I said.

He sighed. "I see."

"No, I really have to check. I'm not sure about my appointments tomorrow. I can let you know as soon as I talk to my shop manager." I didn't want to sound too desperate for a date, so I left it at that, even though I probably could rearrange a client if necessary.

Bixby turned around, holding a metal clipboard with my folder on top of it. "That would be fine," he said, all professional now, but he gave me a wink as he pulled the curtain back and walked out.

I had a clear view of the frosted sliding doors from my

angle, but I couldn't see Frank DeBurra hovering anywhere. I took a deep breath, hoped that he wasn't close by, that he hadn't heard my exchange with Bixby.

The back of the bed was up, and I leaned back on it, closing my eyes. I wondered whether I could sneak over and see how Tim was doing.

I opened my eyes and sat up straighter. I swung my legs over the side of the bed. What could they do to me, except send me back here?

I had taken a couple of steps toward the curtain when the frosted doors slid open. I froze, worried it was DeBurra again.

But it wasn't.

It was none other than Lester Fine, actor turned politician.

Chapter 25

A young woman in a conservative black suit and white blouse was with him, along with a camera crew. June was behind them. I could hear her saying firmly, "You are not allowed back here, especially with those cameras."

Lester Fine turned his head and said something to her, flashing his trademark smile, but June was not daunted.

"You have to leave now or I'll call the police."

I didn't think it would be prudent to mention that besides Tim, there were four other officers in here being monitored as well as that condo security guard. And Frank DeBurra was probably not the only one with Metro Homeland Security who was trying to have words with all of us.

Dr. Bixby appeared from the other side of the center station, where the nurses were whispering among themselves as they stared at Lester Fine. Granted, celebrities are a dime a dozen in Vegas. But we usually don't see them defy all rules and bring a camera crew into an emergency room.

Bixby was pointing to the cameras, indicating that they needed to leave. Two big, burly security guards flanked the doctor and stepped forward to show that they meant business.

The cameramen shrugged at each other, admitting defeat, and seemed to apologize to Lester Fine just before disappearing back to the other side of those frosted sliders.

I was still peering around my curtain when Lester Fine looked over and straight at me. His eyes settled on my face, and I felt a shiver shimmy up my spine. And not in a good way.

I took a step back behind the curtain, out of sight, but peeked through the space between my curtain and the one next door. Bixby shook Fine's hand and smiled and nodded. That sort of smile and nod you give people when they've told you something and you're not really listening. I could see Lester Fine's lips moving, but since I can't read lips, I had no idea what he was saying. Bixby continued to smile and nod as he jotted something down on the papers on his metal clipboard.

Bixby indicated that Fine should follow him, and uh-oh, they were heading this way, tailed by that young woman, who was obviously some sort of flack of Fine's. I ducked back behind the curtain and hopped up onto the bed.

They passed me, Bixby glancing briefly toward me and smiling; Lester Fine didn't look anywhere but straight ahead.

I got back down off the bed, keenly aware that there was nothing underneath this johnny coat as a slight breeze from the air-conditioning shimmied up my bare legs and over my torso. Hugging the cotton jacket closer and hoping those snaps stayed put, I looked out at the bustling nurses and doctors at the center station. There was no sign of Bixby and Fine.

A face appeared next to mine, and I jumped. Tim laughed.

"What are you doing?" he asked.

"Just checking things out," I said.

"You're spying on Dr. Handsome and Lester Fine, aren't you?"

"Who?" I tried to act all innocent, but he didn't buy it. He knew me too well.

"They went out a door over on the other side of my curtain. Frank DeBurra went with them."

"Really? Why do you think Lester Fine is here?"

"He's running for office."

"No kidding. But what does that have to do with—"

"He heard about what happened over at the Windsor Palms. He wants to try to make some sort of statement, get on TV, the sort of crap all those politicians do." Tim hesitated a second, then said, "But I think there might be something else. I did a little poking around into Wesley Lambert after you showed me that sketch."

"He and Lester Fine knew each other," I interrupted.

Tim looked surprised. "How did you know that?"

"I Googled that Queen of Hearts Ball—you know, the AIDS fund-raiser about a year ago? Well, there were drag queens there, and Wesley Lambert was Shanda Leer. There were pictures of him and Lester Fine."

"Were there pictures of them together?"

I thought a second. "No, but there was a picture of Wesley Lambert with Charlotte."

The instant I said it, I wanted to take it back. Tim got that cop look about him, the one that was all excited because there might be a break in the case. Although what that break could be, I wasn't exactly sure.

"Do you think Charlotte was part of the ricin plot?" Tim asked.

"What ricin plot? Was there a plot?"

"Brett," Tim said, his tone condescending, "ricin is a poison used by terrorists. And you don't whip up a batch in your bedroom just for giggles. Wesley Lambert was going to use that for something. We should just be happy that he wasn't Mr. Wizard, and it took him down first."

My instincts were screaming that Lambert wasn't the only victim.

"Tim, Lambert was poking around Chez Tango the other night; then Trevor gets really sick and dies. He gets stomach sick. You know, it seems really similar to the symptoms Dr. Bixby mentioned." I paused a second. "DeBurra thinks so, too. Remember how he said this puts 'that queen's' death into question? He must have come to the same conclusion."

"You think somehow Lambert poisoned Trevor McKay at that club."

"Yeah, I think so. He was looking for Trevor backstage. Eduardo saw him, but I don't know how long he was there. Maybe he got into Trevor's things—his makeup case, maybe—before Eduardo showed up."

"You think he poisoned the makeup?"

I thought a second. "Trevor had his makeup on already when Lambert was backstage. So I don't know."

"Don't those guys refresh their lipstick or something?" Tim wasn't making a joke; he was totally on the same page with me on this.

"He might have."

"Where's that makeup case now?"

"Charlotte brought it to Trevor's house." As the words came out, again I regretted them. But Charlotte was becoming the most common denominator in this whole mess.

"And she had access to that condo where Wesley Lambert had his little science experiment going on," Tim said, running his hand through his hair and nodding. "You really don't know where she is?"

"No one does. Not even Ace, and she was with him yesterday." I didn't tell him that Charlotte had spent a lot of time with Trevor before the show. But I did think of something else. "You know, if Charlotte wanted to do Trevor some harm, why not when he got his tattoo at our shop?"

"Who did the ink?"

"Ace." I could see what he was thinking: Ace and Charlotte were close enough so she ran to him when she was in trouble. I quickly said, "But that's not what happened, because we gave those guys their tattoos four weeks ago. Trevor would've been dead long before now."

It was a strange sort of logic. No, Trevor's demise was precipitated the other night at Chez Tango. It made more sense.

Tim was staring at me.

"What?" I asked curtly.

"What's going on with you? What are you thinking?"

I told him about Rusty Abbott, Lester Fine's assistant.
How he had that queen-of-hearts playing-card ink like the
guy who shot the cork at Trevor. "I have no idea how all
these people are linked, except that they all were at that ball
together." I had another thought. "And then there's Trev-
or's pin. A jeweled one with the queen of hearts on it. He
said he got it from Lester Fine. And he pawns it occasionally for cash, then buys it back, which is what happened just
before Wesley Lambert came around looking for Trevor,
saying there was a mistake or something with buying the
brooch back. Then the pawnshop guy says the brooch is
stolen. Maybe that was the mistake. But now Lambert and
Trevor are both dead, so we might never know." I paused
for a second, another thought crashing into all the others.

"Do you think Lester Fine had something to do with
all this?" I asked Tim. "I mean, he gave Trevor the pin, he
knew Wesley Lambert, he's Rusty Abbott's boss, and now
he shows up here for 'publicity' reasons." I made little quo-
tation marks with my fingers. "Maybe he's here to find out
what we know, find out whether anyone's on to him."

Tim chuckled. "*On to* him? You think he's the master-
mind of whatever's going on, Brett?" But then his smile
disappeared and he shrugged. "Then again, if all fingers
point in one direction . . ." His voice trailed off.

This was becoming like that magic trick where you hide
a ball under one of three cups. Mix them up and see if you
can find the ball. But what it was we were supposed to find
was eluding me.

My eye was way off the ball now, since Bixby was coming back toward us with Lester Fine and his flack in tow.

Chapter 26

They stopped right in front of us.

"Excuse me?" Lester Fine, I noticed now, was about as tall as I was, maybe a hair taller. He wasn't as good-looking in person as he was in the movies or on TV; he had some acne scars on his jawline and neck that probably were disguised by makeup when he was acting. "Are you the victims of the incident this morning?"

I looked around. Victims? What victims?

Then I saw he was looking at me and Tim.

"Who, us?" I asked.

Bixby was trying to push Lester Fine along without actually touching him. It didn't work. Fine opened his mouth to say something else, but before he could, we heard the frosted sliders open and turned in unison to see Bitsy carrying a tote bag that was almost bigger than she was. June was hurrying after her.

"You can't be in here," June said loudly.

Bitsy saw me, waved, and turned to June. "I'm just dropping this off," she said, indicating the tote bag, in a tone that clearly said, *Don't mess with me.*

June looked up at Dr. Bixby and shrugged. Bixby nodded, as if to say it was all right. June turned and went back out the doors. Bitsy continued toward us.

Bitsy grinned, reveling in the fact that everyone was watching her.

"What's up with the door Nazi?" Bitsy demanded. "Like this is some sort of *prison*."

Being a little person, she had no problems being a little politically incorrect.

I, on the other hand, wanted to shrink into the floor and disappear. Although not as much as I did just a second later, when Bitsy pointedly looked up at Bixby and winked. "He's cute," she said, handing me the tote bag.

I felt my face grow hot.

The bag weighed a ton. I wanted to see exactly what Bitsy had brought. Maybe a saw, so Tim and I could break out of this joint.

Bitsy was the first to break the ice.

"You have to stay here all day?"

I was keenly aware that we'd already been here a couple hours, that it was now past noon, and that I was hungry. I was starting to hope Bitsy really did put a saw in that bag, or at least something that would give me an excuse to leave.

"Just to monitor them," Dr. Bixby said.

"The TV crew is just outside. I don't see why this is a problem." Lester Fine obviously had moved beyond the current conversation. He was completely ignoring his lackey, who stood behind him, shifting uncomfortably from foot to foot. I tried to catch her eye, but she was staring at the floor, her head down like a good servant. I felt bad for her.

Bixby shook his head. "I'm sorry, Lester, but cameras are not allowed back here. HIPAA laws, you know."

Ah, patient privacy rules. I liked the sound of that.

But Lester Fine was not one to give up easily. "We could take them outside and talk to them there, and then they can come back."

Take who outside? He was staring at me and Tim. Oh, right, the "victims." But before I could say anything, Bitsy jumped in.

"Just who do you think you are?" Bitsy's voice bellowed louder than her small stature would imply. "Are you looking for some photo op that would make you look good to voters?"

Lester Fine looked at Bitsy then, a snarl creeping around his mouth. "And just who do you think *you* are?"

Uh-oh.

"I am one of those voters. You should speak to me with a little more respect. I am also this woman's friend, and she's been through a horrible ordeal today, and you can't exploit that for your own personal gain. Maybe I should go out there and tell those reporters the kind of person you are."

I wanted to applaud, but it might not go over well.

Lester Fine's face had turned a bright shade of red. He took a deep breath and stood up a little straighter. He pulled down on his suit jacket, held his head high, and stormed off around the center station and out the frosted doors without a response. The woman shuffled off after him.

Bixby was smiling at Bitsy. "Thanks. He wouldn't listen to me."

"You have to know how to talk to some people in just the right way," Bitsy said, turning her charm on.

"How many TV crews are there out there?" I asked, eager to interrupt.

"I counted three trucks," Bitsy said.

"Detective DeBurra said he'd deal with them," Bixby said. That must be where he was, then. Dealing with the media. Of course now Lester Fine had gone out to show off his pretty face, so even without the "victims" they'd still get a story.

Tim had taken the tote bag from me and was rifling through it on my bed. He took out a pair of jeans and a button-down shirt, a pair of socks, shoes, and boxers. He started for his own curtained area, but Bixby put his hand up.

"You can't change yet. We can't release you for another couple of hours."

Tim stared him down. "You said yourself that we're probably okay."

"Probably. Not definite." Bixby took the pile of clothing. "We'll keep this safe, and you can change later."

"It's cold in here," I said.

Bixby took out the boxers and socks and handed them to Tim. He looked at me and said, "You can put something on, too, but you have to keep the johnny coat on."

Great. But it was better than nothing.

Tim, clutching his clothing, went behind his curtain.

Bixby turned to Bitsy. "You can stay for five more minutes, but then you have to leave."

She nodded and smiled. Bixby smiled back, as if he couldn't help himself.

"He's really cute," she whispered, pulling my curtain closed.

"I know," I whispered back. I took a pair of underwear out of the bag and slipped them on. The bra was a black lacy one, a Victoria's Secret purchase from when I was dating Simon Chase the playboy. I raised my eyebrows at Bitsy as I held it up, and she chuckled.

"It's for the doctor," she said innocently.

I took off the johnny coat and put the bra on, wishing it covered up more than it did. It was one of those bras that make you look like you're a lot more endowed than you are, because it squeezes everything together.

It was not comfortable.

I gazed longingly at the stretchy slim black T-shirt in the bag. I made an executive decision and slipped it over my head. Without debating with myself, I also put on the skinny dark jeans and the Tevas and wadded the johnny coat up and threw it in the corner.

Bitsy just stared. "You're not supposed to change," she admonished, but in a whisper.

"I'm getting out of here. We need to find Charlotte."

"I don't know where she is," Bitsy said. "Joel and Ace and I have called all over."

"She's got to be somewhere, and I hope she's not sick," I said, peering out through the crack in the curtain. Bixby was nowhere to be seen; the nurses were busy tending to other patients.

"So what's the plan?" she asked.

"You're going to have to go out there and make some sort of diversion so I can slip out unnoticed."

"Like maybe I should fall or something, make a racket, and tell them I'm going to sue?"

"Sounds good to me."

Bitsy cocked her head in Tim's direction. "What about him?"

"What he doesn't know won't hurt him." Even as I said it, though, I felt a bit guilty. And a little nervous. He wouldn't be happy once he knew I left without authorization. I tried to convince myself that I felt fine, and no one had committed me here. I was a free agent.

I could probably kiss any sort of date with Dr. Bixby good-bye.

Bitsy handed me a set of keys. "My car is in the parking garage, level three. It's right near the elevator. You can't miss it. I'll meet you there."

I gave her a quick kiss on the cheek. "You're the best, Bits."

"You do know I expect a raise for all this?"

I couldn't tell whether she was joking. I watched her go out around the center station and through the frosted doors. Within seconds, a loud thud shook the floor, and I heard a cry. I hoped she really hadn't hurt herself.

Clutching the keys, I stepped out into the main area among the nurses who were heading for the waiting room to see what had happened. One stopped me.

"Where are you going?"

I indicated the bathroom. She nodded her approval and continued past me. I stopped in front of the bathroom door, glancing around for Dr. Bixby, but didn't see him. I did see Tim, looking out from behind his curtain.

I gave him a little wave and a nervous smile, and just as he took a step toward me, I bounded out the frosted doors. Bitsy was on the floor, four nurses and June surrounding her. She gave me a wink as I caught her eye, and I kept walking.

The door to the parking garage was just to the left; I

could see the media circus outside, Lester Fine preening and Frank DeBurra scowling.

I pushed open the door that led to the garage; the heat hit me squarely in the face. The elevator gods were with me, though, because when I pressed the button, the doors slid open immediately. I went inside, hit three, and watched the doors close in front of me.

Chapter 27

I scrunched down in the front seat of Bitsy's MINI Cooper as well as I could. The car was made for a little person, not for someone almost six feet tall.

As far as I knew, no one had followed me.

But then I had a thought: What if they demanded Bitsy stay and be "monitored," too? Just so they could avoid a lawsuit?

A little flaw in what we'd thought was a perfect plan.

My leg fell asleep, and when I moved it, pins and needles tickled my muscles. I wondered what time it was; Leslie had taken my watch along with my earrings. I rubbed my earlobes. They were naked.

Ah, brilliant idea. I shimmied around and stuck the keys in the ignition, turning it until the clock lit up like a Christmas tree.

Two o'clock.

I debated turning on some music but decided against it in case someone came by and heard it and wondered why the radio was on in a car that was apparently empty.

I counted the seconds and watched the numbers slowly change on the clock. One minute, two minutes, three minutes . . . This was going to get old really fast.

Footsteps outside. I peered up at the window and saw a hand reaching for the door. Every muscle got tighter.

Bitsy climbed in and gave me a grin as she put on her seat belt and turned over the engine.

"You look like origami gone bad," she said.

"How'd it go?" I asked, ignoring her.

"Oh, I made a fuss, then got up and showed them my miraculous recovery." She paused and looked down at me. "Dr. Bixby saw you leave."

"How do you know?"

"He walked me to the elevator and said if you show any symptoms at all, you have to come back. He also said he'd have to alert the authorities."

Either he was on my side or he wasn't. He couldn't be on the fence. That didn't bode well. Especially since "the authorities" would undoubtedly be Frank DeBurra, who was already mad at me because I hadn't yet answered any of his questions.

Bitsy stopped at the garage cashier and handed over a few dollars.

"I expect to get reimbursed," she said grimly as we pulled out into the sunshine.

"Yeah, yeah, yeah," I said and started to stretch out.

"Not yet," Bitsy warned as the car turned.

Sirens sounded from somewhere.

"They're behind us," she said.

"How far back?"

"Far enough."

"Are you sure they're after us?"

"No. But I don't want to do anything that would make them suspicious, so stay low and I'll take care of it."

Bitsy was very good at taking care of things, but she also could take things too far. As I felt the car speed up, I got a little worried.

"I can lose them," Bitsy muttered to herself.

The car turned this way and that, and I had to hold on to the center console to keep from getting bumped around. I gazed longingly at the seat belt that dangled just over my head. The pins and needles were worse now.

A few more turns and we could no longer hear the sirens.

"I think you can get up now," Bitsy said.

Easier said than done. I finally managed to get into the seat, reaching over my arm for the seat belt and securing it.

I didn't recognize where we were. It looked as though we were in an alleyway.

"Where are we?" I asked.

"You'll know soon enough."

I knew better than to question her further.

Finally she pulled up against the curb and stopped the car. She turned to me.

"Do you think you can find Charlotte?"

"I don't know."

"You don't think she killed that guy, do you?" Bitsy asked.

I'd briefly asked myself the same question but pushed it aside. I'd seen Wesley Lambert's body and its environs. It seemed as though he'd just died from getting sick from the ricin. Nothing had been mentioned about the possibility of him being murdered. "No." I paused. "I don't know how long I'll be." I thought about my clients. "Can you reschedule my afternoon?"

Bitsy smiled. "Already did. And I'm not kidding about the raise."

"I know."

"And you'll have to pay me back."

"Two dollars for parking?"

She was handing me a bunch of bills. "You're going to need something so you can get around."

I took it, quickly counting out fifty bucks. "Thanks. You'll get everything back and then some."

She smiled. "I know. Call later and let us know what's up."

I got out of the car, then leaned down and asked, "Where are we, anyway?"

"In a safe place," she said.

I shut the door and she took off. I watched the back end of the MINI Cooper until it turned right and out of sight.

Looking around, I suddenly became aware of a stink that was emanating from a Dumpster just a few feet away. Mixed in with it was the odor of Chinese food. Steam was pouring out of a vent in the building to my left. A Mexican guy wearing a stained white chef's coat was sitting on a plastic milk crate and smoking a cigarette, talking to a guy who had his back to me. Smoke curled up from the cigarette dangling from the guy's fingers.

The salt-and-pepper buzz cut and the ink on his arms told me where I was.

In the alley behind Murder Ink.

Chapter 28

Jeff Coleman turned around and lifted the cigarette to his lips. He took a drag, blew out the smoke, and said, "Took you long enough, Kavanaugh."

The Mexican stamped out his cigarette on the concrete, nodded at me and Jeff, and went inside.

I walked over to Jeff, who'd started for the back door to Murder Ink.

"How did you know I was coming?"

"Bitsy called."

"Did she tell you what was going on?"

"Said you needed some help. Why she thought of me, I don't know."

I knew. No one would think to come here, not Tim, not Frank DeBurra.

I was definitely giving that girl a raise.

"What's going on?" Jeff asked, holding the door open for me.

As we went inside, I told him how Bitsy and I had escaped the hospital—and the police.

"And why did you need to escape?"

"Have you seen the news today?" With all the camera crews outside the emergency room, it must be all over TV.

"I don't exactly have time to be watching *Oprah*. Why don't you tell me what's going on?" He shoved a chair on wheels in my direction, and I stopped it with my foot and sat down. He settled into a worn black leather chair and stuck his feet up on the desk, on top of a pile of stencils.

I started at the beginning and told him the whole thing.

When I was done, his mouth was hanging open.

"You do manage to get yourself into all sorts of predicaments, Kavanaugh."

"It wasn't my fault. Charlotte—"

"Got you into trouble," he finished for me. "That girl *is* trouble. Have you stopped to consider that maybe she's part of all this?"

I frowned. "No."

"That's because you're way too trusting, Kavanaugh. The world hasn't chewed you up and spit you out yet."

"Oh, is that why you look the way you do? Because you've been spit out?"

He stared at me a second, and then chuckled. "You really need to lighten up."

"I really need to find Charlotte and make sure she's okay."

"Don't you think the cops are out looking for her? Why would you be able to find her first?"

Good question.

I heard a buzzer in the distance.

Jeff looked up at a clock on the wall. "That's my client." He got up and shoved the stencils around, grabbing one.

"So you're just going to leave me back here?" I asked.

He shrugged. "You can stay or you can go." He reached into the front pocket of his jeans and pulled out a set of keys. "If you promise to drive safe, you can borrow my car." He tossed me the keys.

I reached out and caught them with my left hand.

He grinned. "Good catch. Car's in back. Gold Pontiac." He started for the front of the shop, then paused, turning back for a second. "Be careful, Kavanaugh."

"Why are you being so nice?"

"Because maybe I'd like to think that the girl's not guilty, either. And no cracks about me having a heart or anything."

He disappeared through the sixties-style colored beads in the doorway.

I eyed the keys in my hand. He didn't have to know that I didn't have my driver's license on me. Did he?

I shoved the back door open and found his car just up past the Chinese restaurant.

"Gold" was an understatement. It was as bright as a new penny. I certainly wouldn't be undercover in this. But who would think to look for me in a gold Pontiac anyway? As I climbed into the driver's seat, I started to feel a little invincible.

But just a little.

The car smelled like cigarettes, and I had a sneaking suspicion that I would, too, once I emerged. The ashtray was overflowing with butts, and I pulled it out and took it over to the Dumpster, where I emptied it.

I started the car and pondered where I should go. Tim would argue that I should go back to the hospital, answer DeBurra's questions, and apologize for running out on Dr. Colin Bixby. That would be the right thing to do.

Instead, I turned north on Las Vegas Boulevard.

If Charlotte wasn't at Ace's, like yesterday, and she probably wasn't home because the police were sitting on top of her apartment, then where would she go?

She might be at Trevor's.

I didn't know where Trevor lived, but I did know where Chez Tango was, and maybe Kyle was there. He might know where Trevor's place was.

I continued along Las Vegas Boulevard, crossing over Fremont Street. The neon still flashed in the daytime, luring the tourists and the gamblers. It was that shiny object that tantalized and tempted. The city had turned this portion of Fremont into a pedestrian walkway, like it was some sort of family attraction. As if poker and slots and strip shows were child's play.

I left Fremont Street behind and continued a couple of blocks until I turned into Chez Tango's parking lot.

It was a little jarring to see Chez Tango in the bright

light of day. It was a short, squat, stucco building that
spread along half a block. At night, white and gold Christmas lights twinkled along the outline of the roof and
around the entrance, making it festive and almost magical.
Now the string of lights hung slackly, like an old woman's
breasts.

I pulled in next to an old pickup truck.

I'd seen that truck before.

Outside Cash & Carry.

I gripped the steering wheel. Rusty Abbott had gotten
into that pickup yesterday. As he ran from me for the second time.

I thought about what Jeff Coleman had said, that Rusty
Abbott said accidents happen.

Would he run again if I approached him here?

I was tired of the game, but just as I figured I had nothing to lose, I thought about how it might be better to meet
up with him in a public place. Certainly not a mostly deserted Chez Tango. My idea about going inside quickly dis-
integrated. I wasn't going to be that stupid.

The sound of a car pulling into the lot startled me. It was
a dusty blue Honda CRV, and it came to a stop on the other
side of the pickup, out of my line of sight.

I heard a door slam; then a figure walked around the
front of the pickup.

Kyle Albrecht, aka MissTique.

Ah, a friendly face.

I got out of the car. "Hey, Kyle," I said.

When he saw who I was, he smiled. "Brett, what are you
doing here?" Then the smile disappeared and he said som-
berly, "Awful about Trevor, right?"

I nodded. "Yeah. I'm so sorry."

"Is that why you're here? About Trevor?" he asked, his
curiosity obvious.

"Sort of." I glanced at the pickup. "Do you know the guy
who owns this truck?"

Kyle studied the truck, then shook his head. "No.
Should I?"

"No, guess not." I paused. "I'm actually looking for Charlotte. She could be in trouble."

Concern flooded Kyle's face. "What's wrong?"

I tried to make light of it. "Some police detective thinks she might be in some sort of danger." I attempted a laugh, but it came out a little twittery and not all too human. "This morning she called me, said she needed my help. Asked me to meet her at a condo off the Strip. When I got there, Wesley Lambert was dead. Ricin poisoning. She was gone already, but I know she was there earlier. She might be sick." I figured I would play on his sympathy.

But he was still wrapping his head around the whole story and didn't seem to be able to concentrate on one thing, until: "Wesley Lambert? You're kidding, right?"

"Not kidding, Kyle."

"And Charlotte might be sick? How?"

"Just by inhaling the ricin. It was spilled all over."

He gave me a long look. "You don't think she killed him or anything, do you?"

Bitsy had asked the same thing, and I gave him the same answer I gave her, although admittedly I couldn't help wondering the same thing. "No."

"How do you know she was at Wesley's?"

I told him about the pink hoodie, which reminded me . . .

"Did you ever find out who owned that gray sweatshirt we found at the club the other night?"

Kyle nodded absently. "Yeah, it was Stephan's. Where do you think she went?"

"I thought maybe she might go to Trevor's place to hang low, but I don't know where Trevor lives."

Kyle cocked his head at the Pontiac. "That your ride?"

I hated to admit it and nodded reluctantly.

He walked around to the passenger side. "Let's go."

Chapter 29

Trevor lived in an apartment complex on Charleston Boulevard, going west toward Red Rock. The gray mountains rose in the distance as I drove past office buildings, gas stations, hole-in-the-wall eateries, and condominiums.

Kyle was asking about ricin.

"It's made from castor beans," I said, one of the few things I knew about it myself.

"How?"

I had absolutely no idea. "I bet we could find out online."

"We can find out how to build a nuclear bomb online," Kyle said.

I thought about what Tim had said about ricin being a weapon of terrorists. "We'd probably get on some sort of government list if we looked it up," I said.

He laughed and batted his eyelashes. "Honey, we're probably already on some government list."

He was right about that. I bet Frank DeBurra had the Secret Service out looking for me right this very second. It probably didn't help that I was driving a car that the bad guys on *Miami Vice* would find cool. I just hoped that Jeff Coleman didn't have any sort of outstanding traffic tickets that would alert the cops and get us stopped.

I wasn't one to speed and I rarely even ran yellow lights, so I knew my driving habits wouldn't draw attention.

Kyle pointed to an apartment building that looked like something out of Tudor England. It was out of place among the stucco and banana yuccas.

"Turn here," he instructed.

I did as I was told, and I pulled around the building, which I saw now was raised, with parking spots underneath. Kyle directed me to a spot that he said was just under Trevor's apartment.

I made sure to lock up the Pontiac. Not that there was anything in it to steal, except maybe the car itself. This definitely looked like a gold Pontiac neighborhood.

We climbed a staircase up to the walkway that ran along the perimeter of the building. The apartments were lined up along it like little wooden soldiers.

Kyle stopped at the one closest to the stairway, took out a key, unlocked the door, and opened it.

Trevor's apartment was a mess. At first I thought maybe someone had tossed it on purpose, but Kyle didn't seem to notice anything out of the ordinary.

"Charlotte?" I called, then turned to Kyle when no one answered. "Was he this messy?" I asked, noting the piles of beauty and celebrity magazines next to the flowered sofa and more cardboard boxes than I could count. "Or was he moving?"

Kyle grinned. "Our Britney loved the QVC." He pointed out the exercise equipment taking up the corner of the room and the wigs hung suspended from it. It looked like a character from some creepy Tim Burton movie.

I stepped over piles of sequined clothing and stiletto shoes toward the galley kitchen. Dirty dishes were stacked in the sink, and it smelled like that Dumpster behind Murder Ink. I wrinkled my nose. "How did he live like this?" I asked.

Kyle held up a pair of nylons. "These are in good shape," he said, stuffing them in his front pocket. He picked a silk top up off the floor and held it up in front of his chest. "Is it my color?"

"You know, Kyle, Trevor's dead. Do you think he'd want you rifling through his things?"

Kyle chuckled. "Trevor would be the first one to clean this place out, girl. Nothing should go to waste."

I pushed aside heavy curtains, letting the sun in, and opened a sliding glass door that led to a small balcony overlooking the front entrance to the complex. A small breeze wafted in, and I wondered whether it would be enough to air this place out.

The bathroom was in worse shape than the kitchen: makeup everywhere. Kyle started pawing through it, picking up mascara and taking out the wand to make sure it was still fresh. He wiped some foundation on his face with a cotton ball and turned to me.

"Too dark, right?"

Kyle's skin was very pale, as compared to Trevor's darker, tanned complexion. I nodded, moving toward the bedroom.

More of the same. I didn't even bother going farther than the doorway. It was starting to get to me, how sad it made Trevor's life seem, living in this mess.

"She's not here," I said as I passed the bathroom. Kyle was still playing with the makeup.

I went back out onto the balcony to collect my thoughts. There was a white plastic chair there, with a matching table. I sat down and looked out at the street through the slats in the balcony wall.

"Didn't Charlotte say she was bringing Trevor's makeup case here after the show the other night?" Kyle asked, startling me. He'd put on one of Trevor's wigs, a dark, flowing mess of curls that actually looked pretty good on Kyle. The dress he'd donned was purple lamé, and it would be clingy in all the right places if there were any of those places to cling to. But Kyle was just playing dress-up and had forgone any semblance of breasts.

Still, he was a fine-looking woman.

"Isn't his makeup case in there?" I asked, indicating the bathroom.

"Not the one he used for shows. I can't find it anywhere."

I frowned. That was funny. Charlotte had taken the case that night. And as I thought about the case, I remembered that Dr. Bixby had the brooch. He'd said it was the only item Trevor had on his person when he went to the hospital. Somehow the brooch had gone from the case to Trevor, but where was the case?

I leaned over and put my elbows on my knees and my head in my hands, closing my eyes. I needed to make sense of all this.

Unfortunately, my brain was all mixed up right now.

"What about this?"

I looked up to see Kyle posing in a shimmery satin minidress and thigh-high white patent leather boots.

"Very Donna Summer," I said.

Kyle grinned. "And this isn't the best part."

I wondered what that would be: Another wig that would hit the ceiling? Huge round rhinestone sunglasses?

"Guess what I found in the boots."

I didn't want to know. From the state of Trevor's apartment, there could be a family of small rodents playing house in those boots. There was certainly room enough in them.

But when Kyle held out his hands, instead of mice, they were filled with bills. As in money. As in the most cash I'd ever seen in one place besides a casino.

Chapter 30

My mouth hung open as I stared. "How much?" I managed to stammer.

Kyle chuckled. "This isn't all of it. There's money stashed in all the boots, and that girl loves her boots."

I followed him into the bedroom, which I'd dismissed before as just another room where a hurricane had blown through. Now, though, I watched as Kyle pulled boot after boot out from under the bed, sticking his hand inside each one and taking out wads of bills, dumping them on top of the unmade bed.

I peered around the closet door. "Any in here?"

"He seems to have kept all the boots under the bed, for some reason."

The boots were all thigh high and patent leather, and in all the colors of the rainbow. There were ten pairs, when all was said and done.

"Didn't Trevor believe in banks?" I asked.

"These might be tips," Kyle said, his tone matter-of-fact. "This is the cash we don't want Uncle Sam to know about."

"What was he doing to get tips like this?" I asked, noting that most of the bills were either hundreds or fifties. I started counting.

Kyle was counting on the other side of the bed. We were silent for a while as we kept the numbers in our heads. Finally, Kyle said, "I've got twenty grand."

Our eyes met. "I've got thirty grand."

Kyle blew a low whistle. "This ain't tip money," he said. "No one's that good."

"I thought Trevor didn't have any money. That's why he kept pawning that brooch."

"If you listened to him, he never had any money." Kyle surveyed the bills, which we'd arranged neatly in piles. "What a con."

"Maybe it's not his," I said softly.

"It's in his boots," Kyle said.

He had a point. But something was nagging at me. "It seems like a coincidence that Wesley Lambert was poking around Chez Tango the other night. Now Trevor's dead, and Lambert is dead. Maybe it's not so much a coincidence."

We mulled that a few minutes.

"I wish I had my laptop," I said. "I really want to go on-line and look up ricin."

"So use Trevor's," Kyle said. "It's in the living room."

How he could spot things in this place was beyond me, but he disappeared and came back toting a laptop that was maybe a couple years old.

I didn't want to sit on the bed—who knew what was under those covers?—so I took the laptop out onto the balcony and set it on the small table. I flipped up the top and turned it on, keeping my fingers crossed that there was wireless.

Trevor didn't have it, but someone by the name of Priestly didn't have a secure account. Fortunately, Priestly wasn't online at the moment, so I accessed the account with no problem. I might not run yellow lights, but I have no scruples when it comes to stealing Internet connections.

Priestly would think it was Trevor's ghost anyway.

I Googled ricin and found a slew of news stories, a few from right here in Vegas. Some guy making ricin in a hotel room a couple years back. He died, too. The stories gave the symptoms, just like Dr. Bixby had related them to me.

I took a second to try to be aware of how I was feeling. I didn't feel nauseated, and I was breathing just fine.

A link caught my eye. Some guy in London in the seventies. Stabbed with the end of an umbrella, which was fitted with a small pellet of ricin. The guy died after exhibiting flulike symptoms.

A thought started to form. I didn't much like it, but it would explain things.

Kyle was staring at me. "What?" he asked. "What did you find?" He'd found time to apply about three layers of fake eyelashes, and he batted them at me.

"I think Trevor was poisoned," I said slowly.

He snorted. "How? At my club?"

I nodded. "The champagne cork. I think it was laced with ricin."

Chapter 31

We took Trevor's laptop with us after stuffing the money back in the boots. Kyle wanted to take it, but I didn't want to have that much cash on my person. I already had Rusty Abbott warning me about accidents, and with that kind of money on me, accidents could most definitely happen.

I was also convinced now that Rusty Abbott was the champagne shooter and somehow he was involved with Wesley Lambert.

It was the ink.

Granted, Jeff Coleman had said two other men had gotten the tattoos the same night, too. But I hadn't seen anyone else with one yet. So it was easy to place blame.

I'd definitely have to ask Jeff for the other two names when I brought his car back.

I hated to admit it, but it rode well. Not as well as my Mustang Bullitt, but well enough so I wasn't uncomfortable like I was in Bitsy's car. I'd been folded up like a pretzel in hers, but even when I wasn't, my head hit the ceiling.

"So you think someone put ricin on that cork and deliberately shot Trevor with it?" Kyle asked. He hadn't taken off the dress, the wig, the boots, or the eyelashes, so I supposed I should address him as Miss Tique.

Who knew I'd be driving a drag queen around in a gold Pontiac? Just call me Huggy Bear.

I nodded. I remembered something else, too. How De-Burra had told me at the scene that no one could find the cork that hit Trevor. Maybe somehow the shooter had managed to get the cork before anyone else could touch it and get contaminated. That way it would seem like a coincidence when Trevor got sick.

"Do you think Charlotte had something to do with it?" Kyle asked.

I sighed. It all kept coming back to her. She was buzzing all over that stage after Trevor got hit. And she did know Wesley Lambert.

"So where do you think she might be?" Kyle interrupted my thoughts.

"I don't know where to look now," I admitted. "I really thought she'd be at Trevor's."

"Maybe she was there, then left."

"But where's Trevor's makeup case? I'm more inclined to think she was never there in the first place."

We mulled that over a few seconds as we finally reached Chez Tango. The pickup truck was gone, Kyle's Honda CRV the only vehicle in the lot.

"Want to come in?" he asked.

"I could use a phone," I said, thinking I should call Bitsy at the shop and see how angry Tim was. And if Frank De-Burra was ready to lock me up and throw away the key. I still hadn't answered his questions, and now I was AWOL.

Kyle, or, rather, MissTique, sashayed across the parking lot to the back door at Chez Tango. He unlocked the dead bolt and held the door for me as I went inside.

It was so dark, I couldn't even see my hand in front of me.

"Lights?" I asked, and as I spoke, the hallway lit up like a chandelier.

Kyle moved past me, and I followed him into the dressing room behind the stage. Racks of sequined and lamé dresses stood sentry next to the row of mirrored dressing tables. As opposed to the other night, the tables were neat and uncluttered, the floor swept and clean.

"Is there a show tonight?" I asked.

Kyle nodded, taking a couple of dresses off the rack. He held up a gold sequined halter dress in front of him, his eyebrows arched high. "What do you think? It was Trevor's favorite. I think it's fitting I wear it tonight. We'll do a tribute to Britney." He wiped his eye and smiled.

"Trevor would love it," I said.

He sighed and pointed past the dressing tables. "The phone's in the office."

"Thanks." I left him trying on a wig of blond tresses similar to Britney's.

The office was dark, and I found a light switch. The dull yellow glow made me wonder when they had last changed the bulb. Or maybe it was one of those newfangled energy-saving bulbs. I'd gotten some for the house, and Tim kept complaining the light was too dim. I argued with him about it for the sake of energy conservation, but secretly I didn't think they were as bright as the old ones, either.

An old black rotary phone sat on the desk. Brought back memories as I dialed.

"The Painted Lady."

"Bits, it's me."

"Would you like to make an appointment?" Her voice was crisp, businesslike.

"Someone's there?"

"Tuesday at three sounds fine."

This wasn't very productive.

"Is it the cops?"

"Yes."

"They're looking for me?"

"Yes."

"Have you talked to Tim?"

"Yes."

"On a scale of one to ten, how mad is he?"

"Ten o'clock would be good, too."

Uh-oh.

"I guess I shouldn't go home for a while, huh?"

"No."

"I'm at Chez Tango. With Kyle. He went with me to Trevor's. Haven't found Charlotte. I'll keep you posted. Thanks for everything. I really mean it." I hung up. There was little more I could do.

I sifted through some papers on the desk. Invoices for booze, electrical bills—those might go down if they had the new lightbulbs—a pawnshop ticket.

I glanced quickly at the door to make sure Kyle wasn't coming.

The pawnshop ticket was from Pawned, the second place I'd visited yesterday and the place where Charlotte had gone. The item listed was a "jeweled pin." The seller? Trevor McKay. The date on the ticket was two weeks ago. And according to this, he'd gotten a hundred bucks for the brooch.

I turned the ticket over in my hand, looking for answers. But there was nothing there. I contemplated the office, which somehow seemed smaller today than it had the other night, when I did the drawing for Eduardo.

Thinking about that sketch, I realized I hadn't shown my drawing of Rusty Abbott to Kyle. I hadn't even asked him whether he knew the guy. They may have met at that ball.

Kyle didn't have a queen-of-hearts tattoo, though, so he wasn't one of the guys who'd gone with Abbott to Murder Ink.

I was so engrossed in my thoughts that I didn't hear him approach.

"What do you have there?"

I jumped. Not like a rabbit, but more like a little jolt. I shoved the pawnshop ticket under a stray piece of paper. "Do you know Rusty Abbott?" I asked.

Kyle, who had truly morphed into MissTique now with the addition of fake boobs, said, "He works for Lester Fine."

"So you know him?"

"I don't know him well. I met him at the Queen of Hearts Ball. He came to the club a couple times."

"He came to see a show?"

Kyle nodded.

"Did he come with Lester Fine?"

Kyle barked out a laugh. "Girl, Lester Fine wouldn't be caught dead in my club. He's running for public office. The headlines would tear him apart."

"Did you see Rusty Abbott around here the night Trevor got hit with the cork?"

He hesitated a second, then said, "I don't think so." The light was too lousy to see any real change in his expression.

"I think it was his truck that was outside earlier," I said.

He shrugged. "That was his truck? Then why did you ask me if I knew who it belonged to?" Suspicion crept into his tone.

I wasn't quite sure what to say. I had no idea what I was looking for.

Kyle sighed. "Brett, you've had a long day. You're tired and looking for conspiracies where they probably don't exist. Maybe you should just go home now and fess up to your brother that you went out looking for Charlotte and couldn't find her."

He was trying to get rid of me.

I was ready to be gotten rid of.

I wasn't exactly sure what was going on, but I did know that I suddenly felt very alone here at Chez Tango, and that wasn't a good thing.

"You're right," I agreed.

Before I left the dressing room, I turned around. Kyle had followed me out of the office and was standing with his hand on one hip.

"Thanks for everything."

"Will you tell your brother about the money?" he asked.

I nodded. "Yeah. I think I have to."

I started out again.

"Be careful, Brett," Kyle said to my back.

"You, too." I didn't turn around. Just kept walking.

The parking lot was still deserted except for the gold

Pontiac and the Honda. As I walked toward Jeff's car, the key in my hand, I knew something was wrong, but I couldn't put my finger on it.

When it hit me, I stopped. Stared.

All four tires were flat.

And when I stooped down to check them out, I saw why.

Someone had slashed them.

Chapter 32

I looked around, but I didn't see anyone except a woman walking down the sidewalk on the other side of the street. A few cars passed, but no one paid any attention to me or Chez Tango. One guy in a Ferrari did honk his horn and shouted something at the woman, who was now passing the Bright Lights Motel. She gave him the finger, and he sped past.

I caught her eye for a second, but she just shrugged and kept going. From the looks of her outfit—short, tight dress and stiletto heels—she was probably a working girl. If I asked her whether she'd seen anyone here, she'd most likely give me the finger, too.

I turned back to the car. Jeff was going to kill me.

I didn't have my bag on me, which meant I didn't have my AAA card. I didn't have a phone, either.

I had nothing. Except keys to a car that wasn't going anywhere. And about fifty bucks, thanks to Bitsy.

An inspection of Kyle's Honda indicated that whoever had done this might have been sending me and only me a message. Because the Honda's tires were intact. Who didn't want me to leave? Or, more likely, who didn't want me to keep moving forward with my little amateur investigation?

I thought about asking Kyle if I could borrow his Honda, but considering the state of Jeff's car, he might not think I was a safe bet. But I had to do something.

I went back into Chez Tango, pushing open the metal door, hearing it slam behind me with a heavy thud.

"Who is it?" I heard Kyle call out.

"It's just me," I said loudly as I made my way toward the stage, where Kyle was practicing a dance step. "I need to use your phone again."

He curtsied, then shimmied across the stage, his fake bosom shaking.

"Someone slashed my tires," I said as I climbed the steps up to the stage floor.

Kyle stopped short and pulled himself up straight, but his wig wasn't on properly and it moved by itself into his forehead. He shoved it back. "What do you mean, someone slashed your tires?"

"Just what I said."

"My car?"

"Is fine," I told him. "I just need to call a garage to come tow mine."

"*Mi teléfono es su teléfono*," Kyle said in mangled Spanish. Eduardo should teach him a few phrases.

I found myself back in the little office. I didn't have a phone book, but I figured I should face the music, so I called Jeff to see where he'd like me tow his car to.

"Murder Ink."

"Hi, Jeff," I said, trying to sound casual, but it came out a little funny.

"Kavanaugh? What's wrong?" Concern laced his voice. This wasn't going to be easy.

"Well, there seems to be a little problem," I started.

"Don't tell me you crashed my car. Please don't tell me that."

"I didn't crash your car."

I heard a heavy sigh of relief. "That's good."

"But someone slashed your tires."

A sharp intake of breath. "What?"

"The car was parked at Chez Tango. I was inside for maybe fifteen minutes. When I went back out, the tires were slashed. I have no idea who did it. Of course I'll pay for new tires. It was on my watch. So if you just tell me the name of the garage you want me to have it taken to, I'll get that done right now. I'm really, really sorry about this, Jeff." The words spilled out faster than water going over a New Orleans levee.

I could sense Jeff struggling with what to say. Finally, "I'll call the garage. Do you need a ride?"

I didn't want to impose any more than I already had, but I could hear the drag queens arriving and knew Kyle wouldn't have time to chauffeur me around.

"I do."

"I'll take care of it. Just go in the parking lot and meet the tow truck, okay?"

"No problem."

I was about to hang up, but he wasn't done yet.

"Kavanaugh, it's a good thing I like you."

Then he hung up.

I stared at the receiver in my hand. He liked me? What did that mean? That he *liked* me, or that he just liked me? I hoped it was the latter. I told myself it was the latter. I was the sister he didn't have. Or maybe another sister. I didn't know whether he had a sister or not.

I wandered through the dressing room. Stephan Price, wearing a nylon cap over his hair, carefully outlined his eyes with black eyeliner, preparing to bring Miranda Rites out for the night. He spotted me in the mirror and put the wand down. He got up and came over to me, put his arm around my shoulders, and squeezed.

"Hey, girl. Sad about Trevor, isn't it?"

I nodded. "Yeah, it is."

"Charlotte must be torn up, huh?"

All the stress of the day chose that very moment to come out. "Maybe she is, maybe she isn't. I can't find her. I talked to her this morning before I found Wesley Lambert's body. I don't know what sort of game she's playing." My tone was harsher than it should have been; I shouldn't take my frustrations out on Stephan, especially since he had nothing to do with anything that was going on.

"Wesley Lambert?"

For some reason, his brain seemed to have stuck on those two words, as if the others hadn't registered.

I nodded. "Yeah. He's dead. He was making poison in a condo on the Strip and managed to kill himself with it."

"Poison?"

"Ricin. And because of him, I ended up in the emergency room, stripped to my birthday suit, and getting interrogated by Lester Fine, of all people." I was rambling. I couldn't stop myself.

"Lester Fine?"

"He called me a victim; he was trying to get me on TV." I was a lost cause. I wasn't making any sense.

"Honey, you need a drink." Stephan leaned over to the dressing table, picked up a glass that was filled with ice and what looked like water, and handed it to me.

I chugged it. Felt like I was in college again. I didn't even choke when I realized it was vodka. Not my drink of choice, but the moment called for it. I handed Stephan back the empty glass and thought I was going to be sick.

He got me into a chair and told me to put my head between my legs. Go figure, it worked.

"So Wesley's dead?" Stephan asked.

I nodded as well as I could in my position. I felt Stephan's hand massaging my scalp. It felt good.

"I knew he'd get into trouble someday. But what does Lester Fine have to do with it?"

"Nothing. He was just trying to drum up the sympathy vote, I think." I raised my head and didn't feel sick anymore. Actually, I was feeling rather warm and fuzzy. A glass of vodka would do that to you.

I had another thought.

"But somehow his personal assistant, Rusty Abbott, is part of all this. I just know it. He's got the queen-of-hearts tattoo, you know, on his inner forearm. He could be the one who shot Trevor with the cork. I saw the ink with my own eyes."

Stephan laughed and sat in front of the mirror again.

He started spreading bright purple eye shadow under his eyebrows. "He's not the only one with a queen-of-hearts tattoo, you know."

I sat up straighter. "No, I don't know. Who else has one?"

"Wesley Lambert."

Chapter 33

I hadn't had a good view of Wesley Lambert's body when he was on the floor in that condo, and because of the vomit, I hadn't been inclined to study it, either. And then there was all that decontamination and emergency-room stuff afterward that I didn't even think to ask any questions about the scene or Lambert, either.

If he had a tattoo like Rusty Abbott's, and he'd been hanging around looking for Trevor and saying he'd "send him a message," then it was likely that Lambert was the guy who shot the cork at Trevor that night.

Mystery solved.

Maybe.

There was still that little matter of all that cash in Trevor's apartment.

And then there was Charlotte. She'd gone underground for some reason.

This wasn't over yet.

Marva Luss was sashaying around the dressing room in front of me, but she was only partially put together, too. She had a pair of nylons on and started to pull up a pair of Speedos that were about three sizes too small. I turned away. I couldn't watch. I didn't want to know what was going on there.

An unfamiliar queen was layering foundation on her face. It was thick, as brown as chocolate. She caught me staring and grinned.

"You don't need this much makeup, do you?"

I never wore foundation. My skin was as pasty as a white cotton sheet, except where I had my ink, of course. I wore only mascara, a little blush, and occasionally some lip gloss. I couldn't imagine caking it on like these guys—girls?—did.

She leaned over and held out her hand. "Just call me Chitty," she said.

I took her hand. She had a grip like a vise. I coughed out a short laugh. "Chitty?" I asked.

"Chitty Chitty Gang Bang."

I pulled my hand away. This was getting a bit too surreal for me. I needed to go out and wait for the tow, like Jeff had said.

I stood, gave Stephan an air kiss, and started out.

"Brett?"

I turned to see Stephan looking at me through the mirror.

"Yeah?"

"When you find her, tell Charlotte Trevor thought the world of her."

I nodded and smiled. "Yeah, I will."

Kyle was pirouetting across the stage. He flipped his hand up at me.

"We'll talk."

"I'm sure we will," I said.

The tow truck beat me to the parking lot. The tow guy already had the car up on the flatbed, ready to take it away. He frowned at me, a clipboard in his hand.

"You Kavanaugh?"

Great. Jeff Coleman was going to get everyone to call me by my last name.

"I am."

"I'm dropping you off." He indicated that I should climb up into the cab, so I did.

"So how do you know Jeff?" I asked, trying to make small talk and ignoring his stare.

"Did Jeff do your ink?" he asked.

"No. Had it done in Jersey." Except for Napoleon on

my calf, but he couldn't see that because of my jeans, and I wasn't going to volunteer information if I didn't have to.

"Nice," he said, turning back to the road.

We rode in silence through the city streets until he pulled up in front of Murder Ink.

"Here you go."

I'd hoped Jeff would have him drop me at the Venetian, but no such luck. I thanked the guy and got out of the truck. He took off before I could get to the door, the gold car glimmering as the sun hit it.

Jeff Coleman was nowhere to be seen. His mother, Sylvia, was inking a girl's hand. I got closer and saw it was a skull. Peering into the girl's face, I figured she was eighteen at most. She might regret that skull in a couple of years. Or maybe even next week. I might have tried to talk her out of it. If I knew Sylvia, she'd talked her into it.

"Hello, dear," Sylvia said without looking up, her machine whirring seamlessly as she drew.

I didn't know exactly how old Sylvia Coleman was, but I guessed she was in her seventies, maybe even early eighties. She'd run the shop for years and then turned it over to Jeff when she "retired," although it seemed her retirement just meant she came to the shop for half a day instead of a full day. Sylvia wasn't the golfing type. Or even the traveling type. She was an old-school tattooist, having learned the trade from her husband, who had died of pancreatic cancer about ten years ago. Sylvia had tattoos all over her body, except for her face, and I knew this because the day I showed up for my Napoleon ink, she stripped to her birthday suit and gave me the grand tour.

Most people might have been a little freaked-out by that, but each tattoo has a story, and she told those stories so well that I forgot she was naked underneath that ink.

"While you're here, you might as well pick something out," Sylvia said, waving the machine toward the flash on the wall. "Jeff says you might be here a while."

He did, did he?

I pulled up a chair. "Thanks anyway, Sylvia, but I don't

know how long I'll be here." I watched her outline the skull, then looked back at the girl's face. One tear was crawling down her cheek; her mouth was set in a grim line.

It hurt. It hurt like a thousand bee stings. But for most, the hurt evaporated when the endorphins kicked in. Not for this girl.

She was regretting this already, but she wasn't going to admit it.

And it was too late now. If she told Sylvia to stop, she'd have half a skull on her hand. Might as well go for the whole shebang.

A voice from behind me made me jump.

"It's about time you showed up."

Chapter 34

Jeff Coleman came out from the back of the shop. For "liking" me, he didn't look too friendly at the moment. He jingled a set of keys.

"Come on."

"Where are we going?"

"You're going to see your brother, dear," Sylvia said without looking up from her work. "You need to come clean."

Easy for her to say.

"Do you have another car here?" I asked as I got up.

Jeff had already started out the back again, and I sped up a bit to keep up. He didn't say anything, just led the way through the office and out the back door.

If I'd thought the gold Pontiac was outdated, then the purple Gremlin that sat against the curb was a dinosaur. I might not have even recognized it if it weren't for a silly book Tim had brought home about the worst cars ever. I couldn't remember where the Gremlin was in the lineup, but I did think it got a better rating than the Pinto, which apparently tended to catch fire spontaneously.

Those cars were in and out again before I was even born.

Jeff Coleman, however, was about ten years older than me, if I could hazard a guess, and he probably had some sort of nostalgic warm feeling about this funny-looking car with a long snout and a back end that looked like it had its tail chopped off.

"Whose car is this?" I asked as Jeff opened the passenger door for me. Chivalrous. Who knew?

I had to wait until he got into the driver's seat before he said, "It's my mother's."

This made sense. Somehow I could see how this car's quirkiness would appeal to someone like Sylvia. A vintage car for a vintage woman.

"Are you really taking me to Tim?" I asked.

"I'm taking you home. If he happens to be there, then I guess, yeah, I'm taking you to Tim."

Home. Immediately I thought about my queen-sized bed with the fluffy white cotton sheets. Now I wanted nothing more than to crawl under the covers and sleep for about three days. I felt like I'd been up for a month. And that vodka I'd had at Chez Tango had made me sleepy without my even realizing it.

"Sorry about your tires," I said.

"What did you do?"

"Hey, I didn't do it," I argued.

"No, I know that," he said, taking a cigarette out of his breast pocket and sticking it in his mouth.

"Can you not smoke in here?" I asked.

He gave me a quick glance before looking back at the road again. He kept the cigarette in his mouth but didn't light it. Security blanket, I guess.

"I mean," he said, the cigarette wobbling between his lips, "what did you get into that someone had to slash my tires?"

I sighed. There had been so much all day that it could've been any number of things. And for some reason, my brain settled on Frank DeBurra. Maybe he'd found me after all and was mad I'd ducked out on him at the hospital.

No, he didn't know to look for a gold Pontiac.

He certainly didn't know to look for a purple Gremlin.

Why the heck would a car company call a car a Gremlin?

"Earth to Kavanaugh," Jeff was saying.

"Oh, yeah, sorry. I'm a little tired."

I saw his hand twitch on the steering wheel, like he wanted to maybe reach out and touch me but stopped himself in time.

I studied his profile. Even though he was a couple inches shorter than me and possibly way too old, he wasn't a bad-looking guy if you looked close enough. The salt-and-pepper buzz cut made him look a little military. Hmmm.

"Were you in the army?" I asked.

His expression changed slightly; he clenched his jaw and his eyes narrowed, but he kept staring straight ahead at the road.

"Marines," he said, so softly I had to lean over to hear him. "Gulf War."

Suddenly this was way too much information.

"I found fifty thousand dollars in Trevor McKay's boots," I volunteered, eager to change the subject.

Jeff slammed on the brakes, and my body jerked forward, only to be jerked back again by the seat belt.

"Hey!" I said, clutching the dashboard.

He pointed up. "Red light. Sorry. So what was this? Fifty thousand dollars? Boots? Kavanaugh, it's no wonder someone's trying to ground you. Where's the money now?"

"I left it there."

He did look at me now, with an expression of such incredulity that I started to laugh. "You should see yourself," I said.

His face didn't change. "You left fifty thousand dollars in some guy's boots in his apartment? And he's dead? And you found a dead guy this morning? And my tires got slashed? What else?"

I managed to ease down to a couple of chuckles. "What else? What do you mean, what else?"

"I've never known anyone who had more things happen to her than you, Kavanaugh."

"Why do you always call me Kavanaugh?" I asked.

He just shook his head and put his foot on the accelerator, and the car shot forward, forcing me this time against the seat back.

"Watch it!"

"Where does this guy live?" Jeff asked casually. Too casually.

I knew what he was up to.

"We don't have a key. Kyle's got it, and he's all MissTique'd up at Chez Tango right about now."

"Do we need a key?"

It was the way he said it that made me take notice. Like he *didn't* need a key. I was exhausted and wanted to go home in the worst way, but at the same time curious about what he had in mind. I wasn't eager, either, to face Tim's wrath. Or possibly find Frank DeBurra parked on my doorstep.

So I told him where Trevor lived.

It was late afternoon and the sun had started to fall, casting a glare across the windshield and causing me to squint. I wished I had my sunglasses, but they were in my bag somewhere with the police. I flipped down the visor, but the rays peeked underneath.

Jeff and I settled into a companionable silence on the way. I was running over all the day's events; I had no idea what Jeff was thinking. I wasn't sure I wanted to know.

I indicated the apartment complex. Jeff pulled into the lot and eased the Gremlin into a visitor's space.

On the way up to the apartment, I stopped suddenly.

"What?" Jeff asked.

"I left Trevor's laptop in the Pontiac," I said. "That was stupid."

"We'll just stop and get it on the way back," Jeff said. How could he be so calm and levelheaded?

We reached the door and Jeff tried the knob. Locked, as I'd said.

"Kavanaugh, you might want to turn around for this," he said, reaching into his back pocket.

He was right. I didn't want to see what he was going to do. I stepped away from the door and leaned my back against the wall just to the left of it, eyeing the Gremlin in the lot. It really was an ugly car, and it had been a rather bumpy ride. The Pontiac was much smoother. But then again, it wasn't half a car.

I was so distracted by the Gremlin that when I heard it, I didn't recognize it for what it was, and all of a sudden Jeff Coleman was on top of me, forcing us both to the ground, his arms around me, my head shoved against his neck.

The second gunshot registered.

Chapter 35

I could feel Jeff's heartbeat against my chest, going in synch with mine. My face was smothered, and he smelled like cigarettes and ink and baby wipes. Comfort smells.

And then I felt his hand in a place where I never wanted Jeff Coleman's hand to be.

I tried to shrug him off, but his grip grew tighter.

"They're shooting at us from inside the apartment," he whispered, his breath tickling the side of my face.

"Who?"

"This is your movie, Kavanaugh, not mine. You tell me."

I had a flash of Rusty Abbott's warning that accidents happen.

But an accident is falling off a ladder, getting hit with a baseball, having a fender bender.

It's not being shot at outside a dead drag queen's apartment.

At least not in my world.

"We have to get out of here." Jeff was still whispering.

"How?" I was afraid if we got up, they'd start shooting again.

Before he could answer, however, we heard the sirens. One of the neighbors probably had heard the shots and called the cops. Of course, whoever it was didn't feel compelled to come outside and see what was going on.

Two police cruisers rolled into my line of vision. We were just one story up, and I could see them between the slats in the railing overlooking the parking lot. They stopped just below us. Right in front of the Gremlin. That wouldn't do.

Another shot rang out, and while Jeff had loosened his grip a second ago, he now clutched me again. But I wasn't caring much at the moment. I didn't want to be in the middle of a firefight.

"You up there!"

It took a second for me to realize one of the cops was shouting up at us.

"Get out of the way!"

Right. Like that would be easy. Didn't he think we'd be out of the way if we could? And I didn't much like it that he was alerting those inside the apartment that we were out here, huddled on the ground.

Jeff started shimmying a little away from the apartment door. I had no choice but to shimmy along with him.

It was awkward. I was on my back, Jeff on top of me, and my movements were crablike, while his were similar to a crawl.

It took us ages to move about six inches. We were closer to the railing now, and I could see the cops barricading themselves behind their cruiser doors. One of them had a bullhorn.

"Police! Surrender!"

It was a little like when the wicked witch told Dorothy to surrender by writing it in the sky. It had the same effect, anyway. Nothing.

At least they'd stopped shooting.

Jeff slid off me onto his stomach next to me. I rolled onto my stomach, too, and we watched through the railing as two of the uniforms dashed out from behind their doors and toward the building. We waited for more shots, but none came.

I pulled myself up onto all fours, rocked back onto my heels, and slowly stood, backing up as I did. Jeff was mimicking me.

There was another stairway just a few doors down. We backed up until we reached it, then ran down the stairs two at a time. My heart was pounding again as we reached the bottom, which led into the pool area.

I took a couple of deep breaths, leaning over and putting my hands on my knees. I felt a hand massaging my back.

"You okay, Kavanaugh?"

I nodded and looked up to see Jeff staring at me with a worried expression.

"This was a bad idea," I said. "I told you we shouldn't come here."

He stepped back and crossed his arms in front of his chest. "Okay, so it was a bad call. But who knew?"

I was about to give him a smart-aleck comment back when movement to my left caught my eye.

Someone was lowering himself off the corner balcony. He wore a backpack and a baseball cap.

"What the—," Jeff muttered.

The guy dropped to the ground, rolled over, and landed on his feet in a total James Bond way. The cap had come off, and I saw dark hair, a raised hand like a wave hello.

I took a step on instinct, but he shot off like the Road Runner being chased by Wile E. Coyote.

Jeff was already shouting at the cops.

I was speechless. Because I'd recognized him.

But it wasn't a him.

It was Charlotte.

Chapter 36

I didn't wait around to explain; I just ran after Charlotte. My sandals gripped the pavement as I ran across the pool deck, leaping over the diving board. The latch in the fence kept me busy long enough for Jeff to come panting up beside me.

"You should lay off those butts," I admonished just as the latch let go and the door swung open. I went through, Jeff on my heels.

But when we got to the other side of the fence, we didn't see anyone except a group of teenagers loping along the sidewalk. Cars whizzed past on the main road, their engines muffling the sound of the fountain in the center of the courtyard.

I turned to Jeff.

"It was Charlotte," I said softly. "That's who came over the balcony."

I looked behind me to see whether any of the cops had come out after us, had seen Charlotte, too, but nothing.

Until another gunshot rang out.

Jeff and I looked at each other. I had been pretty certain that Charlotte was the one doing the shooting, and from the look on Jeff's face, he'd thought so, too. There was no other reason why she would have made such a dramatic escape from the apartment building. Was there?

"Someone else was in there with her," Jeff said.

I nodded. "Yeah. But who?"

We started back through the pool area again and saw cops taking the steps two at a time, their guns drawn.

Jeff took hold of my upper arm. "I think we should stay where we are," he said.

"Sounds fine with me," I said, noting that he did not let go of my arm. I made a point of looking at his hand and then looking at his face. "Do you mind?" I asked.

He pulled his hand away and rummaged in his breast pocket for his pack of cigarettes. He took it out, and I laughed. It looked as though it had been run over by a steamroller.

"Maybe someone's telling you something," I said.

He managed to get a cigarette out of the pack and used his thumb and first finger to try to round it out. He did a fairly good job of it, and then he stuck it in his mouth, using a lighter he took from his jeans pocket to light it.

He sucked on the cigarette, took it out of his mouth, and let out a long cloud of smoke.

I coughed.

"You one of those reformed smokers, Kavanaugh?" he said.

I shook my head. "Never smoked a cigarette in my life," I said.

"Why am I not surprised?" he said.

We could hear banging on a door and shouting not very far away.

"What do we tell the cops about your employee?" Jeff asked after taking another hit off his butt.

"I'm not sure she's still my employee," I admitted. I'd pretty much had it up to here with Charlotte Sampson. She was up to something, something that may have gotten her friend Trevor killed and something that definitely got Wesley Lambert killed. And now she was in Trevor's apartment, with all that cash, with someone who was shooting at us, at the police.

I just hoped it wasn't Ace.

The minute I thought that, I stiffened. What if it *was* Ace?

"Do you have a cell phone on you?" I asked Jeff.

More shouting from above, and now the sound of wood splintering. The cops must be breaking the door down.

Jeff's gaze was somewhere off behind me, and I realized he was checking whether someone else was going to be coming down that balcony route, like Charlotte had. He didn't tear his eyes away even while he dug into his pocket and produced a cell phone. He handed it to me.

"Thanks," I said, punching in the number of the shop.

"The Painted Lady." I had never been so happy to hear Bitsy's voice as I was that minute.

"Bits, it's Brett."

"Where are you?"

"That doesn't matter right now, but what does is where Ace is."

"Ace is here," Bitsy said, and I breathed a sigh of relief. "Do you want to talk to him?"

"Yeah, I do."

A few seconds passed; then I heard, "Brett?"

"Ace, what's Charlotte up to?"

"What do you mean?" His tone was defensive, almost icy.

"I'm at Trevor's apartment building, and she just shimmied down off a back balcony here like she was Spider-Man. This was after I got shot at from inside Trevor's apartment."

"Hold on, Brett, what are you talking about?" He sounded genuinely confused. I was glad to hear it.

"Charlotte, your main squeeze, is involved with something that doesn't seem good for her health or for mine. Where is she hiding out?"

"I ... uh ... I don't know. Really, Brett, I don't. She won't answer my calls; she's not at her place. Bitsy told me what went down this morning at that guy's condo. I'm worried about her."

"That's nice, Ace, but I think we all should have maybe listened a little more to that cop who told me she could be in some sort of danger because of her association with Wesley Lambert. Because you know what? She was, and is, but she's also up to something herself."

"Brett?" Jeff's whisper was hurried. My back was to him, and as I turned around to see what he wanted, a hand came down on mine, the one holding the phone.

But it wasn't Jeff now.

It was Frank DeBurra. And as he wrenched the phone out of my hand and closed it, he said, "Miss Kavanaugh, I think we have to have a little chat."

Chapter 37

I looked to Jeff for support, but he just shrugged.

DeBurra nodded. "And your friend, here, is coming with us, too."

"Hey, I'm just along for the ride," Jeff said as he tossed his cigarette down and ground it with the heel of his cowboy boot.

"We wouldn't be here now if it weren't for you," I hissed.

"Isn't this sweet? A lover's quarrel." DeBurra chuckled.

All the muscles in my body tensed up, and I glared at him.

"You've got no reason to be angry with me," DeBurra said. "But I have all the reason to be angry with you. Maybe if you'd stuck around in the hospital and answered my questions, all of this"—he indicated the apartment house—"never would've happened."

"So it's my fault I got shot at?" I barked.

"Brett, calm down," Jeff said softly.

I shot him a look. Easy for him to say.

"You'd better listen to your boyfriend," DeBurra said. "It's going to be a long night."

At that moment I realized I wasn't going home. I wasn't going to sleep in my comfy bed. I wasn't going to be able to relax.

I was going to be stuck with DeBurra and Jeff Coleman all night.

"He's not my boyfriend," I said, although my gumption was gone.

DeBurra noticed. "Okay, fine. Let's go." He herded us out of the pool area, and now we could see the police cruisers and cops milling around.

"Who was it?" I asked. "Who was shooting?"

DeBurra took a deep breath. "He got out the balcony. Someone downstairs said he saw a guy jumping from balcony to balcony and took off."

"But what about that last shot? The apartment couldn't have been empty then."

Jeff's nudge was too late. I'd spoken too soon.

DeBurra stopped and stared me down. "What do you mean?"

It was time to tell the truth. "We saw it," I said. "That's why we ran out to the front courtyard. We saw her drop to the ground and take off. But I don't know where she went."

"She?"

"It was Charlotte. Charlotte Sampson. But after she ran off, we heard another shot from up there. So she couldn't have been alone."

DeBurra rubbed his jaw thoughtfully and nodded, but he didn't volunteer any information. All he said was, "If you'd talked to me earlier, maybe we could've found her."

"I really haven't known where she's been hiding," I insisted, then added, "At least we know she's not sick."

Sister Mary Eucharista would've said that was like making lemonade out of lemons, or something like that. My brain wasn't working right at the moment.

They put Jeff and me into two different cruisers. He gave me a wink as they escorted him to a car a few feet away.

I fell asleep.

In the interrogation room.

On a stiff, metal chair with my head down on my arms on a stiff, metal table.

I dreamed of Red Rock and my bed, and the soft whirr of a tattoo machine was my white noise.

I'd been at police headquarters for about three hours, interrogated by none other than Detective Frank DeBurra, going over and over and over ad nauseum everything that had happened that day.

Except I left out my first visit to Trevor's. I didn't want to get Kyle in trouble, and did it really matter that I'd been there twice? Sure, DeBurra would string me up if he knew, but I kept to pertinent information, like what had happened at that condo this morning and getting shot at with Jeff.

I hadn't seen Jeff since I'd gotten here.

I hadn't seen Tim, either.

I wondered whether he was still at the hospital with sexy Dr. Bixby.

A thud jolted me out of my dreams and ramblings. I looked up.

"Why are you keeping me here?" I asked Frank De-Burra, who'd slammed the door. "I've answered all your questions. Can't I go home now?"

He smiled. It wasn't a nice smile; it had an edge to it. An edge that told me not to push it.

I sighed.

"What else do you want to know?" I asked, defeated, laying my head back down on my arms and staring up at him with one eye.

"Do you know where Ace van Nes is?"

My head popped up and I took my elbows off the table. "Ace?"

"Yes, Ace van Nes. I believe he works for you."

"He's at the shop," I said. "I talked to him there earlier."

"He's not there now. And Miss Hendricks was not helpful."

I couldn't help but smile. I could just imagine what Bitsy had to say to Detective Frank DeBurra.

"You're with Homeland Security; don't you know where everyone is at all times?" I asked, my exhaustion turning into sarcasm.

He sighed dramatically. "That's what Miss Hendricks

said, too. Do you have employee training in how to respond to a police officer's questions?"

"How did you guess?"

"Where is Mr. van Nes?"

"Maybe he's home." Ace lived in a condo that he sublet from some guy in a band over in Summerlin. "Don't you have his phone number? Why don't you just call him?" I asked.

"You really need to start cooperating."

I stood up and faced him. "I've answered all your questions. I've sat here for hours allowing myself to be interrogated by you. I have cooperated thoroughly. Do I need a lawyer?" I paused. "And it's not my fault my brother had a relationship with your fiancée, so you better get over that, too."

As if on cue, the door opened, and Tim walked in.

DeBurra jumped back, startled. "Oh, Kavanaugh, it's you."

Tim looked from DeBurra to me and back to DeBurra again. "Don't you think you've got enough now? She's tired. I don't know how much more you think you're going to get."

I wanted to know where he'd been the whole time I'd been in this little room. But at least he was here now, trying to rescue me from the clutches of Inspector Clouseau. I turned a smile on him, but he wasn't paying attention to me.

DeBurra looked like he was trying to figure out just what to say, how he was going to justify the past three hours. I'd given him everything he wanted in the first hour.

DeBurra licked his lips, then pursed them together as if he were weighing a life-or-death situation. His eyes settled on me in a very unsettling way. Finally, he spoke.

"Your employee Ace van Nes? He's been dating Charlotte Sampson."

Even the cops knew. Why was I the last to know?

But he wasn't waiting for me. He kept going.

"And late today, thirty thousand dollars was deposited in Ace van Nes's bank account."

Chapter 38

I couldn't breathe. Thirty thousand dollars? Ace? He could barely break a thousand on one of those paintings every couple months. And while he made a good living in my shop, he didn't make that kind of money.

Then I had a flashback. Charlotte was wearing a backpack when she'd jumped off that balcony. She'd been in Trevor's apartment. Where there was about fifty thousand dollars hidden in Trevor's boots.

But I hadn't told DeBurra I'd been there earlier. They didn't know I knew about the money in the boots.

I'd already been at the station house for three hours. If I suddenly came clean, I was looking at an all-nighter.

But if I didn't tell them and they found out later that I knew, I'd be in deep crap. DeBurra I could handle, but I wasn't so sure about Tim.

I sighed. "I was at Trevor McKay's earlier today."

They looked at me like I had three heads.

"We know that, Brett," Tim said softly.

I shook my head. "No, I was there earlier, with Kyle Albrecht. MissTique. He had a key; we went over there to see if Charlotte was there. She wasn't, but we found money. A lot of money. In Trevor's boots. In the bedroom." I paused for a second. "Actually, Kyle found the money. But we left it there. We didn't take any of it."

DeBurra looked like he was going to explode.

I waited for it.

He did not disappoint.

"Did you go back there for the money?" he asked, his face just inches from mine. I could smell burger and onions on his breath.

"No."

"Why did you go back, then?"

I did not go for the money. But Jeff Coleman did. I couldn't rat him out, though, because he'd helped me, what with lending me his car and not getting too upset—at least outwardly—when the tires got slashed on my watch.

"I wanted to make sure Charlotte hadn't gone there after we'd left," I said, hoping he'd believe me. "I've been worried about her all day. She could've gotten sick in that condo. She wasn't decontaminated like the rest of us." I hoped I wasn't laying it on too thick.

He stood up straight and stepped back, studying my face. I willed myself to stare back even though I wanted to look away, put my head back down on the table, and go to sleep again.

Finally, after what seemed like hours but was just seconds, he nodded. "Okay. But you have to tell me everything about that visit to the apartment."

Tim nodded at me, urging me to continue.

I sighed. I knew I'd be stuck here if I told. I might as well just suck it up and tell him everything as quickly as I could. Maybe I could go home and get a couple hours sleep at some point.

Since he already knew about Bitsy rescuing me from the hospital—that conversation lasted much longer than I'd liked—I started with Jeff Coleman's car and going to Chez Tango and meeting up with Kyle. It didn't take me long to run through what had happened.

When I was done, I hoped that would be the end of it.

Then DeBurra held up his hand.

"Okay, so you borrowed Coleman's car. Where is it now?"

Oops. Left that part out.

"When I brought Kyle back to the club, I went in to use the phone, and when I came back out, the tires were slashed. So it was towed to a garage."

"All the tires were slashed?"

I nodded.

"Did you find that unusual?" He was baiting me.

I took it. "Yes. I did find that unusual, Detective." The sarcasm dripped off my words. "I figured someone didn't want me poking around."

"And then when you went back to Trevor McKay's place, you got shot at. You'd just been there and the tires were slashed. Is there a connection?"

"How should I know? You're the detective. Is there a connection?" I had stood up and was shaking with anger and exhaustion. I was one breath away from tears. There it was. The one breath. And there were the waterworks.

My whole body heaved with sobs, but I didn't take my eyes off DeBurra's face. It unnerved him. He began to shift from foot to foot; his eyes skipped over to the door as if willing someone to save him.

And that's exactly what Tim did by speaking up at just that very moment.

"I think that's enough," he told DeBurra sternly. "I'm taking her home. If you want to ask her more questions in the morning, I can bring her back. But she needs some sleep." He put his arm around me, which only made me cry harder. I couldn't stop once I'd started.

Which is why DeBurra let us leave.

I went into the ladies' room and managed to calm down a little, throwing some cold water on my face and running wet hands through my hair. It was a little spikier that way, slicked back over my ears, which were still naked. I fingered them absently, wondering whether I should leave them that way for a while. No. I'd find replacements in my jewelry box at home.

When I emerged, not feeling totally refreshed but at least no longer sobbing, Tim and I went out to his Jeep in the parking lot without saying anything to each other. I was tired of talking, anyway.

The desert air was still, and it had cooled a bit. If I figured right, it was about eight.

"What about Jeff Coleman? Is he still in there?" I asked, cocking my head toward the building as we climbed into the Jeep.

"DeBurra took his statement and let him go after about an hour."

"That's good."

"I had a little chat with him. You know, Brett, he's not a bad guy. Why don't you like him?"

I was glad the sun was going down, so my face was in a shadow. I felt the blush crawl up my neck as I remembered Jeff grabbing me and covering me with his body when the gunshots rang out.

I shrugged. "Yeah, he's not so bad after all, I guess."

"He thinks pretty highly of you."

Really? I was too tired to think about it.

"Do you think Ace is involved in whatever it is Charlotte's up to?" Tim asked. "Off the record."

"No. And until I saw her today jumping off that balcony, I didn't really want to think she was doing anything wrong, either. But now I'm not so sure."

"Did you do a background check on her when you hired her?"

I stared at him. "No. Should I have? She's just a trainee."

"Brett, you should background check everyone you hire, even a trainee."

Something about his tone made me pause. "You know something, don't you?"

He kept his eyes on the road, flexed his fingers on the steering wheel.

"What is it, Tim? What's in her background?"

"I can't say."

"Yeah, but you're the one who said this was all off the record. So you didn't really tell me, okay?"

The Jeep slowed to a stop at a light on the Strip. The Venetian was just to our left in all its Renaissance Italy glory.

It looked exactly like the Doge's Palace, with a sign for Madame Tussauds wax museum stuck like a postage stamp at the end of a ramp. I stared at it for a long second before whispering, "Tim? Please tell me about Charlotte."

The light changed and he gunned the accelerator, causing the Jeep to lurch forward.

"I didn't tell you."

"I know."

He waited until we were sitting at the next light.

"Metro Homeland Security's been watching Charlotte Sampson since last year."

Chapter 39

I tried to wrap my head around what Tim was saying, but the fatigue was too much.

"What do you mean, they've been watching her? What do you think? She's some sort of terrorist?"

When Tim didn't answer, I continued.

"That's ludicrous. She was a student, studying accounting, and she wants to be a tattoo artist. She's good. She's really good. She's not a terrorist."

Tim waited until I paused. "They believe she and Wesley Lambert were partners."

"Partners in what?"

He shrugged. The light turned green, and we shot forward.

"Do they think she was part of the ricin making?" I asked.

"I'm not sure. I just overheard DeBurra saying that it was convenient she called you to come to Lambert's condo and he was dead."

"Do they think she had something to do with his death?"

We stopped again, and the red light cast a glow on the windshield.

Tim nodded. "Yeah, they do."

I mulled that for a few seconds. "Wonder what Trevor's role was." And then I knew. The money. The money must have had something to do with this. I kept flashing back on that image of Charlotte with the backpack.

We were on 215 now, heading toward Henderson and my bed. I leaned back on the headrest and closed my eyes, drifting off.

But a thought made me jolt up.

The laptop. Trevor's laptop. It was in Jeff Coleman's car. I wondered if there was anything on it that could give me a clue as to what Trevor had been up to, and, by extension, Charlotte as well.

I glanced at Tim, who was concentrating on the road. Should I mention the laptop?

Two Sister Mary Eucharistas were sitting on my shoulders. One wore little devil horns and urged me to keep my mouth shut. The one with angel's wings said I should own up.

Exhaustion won out. I justified not saying anything by telling myself I'd let him know about the laptop in the morning. After I got some sleep. I didn't have the energy to answer more questions.

I leaned back again and dozed.

I barely remembered getting into the house and going to bed. But when I woke up, the sun streaming through the miniblinds, I was curled up under my comforter, wearing my cotton pajama bottoms and oversized T-shirt. I had a vague memory of pulling it over my head.

The clock told me it was ten already. I usually got to the shop around eleven. I wondered whether I could call Bitsy and explain that I needed a couple more hours of sleep.

But I'd been gone all day yesterday, she'd saved my butt, and I needed to give her a break.

I dragged myself out of bed, looked in the mirror, and almost screamed.

My hair, which I'd slicked back so nicely at the police station, was standing on end, like Alfalfa's from *The Little Rascals*. I swiped a hand over it, and it just bounced right back up again.

A shower. I really needed a shower.

I turned the water on as hot as I could stand it and let it soak me. I tipped my head back, and the water pounded into my skull. In a good way. I don't know how long I was in there, but when I got out, I was all nice and prune-y, my skin was red from the heat, and I felt almost human again.

A cup of coffee would complete me.

Tim was already gone. He'd left the coffeepot on, and I poured a cup as I read the brief note he'd left me on the counter:

> *Had to go in early. Will call later. Your stuff is on the chair. —T*

Stuff? What stuff?

There, hanging on the back of one of the kitchen chairs, was a supermarket plastic bag that sagged with something heavy inside. I picked it up and dumped it on the table.

I grinned. My keys, my wallet, my sunglasses, my cell phone, even the couple of pens and small pad I kept for notes.

My messenger bag was nowhere to be seen. Since it was made of some sort of fabric, the cops probably figured it could be contaminated, like my clothes, and sent it to the Big Hazard Waste Pile. No biggie. That just meant I could buy a new one.

I toasted a bagel and slathered some cream cheese on it, then took my plate and coffee into the living room and sank down on the leather sofa. I grabbed the remote and turned the TV on.

SpongeBob and Patrick were tormenting Squidward again.

The phone rang. I nearly spit out my coffee.

The phone wasn't in its little cradle, but I found it on top of the refrigerator just as the machine kicked in. I punched it on.

"Hello?"

"Kavanaugh?"

No one else but Jeff Coleman called me by my last name.

"Did I wake you?"

I refreshed my cup of coffee. "No. What's up?"

"How was it last night? You were there late."

"How do you know that?"

"I talked to your brother about an hour ago. I called to see how you were."

I didn't like it that my brother and Jeff Coleman were getting tight. The jury was still out on whether Jeff and I were veering into friends territory or if we were going to just stay acquaintances and colleagues. Again I thought about how his body had felt on top of me yesterday. While he was protecting me, keeping me out of harm's way, putting himself in danger.

I told myself it was just reflex for him. He was a Marine, for Pete's sake. His job was to protect.

"I'm okay," I said.

"I got my car back this morning and I found the laptop—"

"Great," I said, interrupting him. "Can I come by and get it?" Just as I asked, my memory flashed on my car, still at the condo parking garage, if the cops hadn't towed it by now.

How was I going to get to Jeff's, much less to work?

He was one step ahead of me.

"Tim said you were going to need a ride to your car. I can come get you and bring you over there."

This might be going a little too far, but I did need to see Jeff anyway to get the laptop, and I did need to get to my car.

"It's a little out of your way," I said.

"I have to go pick my mother up at the pool anyway," he said. "So it's no big deal."

Pool? Did I miss something?

"Where is your mother?"

"She swims with the seniors at one of the pools in Henderson every other day. She usually gets a ride with Bernie, but he just had hip replacement so I'm her new chauffeur until she can get some other sucker to drive her."

"Why does she come all the way out here?" I asked.

"There are pools closer to her." Sylvia lived in Bo-
nanza Village, a trailer park—excuse me, a mobile home
community—out near the Desert Pines Golf Course. "What
about Garside or Doolittle or even the municipal pool?"

Jeff chuckled. "Because Bernie swims in Henderson."

I hadn't heard about Bernie before. This was interesting.
A little late-in-life romance. I was happy for Sylvia.

"I swim at the competition pool," I offered before I
could stop myself. I might as well keep going. "Is that where
Sylvia goes?" There were only two places that were open
year-round: the Multigenerational Center pools, where I
swam, or Whitney Ranch.

Jeff hesitated, then, "Yeah, that's where she goes."

"I've never seen her there. But then, I go pretty early."
I didn't tell him I hadn't gone there in more than a month.
When the temperatures start to cool off, that's when I head
to Red Rock for my exercise.

"Kavanaugh, you're a woman of many surprises."

"So when will you be here?" I asked, not wanting to get
into "surprise" territory with Jeff Coleman.

"I'll swing by after I pick up Sylvia."

"Hey, why doesn't she drive herself? She's got a car."

Jeff chuckled. "That car's a hazard. We only use it in
emergencies."

He hung up without saying good-bye. That was the Jeff
Coleman I knew and was comfortable with.

Almost immediately the phone rang again.

I picked it up.

"What did you forget?" I asked.

"Forget? What? Brett, it's Charlotte."

Chapter 40

Every muscle in my body tensed up, and I could feel the veins pounding in my head.

"Charlotte?"

"Brett, please listen. You have to trust me."

I snorted. "Trust you. How am I supposed to do that? You set me up with a dead body that might be contaminated with some sort of poison; then you shoot at me and steal Trevor's money. Did I leave anything out? Oh, right. You deposit Trevor's money into Ace's account so it looks like he's some sort of criminal, and now the cops are after him, too. What exactly are you up to, Charlotte?" It dawned on me during this tirade that perhaps I should be nicer to reel her in, get some answers, and then turn her over to the police.

"What about Ace? What do you mean, I deposited money in his account?"

For a second, she fooled me. It really sounded like maybe she didn't know what I was talking about.

"Thirty thousand dollars. In Ace's account. I know there was more money than that in Trevor's apartment. Did you keep the rest? Are you heading for the Cayman Islands or something?" I couldn't keep the sarcasm out of my voice. Not that I was trying very hard.

"Thirty—" She cleared her throat. "Brett, I don't know what you're talking about. Yes, I was at Trevor's yesterday afternoon."

"Why did you shoot at me and Jeff Coleman?"

"I didn't."

"So you were flying off balconies like there was no tomorrow just for giggles?"

"You have to believe me. I wasn't the only one there. I heard someone come in and I went out on the balcony and hid behind the curtain. I didn't see who it was, but when I heard that first gunshot, I figured I should get out of there."

"Why don't you tell the cops?"

"You told them I was there, didn't you?"

"They know, yes." I paused, then, "I know the police are investigating you. It would be better to turn yourself in."

"Investigating me?" Incredulity laced her voice. "Listen, I'll set things straight with Ace. No worries." She paused a second, then added, "Oh, by the way, I'm feeling okay."

She hung up as a tinge of guilt tickled me between the shoulder blades because I hadn't asked how she was.

I stared at the phone and after a second hit star sixty-nine. The operator told me the number I was trying to reach was restricted. We didn't have caller ID on our landline. Tim had issues with that feature. I now had more ammunition to argue the case.

I dialed Tim's cell number.

"Thanks for my stuff," I said when he answered.

"Can't talk, Brett."

"Thought maybe you would want to know I just talked to Charlotte. She called me."

Silence for a second, then, "What did she say?"

"Said I have to trust her. That someone else was shooting at me and Jeff. That she didn't put that money in Ace's account."

A second passed, then, "I'll have to get back to you, Brett, okay? I'm in the middle of something." And he hung up.

I stared at the phone. If I had insecurity issues, getting hung up on three times in five minutes might push me over the edge. But I wasn't going to take it personally. Charlotte was on the lam, and my brother had a demanding job. Jeff—well, Jeff was Jeff.

Speaking of whom, I had to get to the shop. I looked out the window, but there was no sign of him yet. I told myself it would take him longer than that to get here.

I found an old messenger bag on a hook in my closet and tossed all my stuff inside. As I passed the mirror, I noticed that I'd spilled some coffee on my tank top. I pulled it over my head, threw it in the laundry basket, and found a hot pink, tight, stretchy T in my drawer. I needed something cheery, so I put it on. It hung to my hips and clashed nicely with the dark skinny jeans, a different pair from yesterday.

A honk made me grab the bag and dash out the front door, making sure it was locked before climbing into the backseat of the gold Pontiac. Trevor's laptop was right where I'd left it.

"Hey, thanks for this, Jeff," I said, then leaned forward and patted Sylvia on the shoulder. "Hey, Sylvia."

She wore a bright yellow latex bathing cap with little daisies all over it. A peek over the front seat showed me that she was wearing a matching terry-cloth housecoat and flip-flops. Even her feet were inked. Beautiful red roses were entwined with leafy greens. She would look spectacular in her bathing suit. And probably raised a few eyebrows.

"We have to stop off for my car," Sylvia explained. "Someone"—she looked at Jeff—"left it in some parking lot all night."

"We're going back to Trevor's?" I asked Jeff. "Can you drop me first?"

"And miss checking out the scene of the crime? Kavanaugh, I'm disappointed in you." He didn't look at me, but I could see the corner of the smile in his profile.

I sighed and leaned back in the seat. When he put it that way, I couldn't really back out. "Sure, fine. But let's make it quick, okay?" I reached into my bag and took out my phone, punching in the number for the shop.

"The Painted Lady."

"Hey, Bits, it's me."

"How are you?"

"Spent most of the night at the police station."

"Ace is there now."

"I was afraid of that." I told her about Charlotte at Trevor's apartment and the money and how the police thought she might have made a deposit in Ace's bank account but she was denying it. As I spoke, I saw Jeff sneaking looks at me in the rearview mirror. Sylvia bobbed her head to a tune only she could hear. Literally. She had earbuds in her ears and was flipping through songs on a bright pink iPod that matched my shirt.

"I'm not sure who to believe anymore," Bitsy said when I finished.

Her and me both.

"I assume you're home today," Bitsy said.

"No, I'll be in, maybe in about an hour or so. Jeff Coleman's taking me to my car, but we've got a stop to make first."

Just as I said that, we passed the access road that led back to Windsor Palms, the high-rise condominium where my Mustang was still parked. Surprisingly, a chill slid down my spine. Maybe it was a good thing it would be the last stop. I must have underestimated the degree of my freaked-out-ness from the day before.

When I hung up after talking to Bitsy, I spotted Jeff's eyes in the mirror.

"So no one told you what they're investigating Charlotte for?" he asked.

"No."

"I've got some friends I could call. Make inquiries. See what I can find out."

I frowned. Jeff Coleman had "friends." That was interesting. But then I remembered: He'd been in the military. Maybe he was onto something.

"Sure," I said, slipping the laptop into my messenger bag.

We didn't say anything more; I stared at Sylvia's bathing cap and wondered if all the decorations would keep her from moving well through the water. I'd never seen her at the pool; I would've remembered that cap even if I hadn't known her.

The sun was bright, blasting through the car windows as we turned into the parking lot at Trevor's. The Gremlin sat squat with two empty spaces around it. Every other spot was taken. No one probably wanted to park too close to it; it might have something that was catching. Like the rust that was creeping along the frame.

Jeff eased the Pontiac next to the Gremlin, and Sylvia opened her door to get out. But as she swung her body around, Jeff put his arm across her chest.

"No, you're not driving it," he said, and with his other hand he tossed the keys back into my lap. "She is."

I frowned, picking up the keys. "What?"

Jeff was cocking his head at Sylvia and shaking it at the same time. I got it. He didn't want her to drive. I'd wondered whether Sylvia had started a decline into dementia, but Jeff put the kibosh on that.

"You don't have your license with you," Jeff admonished her. "You can't drive in that silly outfit. You'll get stopped by the cops."

"Then it'll all be in the family, won't it?" Sylvia asked, still attempting to get out, but Jeff continued to hold on to her.

"Kavanaugh, get out," he said. "I'll meet you back at my shop, and then I'll take you to your car."

I opened the door and climbed out. Sylvia was still arguing with Jeff, but then I heard, "You better treat that car nice." I assumed that was for me. The door slammed shut, and Jeff gave me a little finger wave as he backed out and the Pontiac moved away.

I stood next to the Gremlin, and I felt another shiver. Twice in one day. Go figure. Getting shot at here wasn't giving me the best karma.

I looked up at Trevor's apartment on the second floor.

A band of yellow crime-scene tape had been slung across the door.

But it was broken. Two pieces of tape hung down on either side like limp ponytails.

The door was open. And someone was coming out.

Chapter 41

I couldn't move. My feet felt as though they were cemented to the asphalt.

It was Rusty Abbott.

He looked down at me, and a look of panic crossed his face. He glanced to the left and to the right, probably trying to figure out which way to run.

I had that effect on him.

But then he surprised me. He started down the stairs. He was carrying something that looked remarkably like Trevor's makeup case. Kyle and I hadn't seen it in the apartment yesterday, so where had it come from?

I didn't have time to ponder that, however, because Abbott's other hand had moved up to his waistband.

The gun glinted as the sun caught it.

I caught my breath and scrambled into the car. I'd been shot at once here. I wasn't going to make it a habit.

I started the car and in the rearview mirror saw Abbott approaching. I shoved the stick shift into reverse and gunned the engine.

He had to jump out of the way. The tires skidded a little as the Gremlin's muffler roared, and I pulled out onto Charleston without even looking.

I was lucky there'd been a lull in the traffic.

My heart was pounding. Why on earth would Rusty Abbott want to kill me? I hadn't wanted to take that casino chip in the first place.

Unless he really was the guy who'd shot Trevor with the cork, and it wasn't Wesley Lambert. Maybe he thought I could identify him.

And what was he doing with the makeup case? Unless he'd known Trevor kept the brooch in it and thought it was still there.

As I sat at a light, I knew I was going to have to find out more about that Queen of Hearts Ball. There was that pin and the tattoos and all those pictures of everyone looking so tight with their arms around each other: Rusty Abbott and Wesley Lambert and Charlotte.

How did Trevor play into all that? Was he the third person who showed up at Murder Ink for a tattoo?

No, he didn't have a playing-card tattoo. That I knew for sure. So who was the third person?

Jeff Coleman wasn't back yet from dropping off Sylvia. Murder Ink was closed up, but I found a key to the back door on the chain with the Gremlin key. I let myself in.

I turned on the overhead light and dropped my bag on the cluttered desk. I eyed the file cabinet in the corner. Jeff had to have some sort of record of those three clients that night.

I told myself he was as interested as I was in all this as I opened the top drawer.

The files were a mess, just like the rest of the place. I couldn't make heads or tails of them. They weren't in any sort of alphabetical order or even arranged by date. It seemed totally random. I flipped through about twenty folders, taking a deep breath with each one, not because I was afraid of what I'd find, but with the exasperation I felt. Bitsy would never let our records be such a mess.

I had reached in to grab another file when the door opened, and I felt my heart jump into my throat.

"Kavanaugh, what are you doing?"

Jeff was next to me, taking the file out of my hand and slipping it back into the drawer.

"You weren't here—"

"So you decided to go through my files. For what? What are you looking for?" Despite our rather up-and-down relationship, this was the first time I'd heard him actually angry with me. He'd teased me before, but this time I'd touched a nerve.

"What don't you want me to find?" I challenged. It was easier to get on the offensive.

But he wasn't having it.

"What are you looking for?" he growled, slamming the drawer shut.

I decided I should tell him the truth. "I just wanted to know if you've got a file on that third guy who came in for the queen-of-hearts tattoo with Rusty Abbott and Wesley Lambert," I said.

His eyes were narrowed, and he studied my face for a few seconds, during which I could totally believe that he'd been in the Marines. He scared me.

But then he gave a low chuckle and started shaking his head.

"Oh, Kavanaugh, you could just ask before you start snooping around. Or do you like playing *Charlie's Angels*?"

I felt my face flush, but I couldn't let that go. "That was one of the most misogynistic shows ever on TV," I said hotly.

"Yeah, maybe, but they were so hot." He turned his back on me as he rifled through the files, then turned around with one in his hand. He waved it in front of me, teasing me. "Didn't every girl want to be a Charlie's Angel?"

"Not me," I said, a little too loudly, my eyes following the file.

"Which one would you be? The smart one or the tough one or the dumb, sexy one?"

I sighed. "Stop playing around," I said.

He laughed out loud. "You know, Kavanaugh, you shouldn't make it so easy to get to you."

I couldn't tell him that he was the only one who brought

out this side of me. Then he'd think he was something special.

"What's in the file?" I asked.

He looked at it as if he were seeing it for the first time. "Oh, this," he said. "This is the file you're looking for from that night."

"How do you know?" I asked. "Those files aren't in any particular order."

"Well, that's where you're wrong," he said. "There is an order. My mother set it up, and it works, so it's staying that way."

If Sylvia set up the filing system, then it clearly wouldn't have any rhyme or reason to it. But if they could keep track, who was I to say anything?

"Do you want to see it?" Jeff said, handing the file to me.

I snatched it away from him and rolled my eyes as I flipped it open.

The name took my breath away.

"Are you sure?" I asked. "This is the right one?"

Jeff nodded. "Yeah. You know who it is?"

I nodded slowly. "I do."

And he'd told me he didn't have any ink because he didn't like needles.

Colin Bixby.

Chapter 42

"This is the guy who was in drag?" I asked.

"One of two," Jeff said. "That guy Wesley Lambert, the one with the ricin in the condo? He was the second one. I checked that out this morning. And Rusty Abbott was the third guy, but he wasn't in drag." He paused. "Who is this Bixby guy?"

"He's a doctor," I said softly. "At the emergency room. I met him."

"Yesterday when you were there?"

"And the day before, when I went to see Trevor. He's the one who told me Trevor was dead. He knows Kyle. Kyle Albrecht. He's MissTique. At Chez Tango." I thought about how I'd suspected Bixby of being gay. So maybe I wasn't so wrong about that.

"Those guys really look like women," Jeff mused.

"It's weird to see them taking off their girl faces and becoming boys again," I said.

"Huh? You've seen that?"

"They're so not shy," I said, but I was still distracted by how I'd misread Bixby. Sort of.

I handed the folder back to Jeff. "I've got to get to the shop," I said.

"Sure you don't want to hang around here and learn how it's really done, Kavanaugh?"

"Doesn't take much to do flash," I tossed back at him,

picking up my bag and slinging it over my shoulder. "Just take me to my car, okay?"

"Say please." He'd put the folder back, shut the drawer, and was standing too close to me, his eyes searching my face.

I stepped back. "Give me a break." I rolled my eyes at him. "Should I just call a cab?"

He dug keys out of his pocket and motioned that I was to follow him back out into the alley, where the gold Pontiac sat. We settled in after he locked up his shop, then headed back down to the Strip.

The sky was a deep cobalt blue. No clouds in sight. The Stratosphere Tower loomed high above us on our right just before crossing Sahara. I spotted the pawnshops to the left, just before the Sahara hotel. Just a little way down, Circus Circus was to our right, its red and white striped big top advertising its theme, and an empty lot sat where the Starburst used to be.

Jeff took a right down Desert Inn Road toward the new Trump hotel, just before Fashion Show Mall. The Windsor Palms was adjacent to it, sort of kitty-corner.

Jeff eased around the entranceway marked by a gigantic palm tree and veered around into the parking garage. He turned to me with raised eyebrows, asking an unspoken question.

"Second level," I said, surprised I could even remember that.

He guided the Pontiac up the ramp and turned the corner to see my Mustang Bullitt where I'd left it. Jeff stopped the car right behind it.

He looked over at me and nodded. "Here we are."

For an awkward second I felt like I should lean over and give him a peck on the cheek. Seemed the least I could do, since he'd been so gracious and all. But then I remembered whom I was with and nodded back.

"Thanks," I said, opening the door.

But before I could get out, I felt a hand on my arm.

"Be careful, Kavanaugh."

I threw his hand off and laughed. "Hey, what more can happen?"

"You never know."

I thought about Rusty Abbott coming out of Trevor's apartment. He was right. I'd have to watch my back.

"Thanks, Jeff," I said again, this time really getting out and slamming the car door shut.

I stepped back just as he took off like Mario Andretti in the Indy 500. A curl of smoke came out of the tailpipe as he turned the corner.

I settled into my Mustang, happy to finally be driving my own car again. The seat was contoured just right, my Springsteen CD was still in the player, and the mirror didn't need adjusting. In honor of this trip, I put the top down, relishing the warm desert breeze, and cranked up the volume on "Jungleland."

I tried not to think about Colin Bixby.

I drove down the Strip, and instead of being annoyed at the lights, I looked up at the palm trees in the median, felt the sun beating down on the back of my neck—oops, forgot the sunscreen—and mellowed out for the first time in days.

I reached the Venetian too soon.

The towers of the fake Doge's Palace beckoned me, and I noticed some activity of the media kind at the entrance to Madame Tussauds wax museum, which was adjacent to the Venetian. Three TV vans were parked along the side of the road.

Curious, I turned into the entrance for valet parking. So I'd splurge—at least until I could move my car in a couple of hours. I wanted to see what was going on.

The laptop slammed against my hip as I slung the messenger bag over my shoulder and handed the valet my key. I cocked my head toward the wax museum.

"What's going on over there?"

"Some sort of celebrity thing," he said, taking the key.

I sauntered over toward the museum and saw that it might be easier said than done to get up the escalator to the museum entrance, because a crowd had formed. I pushed my way onto the moving incline, sandwiched between a young couple with a baby in one of those pouches and an elderly couple wearing far too much spandex.

It was a long ride.

We finally reached the top, but security guards were herding people off to the walkways and away from the museum. I was tall enough, though, to see what was going on.

Reporters hovered, their microphones held out in front of them, vying for the best position to interview the man posing next to his mirror image.

Lester Fine and his wax twin. Great. I couldn't get away from the guy for some reason, and now there were two of him.

In a cynical moment, I had the thought that if he were running for public office, this might not be the perfect time to unveil his doppelganger.

But wasn't it ideal to have this photo op outside, so everyone could see it, rather than just the people who paid big bucks to see all those other wax figures inside?

I mentally slapped myself, glancing down for a second so I wouldn't bump into the spandex-clad woman in front of me. When I looked up and over at Lester Fine again, I caught my breath.

He was staring at me.

I blinked a couple of times just to make sure I wasn't imagining it. But he was. He was staring at me. And then beckoning me to come over.

"There she is," he said loudly to the reporters. "That is the young woman who was involved with the incident at the Windsor Palms yesterday."

I froze as the crowd stepped aside in unison to let me pass.

"Yes, yes, you, dear," Lester Fine said, walking toward me and taking my arm, pulling me toward the wax figure.

I yanked my arm away, but Lester Fine would not be dissuaded. He smiled at me, although there was something behind his smile that totally was not sincere.

The wax figure had been forgotten. I was his new photo op.

I was not a happy camper.

The reporters were shouting at me all at once. I couldn't make out their questions, until I concentrated on the woman standing closest to me. She was blond, familiar.

Leigh Holmes, Channel 6. We'd crossed paths before, and she'd mistakenly thought my brother would give her classified information if she slept with him. She'd had no idea that he just wanted the sex and had no intentions of sharing any sort of information. He was a guy.

"Can you tell us what happened yesterday?" she asked, the microphone bobbing so close to my nose that I stepped back slightly so as not to get hit with it, but I was now invading Lester Fine's personal space. He didn't seem to mind.

"What can you tell us?" Leigh Holmes insisted.

I shook my head. "I'm sorry, no comment."

I could feel Lester Fine's hot breath on the side of my neck. And when he asked, "Where is it?" his voice was so low I knew no one could hear him but me.

"Excuse me?" I asked.

"Where is it?" he hissed.

"What?"

"You know."

"No, I don't."

He blew air through his nostrils. "Miss Kavanaugh—"

The moment he said my name, it reminded me of something. How his personal assistant, Rusty Abbott, had also said my name. Without my ever telling him what it was.

Granted, Colin Bixby could have told him yesterday. Frank DeBurra could have. But I wasn't a hundred percent sure about that. Even though I was having doubts about Bixby right now, those HIPAA laws would have protected me, as he'd told Fine yesterday. And DeBurra, well, he wasn't exactly the cooperating type.

I gave Lester Fine the look I'd given Cory Michaels when he told me he hadn't stolen my lunch money out of my desk.

"How do you know my name?"

The smile was smooth, practiced, and solely for the cameras, while his tone was threatening. "If I don't get it back—"

I snorted. Which might not go over well on the TV. A camera was aimed right at me.

"I have no idea what you're talking about," I said, stepping away.

That's when I saw Rusty Abbott on the moving incline, coming toward me.

Chapter 43

Leigh Holmes wasn't about to let me get away, even though I took another step. She was in my face again with that microphone.

"We understand an employee of yours was involved with the ricin poisoning at the Windsor Palms," she said.

That stopped me. I stared at her for a long second. How did she find out about Charlotte?

"I still have no comment," I insisted.

But she was onto me. She knew that question had sparked something.

"And the police are interrogating another one of your employees as we speak," she said, a hard edge in her voice.

When I didn't say anything, she added, "So what sort of business are you running, Miss Kavanaugh?"

"Maybe you should sleep with my brother again to see if you can get answers to all these questions," I said loudly.

Under the five inches of caked-on makeup, I believe Leigh Holmes turned white. She waved her hand in front of the camera lens frantically, the microphone now drooping toward the ground by its cable.

While she was distracted, I glanced around and saw that Rusty Abbott was almost to the top of the incline. He must have followed me here from Trevor's apartment. I wasn't interested in an up-close-and-personal encounter, so I scrambled through the crowd and got on the incline going back down. I caught Abbott's eye.

He pointed to the bottom of the incline. "Wait for me," he mouthed as he moved his shirt to the side and I saw that gun again.

What, was he kidding?

I swiveled my head to see him start to stride up the incline, and when he got to the top, he turned around to come right back down again. He was gaining on me.

I pushed my way down the incline and caught purchase on the pavement at the bottom. I ran around the fountain and toward the entrance to the lobby of the Venetian.

I usually didn't go in this way. There was no need, since I could get to the Venetian Grand Canal Shoppes through the parking garage around the back. After living in Vegas for two years, going on three, you'd think that I'd be used to the decadent, over-the-top opulence in the resort lobbies by now.

Everything dripped gold. I almost slipped on the shiny Italian tiles on the floor as I bounded through the palatial walkway. Flags advertising *Phantom of the Opera*—I'd never seen the show; somehow watching a man sing with a plate on his face didn't appeal to me—fluttered in the air-conditioning just below the arched ceiling sporting Renaissance-style paintings in gold frames. Marble columns topped with gold stood sentry, flanking the walkway that led to the globe fountain, to which golden statues clung.

It was gold overload.

I turned and started to run through the casino, but a security guard appeared out of nowhere, stopping me with a raised hand.

"What's your hurry?" he asked.

I glanced behind me. "Someone's following me," I said, my breath coming out in spurts. I didn't realize how hard I'd been running.

The guard looked behind me. "No one running but you."

I peered past the fountain to the marble columns. I didn't see Rusty Abbott. Maybe he'd lost interest. I could only hope. I looked back to the guard and nodded. "Okay, fine. I just have to get to the Grand Canal Shoppes."

He pointed to my left, and the escalators were there, ready to take me to my shop. I thanked him and power walked toward them, sneaking looks behind me as I went.

Still no sign of Abbott.

At the top of the escalators, I was in the Great Hall. Talk about over the top. More ceiling paintings, more elaborate theme park–like illusions of actually being in Venice. Without the stench of the canal, of course. I'd been in Venice once, in July, and I thought I'd landed in the middle of a sewage plant. I got over it, or probably just got used to it, as I wandered the streets and bridges.

I was doing the same thing here, skipping past the restaurants and shops. It was like being in Oz, but instead of a yellow brick road, there was a minicanal with gondolas filled with tourists.

As I walked, I pondered what it was Lester Fine thought I had. Did he know I'd been to Trevor's apartment? Did he know about the money? Did he think I took it?

I shook the thoughts away. How would Lester Fine know about Trevor's money? No, it had to be something else. The queen-of-hearts pin, maybe? Rusty Abbott had the makeup case, so he most likely knew now that the pin had been removed. Could he think I'd taken it?

I was circling the runway but had nowhere to land.

The Painted Lady was at the opposite end of the canal, squeezed in between Barneys New York and Jack's Gallery. Across the waterway was a Godiva chocolate place. I needed a little chocolate right about now, so I crossed over one of the footbridges and found myself pointing out various truffles that the kind girl put into a box for me. Armed with sugar, I scooted around the end of the canal and the line of people waiting their turn for a gondola ride and pushed open the door to my shop.

I took a deep breath as the door slowly closed behind

me. Bitsy was sitting at the front desk and looked up at me expectantly. I handed her the box of chocolates.

Her grin was immediate.

"Godiva!" she exclaimed.

Joel's head poked out of his door. "Did you bring Godiva?" he asked.

I nodded.

Bitsy had already opened the box and was popping a truffle in her mouth, *mmm*ing as she savored it. Joel came out of his room a few seconds later and bounced over to the desk, grabbing the box.

"Do you have a client?" I asked.

His mouth was already full of truffle. He nodded. "Needed a break anyway," he said as chocolate smeared across his teeth.

I grabbed one because I knew they could be gone in seconds, and when the chocolate hit my tongue, I sighed again.

"You should get poisoned more often," Joel said, taking three truffles back to his room with him.

Bitsy cocked her head toward his back. "He's off Weight Watchers. Said he gained five pounds and can't afford any more."

"Too bad," I said.

"Yeah."

We both knew he'd join up again in about three or four months.

I had my back to the door, and when it opened, I jumped a little, but it wasn't Rusty Abbott. It was my client.

I was feeling almost normal again as I inked the pinup girl on Herbie Nelson's upper arm. She had unnaturally large breasts with the nipples peeking out of a low-cut shirt and legs that any showgirl would die for. Herbie wanted her to be a blonde, so she had a huge bouffant of yellow curls cascading over her shoulders. When Herbie flexed his biceps, the breasts got even larger. He loved it.

I wasn't so sure. This was old school, the kind of ink Jeff Coleman would do. I didn't do many like this—usually left it to Joel, who was better at it than me. But Herbie was a regular. I'd already inked him five times, and he'd fallen in love with the Japanese geisha that I'd done just a few months back on his other arm. Granted, he'd wanted a more scantily clad geisha, so the kimono was short and open in the front. Herbie liked sexy women on his person. I hated to say it, but it might be the closest he would ever get. Who was I to turn him away? Plus, he paid top dollar, and considering the economy, we needed as much money as we could get in the till at the end of the day.

The gloves were feeling a little clammy, and my hand started to cramp about an hour into Herbie's ink. I lifted my foot off the pedal and the machine stopped. I looked at Herbie's face, and he had tears running down his cheeks. Herbie always cried. I was used to it now.

"A break?" I asked, pulling off my gloves before he could answer.

Herbie nodded, and I handed him a box of tissues so he could clean himself up before round two.

I stepped out of the room. Bitsy was still at the front desk, going over the appointment book. She looked up when I came out. I walked over to her and noticed that the box of truffles was empty. I raised my eyebrows at her, and she chuckled.

"Joel enjoyed them."

"Where is he?"

"He's got half an hour between clients. I think he's out getting something else to eat."

Figured. It was lunchtime. I hoped he'd bring something back for me and Bitsy.

"Oh, by the way," Bitsy added, giving me a sly smile I couldn't read. "A few minutes ago someone came in and made an appointment. He's going to be back in a couple hours to go over what he wants with you."

I nodded. "Okay." I leaned over her shoulder and looked at the appointment book.

When I saw the name she'd penciled in, I froze.

Colin Bixby.

Chapter 44

"You look like you've seen a ghost," Bitsy said. "I thought you'd be happy about this, Dr. Sexy coming in for a tattoo. You might be able to see a part of his body that you've just thought about seeing. And he looks even sexier without that lab coat on. He's got a nice tight butt in those designer jeans." Her eyebrows bounced up and down as she grinned.

I chuckled nervously. "It's just, well, I found out he's already got a tattoo, but he told me in the hospital that he didn't have one, that he was afraid of needles."

Bitsy looked at me like I had three heads, but before I could explain, the door opened and Joel came in, carrying take-out bags from Johnny Rockets.

I prefer In-N-Out Burger, but Johnny Rockets would do in a pinch.

"Lunch has arrived," Joel announced.

I glanced back at my room. I had to get back to Herbie, but my stomach was growling. I reached in one of the bags and grabbed a burger, peeled back the paper, and took a couple of bites. I indicated my room. "Gotta get back," I said, talking with my mouth full. Sister Mary Eucharista would have made me write "I will not talk with my mouth full" on the blackboard fifty times for that.

I took another couple of bites, wadded up the paper, and put it in the trashcan under the desk. "Thanks," I said to Joel before heading back to Herbie.

My head was distracted with thoughts of Colin Bixby as I finished the pinup girl, and he still hadn't arrived by the time Herbie and I emerged from the room. Herbie paid Bitsy, and we sent him on his way. I looked nervously out the glass doors at the canal and to the right and the left, but there was no sign of Bixby.

"You're acting like a girl on prom night," Joel commented as he came up behind me, startling me.

I slapped his arm playfully. "Don't do that," I said. "It's just that I'm not exactly sure what this guy is up to." I told them about the queen-of-hearts tattoo Bixby had had done at Murder Ink a year ago, when he was dressed in drag with Wesley Lambert and Rusty Abbott. "So he lied to me, and I don't think he'll be all that into me, either, since he's obviously gay, like I thought initially."

Bitsy's eyes skirted to Joel for a second, and I knew what she was thinking. We still didn't know which way Joel swung—officially, anyway. He had never come out to us, might never. We always tried to say in front of him that we didn't care who was gay or who wasn't, but it didn't do any good. Sometimes we thought he was just asexual, which was also a possibility.

I looked back out the door, but the scene was the same as it had been a second ago, the last time I checked.

"When he gets here, just let me know, okay?"

I went down the hall and into the staff room, where I settled in at the light table. I had a sketch to do for a client tomorrow, but just as I put pencil to paper, the corner of my messenger bag as it hung over the chair caught my eye. That's right. Trevor's laptop.

I put the pencil down and got the bag, sliding the laptop out and setting it on the table. I lifted the cover and turned it on.

A bunch of folder icons littered the screen when it booted up. They were tagged with dates, nothing else. I clicked on one.

Pictures. Seven of them, of Trevor in various stages of development and finally ending up as Britney Brassieres. A glance at the date on the folder told me that this was two weeks ago. I clicked on a video file, and the movie started. It was a how-to: how to become a drag queen in seven minutes. Although Trevor's narration told me that it really took two hours from start to finish.

Interesting, but I didn't think this was anything special.

I clicked on another folder; this one was dated a week ago.

These looked like Britney Brassieres's publicity shots. She was all dolled up with that long, big, blond wig and eyelashes that curled out about two inches. Each picture had her in a different costume: the Catholic schoolgirl skirt and blouse; a cheetah-print bodysuit; a short, white, sequined dress that rode up high enough so if Trevor's jewels fell out it would create quite a stir.

I closed the folder and opened another one. This one had a date from about six months ago.

Trevor and Kyle and Stephan all as themselves sitting around what was obviously Trevor's apartment, holding martini glasses and mugging for the camera. Clicking on a couple of the other pictures told me these were from a party. I noted that Trevor had actually cleaned up the apartment a little, although the exercise equipment still sported the wigs. Maybe it was just a conversation piece.

I'd like to listen in on that one.

This was getting me nowhere.

I looked in Trevor's documents, but nothing seemed unusual. He had a folder called "taxes," and I clicked on that, just out of curiosity.

The files went back five years, from what I could see. I wondered how long Charlotte had been doing his taxes for him. If, in fact, she actually had ever done his taxes. I was doubting mostly everything Charlotte had told us now. I mentally slapped myself. Of course she'd done his taxes. He'd told us that himself. Then again, if he was in on it with her, then he could lie, too.

I mulled over what they could be "in on" together. I still didn't have a clue.

As I opened the file for this past year, I could almost hear Sister Mary Eucharista telling me I should respect a person's privacy. But Trevor was dead, and someone shot at me. I figured I'd get a pass on this.

I found a Word document with all Trevor's deductions: wigs, costumes, makeup, shoes. I wished I could deduct my shoes.

An Excel document had two lists of numbers. When my eyes adjusted to the little boxes, I focused on the first column and figured they had to be dates, because they were noted as 2/1, 3/1, 4/1. If they were dates, they ran the course of about ten months. The column next to it showed 3,000, 5,000, and one 10,000. A quick add off the top of my head indicated that the total was around 50,000.

I leaned back in my seat for a second. That was about how much Trevor had in those boots. This money came from somewhere, but nothing indicated where.

I touched the pad again, closing the Excel document and eyeing a few PDFs, all of them of Trevor's 1099 wages—money he'd made freelancing his wares. Chez Tango was there, as well as a couple of other clubs. But those weren't the most interesting.

The 1099 from Lester Fine was.

According to this, Trevor made almost a hundred thousand dollars in the previous year working for Lester Fine. I scanned the PDF and saw a notation for "bodyguard."

Trevor? Really? That was a lot of money to pay a skinny little queen to be a bodyguard.

What was Lester Fine really paying him for? Was the money in the boots part of this?

I found the connection to the Internet and opened Firefox. I scanned his sidebar of bookmarks.

I clicked on one for a credit union, hoping it was his account and that Trevor had saved his password. I smiled when I saw the login and password pop into the boxes. I hit return and waited a second before Trevor's accounts showed up. I clicked on the checking account. He had fifty dollars and thirty-three cents. Sad. But there was also a link for a savings account. I clicked.

Forty-two dollars and three cents.

Had Trevor just cashed the checks from Lester Fine and hid the money in his boots? Seemed a little odd, since he had an account and a place to put it. Maybe he was worried about so much going in.

I kept coming back to my original question of what he was doing for Lester Fine to make so much money.

I looked at the bookmarks again.

Hmmm. Facebook. I clicked on it, and the page popped up, complete with Trevor's saved password and login.

I made a mental note to take my passwords and log-ins out of my own laptop. I didn't want someone poking around in my life like I was poking around in Trevor's.

His last Facebook status had been recorded the afternoon before the Chez Tango show: Trevor McKay is all tatted up and ready to go.

A rush of sadness overwhelmed me as I noted his birth date. He'd been only twenty-six. And to be taken down by a champagne cork, well, that wasn't right.

His favorite musicians were Donna Summer, Wham!, Boy George and Culture Club, George Michael, and the Bee Gees. He was only twenty-six? It was as if he'd been living in the late 1970s and early 1980s. Britney Spears was not on the list.

This was a total bust. I started to log out, then paused a second and clicked on Trevor's pictures. I had a feeling I might see something familiar.

I was right. The photos in the folders on his desktop were categorized as photo albums on Facebook. He probably had uploaded them and then forgot to delete the folders.

I glanced over toward the door and could hear Bitsy and Joel laughing about something. Obviously, Colin Bixby had not arrived yet. My watch told me he was late now. I wasn't going to get too upset about it. I really had no idea what I was going to say to him when I saw him.

I absently clicked through Trevor's pictures from his party and smiled at one of Kyle wearing a pair of Trevor's boots and one of the wigs. It might have been the one he ended up wearing home yesterday, but then they all started looking alike after a while.

Just like all the boys.

Except one.

She had a mane of blond hair and wore a sexy white mini-dress that was sleeveless on one arm and had a long sleeve on the other. Her biceps were buff, in a good way, like Michelle Obama's. Her face wasn't as long and thin as some of the others, but the makeup was impeccable. She was gorgeous. But it was none of those things that struck me.

On the forearm that was bare, she had a queen-of-hearts playing-card tattoo.

I took a deep breath. Could this possibly be Colin Bixby? I tried to see him in her but failed. That wasn't a total surprise. These guys transformed themselves so well.

Something about her seemed familiar. I knew I'd seen her before. I shut my eyes and tried to picture her. This was bothering me.

Until it hit me.

This was the woman I'd seen across the street from Chez Tango when I discovered that the tires were slashed on Jeff's car.

Had Colin Bixby slashed the tires? He was scheduled to arrive here any minute. How was I going to react to him now?

Kyle could probably tell me for sure who she was. I wished I could print the picture, but the laptop wasn't hooked up to a printer. I'd just have to ask him to go to Facebook and check it out.

Granted, when Colin Bixby showed up, I could confront him about it, but I'd have to play that by ear. I wasn't sure I was ready to go public with this just yet.

I closed Facebook and opened the folder with the photos in it again. A quick click confirmed the pictures on Facebook had come from here.

Except there was one more folder. I opened it. There was only one picture in it. This one hadn't been on Facebook.

"Brett, he's here." Bitsy's voice made my heart jump into my throat.

I looked up to see Colin Bixby hovering behind her in the doorway, a grin on his face. For a second, my heart jumped out of reflex.

Before I shut down the computer, I took another look at the last picture, just to make sure my eyes hadn't been playing tricks on me. And then the screen went black.

I didn't want to have to deal with Colin Bixby now. I wasn't ready for that. What I really wanted to do now was go back over to see if Lester Fine was still at Madame Tussauds.

Because I was pretty sure why Lester was paying Trevor McKay. For his silence. Trevor was guarding Lester's body all right.

Chapter 45

Bitsy stepped aside and let Colin pass her and come into the staff room. He was wearing a long-sleeved white shirt and a pair of dark jeans that did, indeed, show off that nice butt Bitsy had mentioned. I stood, one hand shutting the laptop, the other in the air to stop him.

"Let's go out there," I said, indicating the hall. I moved past him, trying not to notice his musky scent. He must have poured a whole bottle of cologne on himself. But instead of it being a turnoff, I liked it.

I was getting too desperate if I was caving in to a guy who dressed like a girl. I needed a date.

Bixby followed me into my room, where I indicated he should sit in the client chair. I grabbed a sketchbook off the shelf and picked up a pencil before settling onto my chair. I settled a little too fast, though, and it started to roll. I stuck a foot down to stop it, but my knee connected with Bixby's, and he flashed his sexy smile at me.

I cleared my throat and pushed away, my pencil poised.

"So what is it you want?" I asked, realizing too late that it was a loaded question and could mean just about anything. "I mean, well, what sort of ink do you want? Something small? Since it's your *first* one." I couldn't keep the sarcasm out of my tone.

He frowned. "Did I do something wrong?" he asked.

I sighed. Might as well get this over with. I pointed to his long sleeve on his right arm. "Can you just pull that up? I want to see it."

More frowning. "See what?"

I shook my head. "Just do it, okay?"

He actually looked puzzled, then unbuttoned the cuff and shoved the sleeve up.

I did a double take. Really.

There was nothing there.

I peered more closely, wondering whether he'd had it removed. But I didn't see any signs of laser surgery.

"What's this all about, Brett?" he asked, his tone frosty.

I bit my lip and shrugged. "I thought you already had a tattoo," I said.

"I told you I didn't. And I must really like you, because this isn't something I'd do on the spur of the moment."

He didn't sound like he really liked me at the moment, but I was too busy trying to register what he was saying.

"But Jeff Coleman—" I thought about the folder at Murder Ink, how I'd seen the name Colin Bixby. I wasn't going crazy; it was there in black and white.

"Who's that?" he asked. "Is he your boyfriend?"

I snorted. "Absolutely not," I said with more force than I intended. "He owns Murder Ink. He said you got a tattoo."

Bixby's eyebrows moved so close together, they looked like they'd become one. "I never had a tattoo. I told you that." He looked at my tattoo machine on the counter and sighed. "I'm not thrilled about needles."

"Yeah, yeah, you said that," I said, mulling this new information. If Colin Bixby hadn't been the one at Murder Ink with Wesley Lambert and Rusty Abbott, then who was it? Who was using his name? "You said, too, that you know Kyle Albrecht. Do you know Wesley Lambert, too? Shanda Leer," I added, trying to hide my smirk.

"I do," he said.

"Lambert and a guy named Rusty Abbott—"

"Lester's assistant?"

He knew all the players. How was he involved in all

this? Because even though he didn't have a tattoo, it was all a little too close for comfort.

"That's right. Rusty Abbott, Lester Fine's assistant. How do you know him?"

"What about him?" He was evading my question. I'd have to get back to it.

"Well, Abbott and Lambert and another guy went to Murder Ink after that Queen of Hearts Ball last year and got queen-of-hearts playing cards inked on their inner right forearms. Jeff Coleman told me that the third guy's name was Colin Bixby." I leaned back a little, studying his face to see his reaction.

"Well, it wasn't me," he said loudly. "I have no idea who it was. And I've never gone to a tattoo parlor with anyone, anytime." He paused. "Except right now."

I had to ask. It was eating me up inside.

"How do you know Kyle and Wesley? Are you a drag queen, too?"

His eyes grew wide, shock crossing his face. "You think . . ." His voice trailed off into a sort of cough.

"I don't know what to think," I said.

Bixby took a deep breath and forced a smile. "Brett, I'm not a drag queen. I'm not gay. I know Kyle because he's my cousin."

His cousin?

"But why would someone use your name when getting a tattoo?"

He shrugged. "Who knows?" But his jaw had tensed, belying his nonchalant tone.

"Wouldn't it be easier to say your name is John Smith or something?" I was talking off the top of my head now and didn't exactly expect an answer.

"Rusty Abbott and I don't get along very well. Maybe it was his idea of a joke."

The mention of Abbott veered my thoughts onto another track. "So how do you know him? Is it through Lester Fine?"

"That's right."

I had another thought. "You called him Lester. That's pretty familiar for someone it seemed like you met just yesterday at the hospital."

Bixby bobbed his head a little in a sort of nod. "I know Lester. I don't advertise it because he's a celebrity and all, and I don't want to come across as name-dropping or anything. But I met him several months back when he came into the hospital for a . . . well . . . a procedure."

I grinned. "A face-lift?"

He shook his head.

"Eye work?"

He shook his head again. "I can't tell you. HIPAA, you know."

Yeah, I knew. "But you're an ER doctor. Emergencies only. Do you do procedures?"

Bixby chuckled. "You can't cut a guy a break, can you?"

"I just like to find out as much as I can about someone before I ink him." I almost said "when I like him," but managed not to slip up.

"Did you Google me yet?"

Hmmm. That was an idea. I was so wrapped up with Trevor and Lester Fine and Wesley Lambert that I didn't think to Google Colin Bixby.

"Is that a no?" he asked.

I shook my head, happy I could be honest, although later I'd take a quick look. He seemed to know what I was thinking, and he leaned over and put his hand on my knee.

"I came here today because I like you," he said softly.

I let myself get lost in his eyes for a second, and it was an extremely pleasant place to be. But then he sat back again, his eyes leaving mine and skipping all around my room. "Can we get this over with?" he asked.

"With that sort of attitude, I'm not sure it's a good idea," I said.

He flashed me a smile. "A Celtic knot. Small." He unbuttoned the top three buttons of his shirt, and I tried not to catch my breath. He pointed just above his left nipple. "Here."

I smiled back, despite myself. "You've been thinking about it."

"I didn't want to go someplace where I'd get hepatitis, or worse," he said, waving his hand around to indicate my room. "This looks pretty good. I feel safe here."

"I'm glad you feel safe," I said, sketching out a Celtic knot on my pad. I could do one of these with my eyes closed. But I wasn't going to tell him that. He might think I would actually close my eyes, and then he'd get spooked. "What about this?" I asked, showing him my sketch.

He nodded slowly. "That's exactly right."

"You can make an appointment with Bitsy and leave a deposit," I said, standing.

Bixby reached out and caught my hand with his. "Now. It has to be now, or I might never come back." He paused. "I took a Xanax."

I laughed out loud. "Let me check with Bitsy, make sure I'm free for an hour. That should be all it'll take. I need to make a stencil. I'll be right back."

I could still feel the pressure of his hand on mine as I scurried out to the front desk.

"Someone looks happy," Bitsy teased.

"He wants me to do it now."

"I like a man who's decisive," she said, looking at the book. "Go ahead. You don't have anyone coming in for another couple hours."

I had started back toward the staff room to make the stencil when I heard her say, "Oh, by the way, Jeff Coleman just called. He wants you to call him right away."

"What did he want?"

"I don't know. He wouldn't say." She rolled her eyes at me. "Maybe he wants to make an appointment, too."

I made a face at her, and when I went into the staff room, I grabbed my cell phone out of my bag. I could multitask with the best of them, but I'd have to call Jeff before I started Bixby's ink.

"Murder Ink."

"Jeff? It's Brett. What do you want?"

"No foreplay, Kavanaugh? You disappoint me."

"What do you want?" I repeated. "I haven't got all day."

"You might want to make time for this. I made a few calls. About Charlotte. Asked what Homeland Security was investigating her for."

My heart started to beat a little faster, and I put my sketch down. "What was it?"

"She's not being investigated."

I thought about what Tim had said. Was he wrong? "What do you mean?"

"She's working for them. Undercover. Has been for almost a year now."

Chapter 46

Charlotte? Working for Homeland Security? "What's she doing for them?"

"She's been getting them information about that Lambert guy, the one you found dead in that condo."

"It's the ricin, right?"

"He's involved with some sort of militia out in the desert."

So it wasn't drugs. It really was terrorism.

Jeff was still talking. "There was something about Lester Fine, too, but they got all squirrelly, Kavanaugh. Wouldn't tell me more than that, and they were all nervous about telling me what they did."

"Why did they, then?"

"Why did they what?"

"Tell you."

I could hear a low chuckle. "Well, if you really want to know, one guy doesn't owe me money anymore, and I've got a date for Saturday night."

I didn't want to know about Jeff's social life. "Are they really looking for her, or is that all a ruse, too?"

"That's all I know, Kavanaugh. The rest is up to you." He hung up.

I sat, staring at my phone for a few seconds.

"Brett?"

Joel's voice made me jump. I turned to see him coming into the staff room.

"Are you aware you've got a hunky guy in your room?"

I nodded. "Yeah, and I've got to get this stencil done." But my hands were shaking and I dropped my sketchpad. Joel leaned down, picked it up, and handed it to me.

"What's wrong?"

I told him what Jeff Coleman had said about Charlotte working for Homeland Security.

My thoughts were more mixed up than clothes in a dryer. And I still had Colin Bixby to deal with. All of a sudden, he was the last thing on my priority list. But I couldn't let him down now. It wouldn't take but an hour.

"Why would she work undercover?" Joel was asking. "Is she undercover here? I mean, she just started working for us a couple months ago. Do you think she's investigating one of *us*?"

I hadn't thought of it like that. Jeff said his people told him it was Lambert. Since he was dead, though, why was she still hiding out?

There were more questions than answers as far as Charlotte Sampson was concerned.

"I have no idea what's going on," I told Joel truthfully as I put the drawing into the thermal fax machine and watched the stencil emerge. I grabbed it and went back to my room.

Bixby flashed a nervous grin at me. "I thought you forgot about me."

"How could I forget about you?" I asked, forcing myself to flirt even though my thoughts were miles away. I told him to take his shirt off as I lowered the back of the chair so he would be more lying down than sitting up. I washed the spot where he wanted the ink and then carefully shaved it. He was watching everything like it was on the Discovery Channel.

Before putting the stencil on the spot, I rubbed a little glycerin-based deodorant on it.

"What's that for?" he asked.

"You'll see," I said, carefully pressing the stencil on his skin and then peeling it back to show the Celtic knot design.

He grinned. "Is that it?"

I turned in my chair to the counter and put a new needle into the machine and dipped it in black ink. I wheeled back toward him and let the machine hover a second. "I assume you didn't want any color."

There was no color in his face as he stared at the machine. He nodded, and I pressed the foot pedal. The soft whir of the machine was hypnotizing—for me, because it pushed everything out of my head except this tattoo; for Bixby, I wasn't so sure. I moved the machine closer.

"It's going to feel like bee stings," I warned.

He closed his eyes. "I'm ready."

He didn't cry, and after a few minutes, he was even watching me draw.

"I'm glad you're my first," he said when I was almost done. He hadn't spoken at all until then, and his voice knocked me out of my zone.

I smiled. "I will tell you that people who get one tattoo usually end up getting at least one more."

"Maybe I'll be back." He cocked his head toward my arm. "Although I'm not sure I'd get anything like that."

"You could bond with the ER patients," I quipped, putting the finishing touches on the tattoo. I took my foot off the pedal and surveyed my work. It was a simple design, but classic.

"Want to look?" I asked. "There's a big mirror in the back, on the wall next to the couch."

Colin Bixby stood up, a little wobbly at first; then he flashed me that sexy grin as he left the room. I put the tattoo machine on the counter and started to gather the instructions for the tattoo's care.

When he came back, he was still smiling, so I figured he liked it. I covered the tattoo, told him to keep it like that just for a little while, then instructed him to take the wrapping off to let it heal, washing it with liquid antibacterial soap and applying an antibiotic ointment. After a few days, he could switch to using an unscented moisturizer.

"It'll be pink for a while, like bubble gum," I said, "and it'll peel like sunburn. Then it'll be fine."

He buttoned his shirt, and I saw his fingers shaking a little.

"Has the Xanax worn off?" I asked.

"No," he said. "I'm just a little nervous about what I'm going to do next."

"And what's that?" I asked absently. My thoughts were turning back to Charlotte and what I'd be doing next.

But instead of answering, he grabbed me around the waist and pulled me to him. His lips found mine, and I couldn't breathe, but in a good way. He tasted like wintergreen Tic Tacs.

When we finally came up for air, we grinned stupidly at each other.

"I guess you don't think I'm contaminated after all."

I couldn't believe I said something so stupid.

But he didn't seem to notice. "I'll call you." He started out the door, but then stopped and turned. He held his hand out.

"I don't know what to do with this. Kyle came and got Trevor's clothes, but he wouldn't take this." He opened his hand, and sitting in the center of his palm was the queen-of-hearts brooch.

I stared at it.

"Isn't there some sort of hospital procedure for stuff like that?" I asked.

"We keep things for the next of kin, but Trevor didn't have family, apparently. That's why Kyle took over. But he didn't want to take this. Said it was bad karma or something."

No kidding. Wesley Lambert was looking for this pin, and the next thing we knew, Trevor was dead.

I reached over and took the brooch from Bixby, turning it over in my hand. Still seemed as garish as the first time I'd seen it. I held it back out for him, but he shook his head.

"How about if you give it to your brother for me? I want

the police to have this. I don't really want to leave it around the hospital. It might get lost or stolen."

I thought about how the pin had been reported stolen already. It probably should be in police hands. They'd most likely give it back to Lester Fine.

Something Jeff had said picked at my brain. Lester Fine's name came up in conjunction with the investigation into Wesley Lambert. Lambert had been poking around for the brooch. There had to be a link there somewhere. I could give the brooch to Tim and tell him what I'd found out.

I nodded. "Sure. I'll give it to Tim." I put it in my jeans pocket.

He flashed me that smile again, the one that made me a little weak in the knees. I almost told him the ink was on the house, but Bitsy wouldn't be happy about that. I consoled myself by not accompanying him to the front desk where the money would change hands, or at least the credit card would be swiped.

I went back to the staff room. Trevor's laptop still sat on the corner of the light table. It reminded me of something, and I went back out to the front, where Bixby was just about to leave. He looked up when I approached.

I tugged on his sleeve.

"Just one question," I said.

"I haven't been interrogated this much since my prom date's father." He grinned.

I wanted to kiss him again but pushed the thought aside. Time for that later. I hoped.

"I saw some pictures," I said. "Trevor had some pictures, and the funny thing is, Lester Fine's in one of them." I didn't want to describe it, so I just stopped there.

It was like someone had switched the light off. Bixby's face grew dark. "Listen, Brett," he said in a tone so low I had to lean forward to hear him. "If you think you saw Lester in a picture and you think it means something, maybe you should just tell your brother and let him handle it in whatever way he feels is appropriate. I don't think Lester would like it very much if you start throwing accusations around."

I was already on Lester Fine's bad side. But Bixby wasn't done yet.

"Rusty Abbott is more than just a personal assistant, Brett. He's taken care of things for Lester for the last couple years." Bixby paused. "He can make accidents happen. Get my drift?"

Chapter 47

Accidents can happen. I remembered how Jeff Coleman had said that was Abbott's message to me.

"How do you know all this?" I asked. "This is more than just him showing up for a procedure, isn't it?"

Colin Bixby traced my jaw with the tip of his finger, and I felt it all the way to my toes. Although I wasn't quite sure if it was in a good way or not, because what he'd said creeped me out.

"I'll call you," he said, leaning over and brushing my cheek with his lips before going out the door.

Bitsy was watching with her mouth hanging open.

"You look like some sort of fish," I said a little too sharply.

"You move fast," she said.

"I just spent over an hour with the guy."

"Yeah, touching him."

"Not exactly. The needle was touching him."

"It's romantic."

I sighed. This was getting us nowhere. "When's my next client?"

"Half an hour."

I needed more sugar. I'd managed to get only a couple of truffles before Joel finished them off. I thought about the gelato place over in the Palazzo shops on the first floor. Usually I didn't go for five-dollar ice cream, but I was in the mood for a little splurge. I went into the staff room and grabbed my bag. On my way out, I tucked Trevor's laptop on the shelf under the light table.

Bitsy and Joel both placed orders, and I made a mental note to call Tim when I got back to find out what was going on with Ace. I recalled Joel's question about Charlotte: Had she gotten the job at the shop to check out one of us? Ace? They'd gotten very close very quickly. And now he had all that cash in his account.

For a split second I wondered if he was somehow involved with all this.

But then I mentally slapped myself. While I did know Ace less than I knew Bitsy or Joel, we'd all been together now for two years. I couldn't see Ace doing something like stealing money from Trevor.

Should I tell Tim about the picture of Trevor and Lester and the 1099s on the laptop? Probably. But then I'd have to tell him I'd taken the laptop from Trevor's apartment. I'd conveniently left that small fact out when I told him and DeBurra about my first trip to Trevor's yesterday. Somehow, I wasn't quite sure how to relay that information without putting myself in a really bad light. It would have to be done delicately.

I'd think about it.

I walked around the end of the canal, where people were waiting for gondolas. Back in St. Mark's Square, I could hear lutes and a harp and some singing. Without even looking, I knew costumed men and women were probably dancing, entertaining the tourists.

I kept walking past the shops and down the escalator to the first floor.

Spray from the waterfall misted my face, and I combed my hair back off my forehead with my fingers. I didn't want to think about how much water was being wasted.

There was a line at Espressamente illy. I stood between it and the escalator, debating with myself. I could go back upstairs and get gelato at St. Mark's Square, but I preferred the gelato here. As I hesitated, someone knocked into me from behind.

I whirled around and saw Frank DeBurra.

Just my luck.

"What do you want now?" I asked wearily.

But he wasn't paying attention to me. His face was screwed up with anger as he addressed a gaggle of twentysomething girls on the other side of him. They were giggling and whispering and hadn't paid attention when two of them bumped into him.

"Watch where you're going!" he said.

He whirled around, not accepting their apologies.

I eyed the escalator, knowing if I'd been just a few minutes earlier or later I might not have had another close encounter with my new nemesis. Since he was probably stalking me again, I figured I should go on the offensive.

"What's going on with Ace?" I asked. "Have you charged him officially with anything?"

"That's none of your business."

I sighed dramatically and threw up my hands. "This is all my business. You won't leave me alone. You won't leave my staff alone. I really don't know what you're looking for, what you want from me. Why don't you ask Charlotte? She's working for you, isn't she? Doesn't she have any answers for you?"

I had succeeded in surprising him. His eyes grew wide, and his mouth hung open. Finally, "How do you know about Charlotte Sampson?"

"So it's true?"

For a second, something flashed across his face that I couldn't read. Either it was dismay that I'd just been baiting him and he'd admitted the truth, or it was disgust that I knew something I shouldn't. Maybe it was a little bit of both.

Finally, he said, "We're just trying to protect her. That's why we need to find her."

His tone seemed sincere, but I was getting tired of going over the same old territory. So I decided we needed a new subject.

"You know, Trevor had a Facebook page."

He looked at me like I had three heads.

"You know? Facebook? Social networking?"

He snorted. "I know it. What does this have to do with anything?"

I shrugged. "I was looking at the pictures he's got there and I saw one of a drag queen who looked familiar."

Something crossed his face that I couldn't read. "What do you mean?"

"Remember when I said someone slashed my tires? I saw a woman walking by. And I think she was the one I saw in the picture on Trevor's Facebook page."

"How can you tell?"

"Looked the same. Even almost the same sort of dress."

"But not familiar?"

"I didn't have time to look that closely at it. I'd have to look again. I can show you. Maybe she's the one who slashed the tires."

"Why would she want to do that if you don't even know her?"

Well, now, that was a good question, wasn't it? "It was just an idea," I said.

DeBurra stared at me for a second, then said, "Why don't you leave the ideas to me?"

So we were back to belligerence. Fine.

"I have to get back to work, Detective," I said, emphasizing the last word as though it were of the four-letter kind.

He studied my face for a second.

"Watch your back," he said and turned and walked away.

I forgot about the gelato and got back on the escalator. Maybe I should've told him about the picture of Lester Fine, too. Maybe then he wouldn't dismiss me so quickly. But to tell him about that picture would mean I'd have to tell him I had Trevor's laptop. I wasn't ready to admit that yet.

My imagination started to go a little crazy: Maybe that money in Trevor's apartment wasn't just bodyguard money.

Maybe Trevor blackmailed Lester with the picture. Rusty Abbott was at Trevor's apartment earlier. Maybe he wasn't just looking for the pin in the makeup case. Maybe he was looking for the laptop, too. Maybe he knew about the photograph.

Lester Fine *was* running for public office, after all.

Chapter 48

Ace was leaning against the front desk when I got back to the shop. Bitsy was leaning toward him from behind the desk, taking in every word. When I pushed the door open, they both turned to me with deer-in-the-headlights looks, as if they were sharing a secret that no one else was supposed to know about.

"Glad to see you back," I said to Ace. "What's going on?" Even though my tone was casual, I was anything but. I wanted to know everything that had gone down at the police station, and he knew it.

"They let me go," Ace said, stating the obvious. "That cop, the one looking for Charlotte, he brought me back."

So that was why DeBurra was hanging around. He wasn't stalking me again. He could've told me, though, when I asked him about Ace.

"What about the money?" I asked, ignoring Bitsy's raised eyebrows. "The money in your account?"

Ace shrugged, his hands moving to his pockets as he slouched. "It's gone."

"What do you mean, it's gone?"

"I guess it was there, and then it was gone. That cop, De-Burra? He kept insisting that I knew where it was." His eyes grew dark with anger. "I kept telling him that I didn't know it was there in the first place."

"So was it?" Bitsy asked.

"Was what?"

I followed what she was thinking. "Was the money really there in the first place?" I asked.

He nodded. "Yeah. I saw it on the computer. And then it was gone. Just like that." He snapped his fingers.

"It disappeared while you were sitting there?"

He snorted. "And they still wouldn't let me go. I didn't even touch the mouse."

"How did they know it was there in the first place?"

Ace ran a hand through his hair and sighed. "I don't know. They got into my account somehow."

"They're Homeland Security," I said.

"What, do they think I'm some sort of terrorist or something?"

Bitsy and I shrugged but didn't answer.

"Where's Charlotte?" I asked.

"I have no idea. Haven't seen her since yesterday. She was a little nervous."

No kidding.

I debated whether I should tell him about seeing her on that balcony. But while I was thinking about it, he spoke again.

"She called me this morning, though."

"What did she say?"

He pulled himself up a little, took his hands out of his pockets. "What is this? The inquisition? I just finished up with that."

I didn't much care. "Did you tell the cops you talked to her this morning?"

He sighed, slouching again as if he couldn't keep up the anger. "I told them everything. Your brother's the one who got me out. He told that cop DeBurra that he had to let me go. It was clear I didn't move that money."

Chalk one up for Tim. I made a mental note to say thank you.

"So what happens now?" I asked.

"Ace has a client coming in later," Bitsy said loudly. "And you've got one coming in, too."

Nice to know life went on. But I was still feeling a little obsessed with everything that had transpired in the last few days.

I looked at Ace. His usual perfect mane of hair was a little disheveled; he had dark circles under his eyes; his mouth sagged at the corners. I'd never seen him look less than handsome. "If you want to go home, you can," I said. "You've had a long day. I'll take your client." I glanced at Bitsy, who was already looking at the appointment book.

"I can switch a few things around," Bitsy said. "Don't worry." This last was to Ace, who looked so relieved that I was happy I'd read him right.

He gave Bitsy and me a wan smile. "Thanks," he said, and we both smiled back as we watched him head out.

I turned to Bitsy when he was out of sight. "I do wish he'd been a little more forthcoming about Charlotte."

"You shouldn't badger him, though. Just before you came in, he was telling me how she broke up with him in that phone call this morning. Said she didn't want to cause him any more trouble, that he was better off without her. He's pretty broken up about it."

I had the sense that Ace had told her this in confidence, but he should have known by now that you can't count on Bitsy to be discreet.

I didn't get a chance to continue the conversation, however, because at that moment, Ace's client came in. Bitsy explained that Ace was out sick, but that I could take him, if he was okay with that. The guy looked remarkably like Tony Soprano, and he gave me a look that made me wish I hadn't been quite so generous after all. He was perfectly okay with me taking over.

Fortunately, he was just in for a New Zealand tribal tattoo on his biceps, which didn't take much effort at all. I could understand why Ace had issues with "sacrificing his art." As I worked, I tried to push everything that was going on out of my head, but I kept wondering about that money. If Charlotte hadn't taken it, like she said, then who did? Was it the unknown person in Trevor's apartment who shot at us? Or had someone gone in after I'd been there with Kyle and before I went back with Jeff? What about Rusty Abbott?

When I deposited Ace's client with Bitsy to deal with payment, I went straight into the staff room. While I was thinking about the money, my thoughts had wandered back to Trevor's laptop and that picture of Lester Fine. Finally free for a little while, I took the laptop out from under the light table where I'd left it and booted it up.

I went back to Facebook to look at those party pictures again. Maybe Trevor had posted a picture of Lester without realizing it. Then I could tell Tim that there was something on Facebook rather than tell him I'd been snooping.

I clicked on the photo albums link.

There was only one problem.

All the pictures were gone.

Chapter 49

How could this be? As far as I knew, only Trevor—and me, now, because I had his password—could delete any pictures. I began to wonder what the rules were with Facebook when someone died. Did Trevor's page just stay up there indefinitely?

Then I remembered that I'd told Frank DeBurra about that picture. Maybe he actually took me seriously. That would be a switch.

I decided to give him the benefit of the doubt and made a mental note to ask him whether he found out anything from the pictures.

I heard Springsteen warbling "Born to Run" from inside my bag. I got up and took out my cell phone, flipping it open even though I didn't recognize the number on the screen.

"Yes?"

"It's Kyle."

His words were rushed, his voice lower than usual.

"Do you have a cold?" I asked.

"It's Charlotte. She's sick."

Panic rose in my chest. "Sick?" I thought about Wesley Lambert on the floor of his bedroom, dead from ricin poisoning, and Charlotte's hoodie in the living room. Granted, I'd seen Charlotte between then and now, talked to her, but it was possible that it just took that long for her to get sick. "Where is she?"

"Chez Tango."

"Can I meet you at the hospital?"

"Here."

I looked at my watch. My client would be here any minute. "Just take her to the hospital."

"No. Here."

This sounded a little too familiar. "Last time she wanted me to meet her I ended up alone with a dead body."

"Not kidding. Please." The last word was said with so much emphasis that I couldn't ignore it.

I sighed. "Fine. I'll be there in a few."

He'd already hung up, so I closed my phone and stared at it a second. She must be really sick. Kyle was such an upbeat guy, but he sounded defeated, so unlike himself. Almost like he was sick himself.

I didn't like the idea of Charlotte not going to the hospital right away. Then I had a thought. Colin Bixby. He was a doctor. He might know what to do. And I had his card somewhere. Where had I put it? I grabbed my bag and rifled through it. Had Tim returned the card with all the other things? I couldn't remember.

Finally my hand settled on something that felt like a business card. Yes, this was it. I punched the number into my phone.

"Hello?" he asked hesitantly. Oh, right, we hadn't exchanged phone calls yet, so he wouldn't know my number offhand.

"It's Brett," I said, and before he could respond, I told him what was going on.

"You should call an ambulance," he said.

"Are you free right now? Can you meet me there, and then we can see what's up?" I asked. "Kyle's with her. I think if it was that bad, he would've called an ambulance even if she said not to."

"I hope so," he said slowly.

"Can you get there?" I asked. "I'm sorry to ask, but you were the first person I thought of."

"I like the sound of that," he said, and I could hear the

smile in his voice. "Yes, I can meet you. I can be there in about fifteen minutes."

I thanked him and hung up.

For about a nanosecond I thought about calling Frank DeBurra, too, but if Charlotte really was that sick, then we could call him when we assessed the situation. It might not even be the ricin. I hoped.

I was walking out when my client walked in. She smiled shyly at me. Shoot.

"Oh, Susan, I'm really sorry, but I have an emergency," I said quickly.

Bitsy looked up with a frown. I hadn't told her yet.

"Is Joel here?" I asked, and Bitsy nodded, although I could see that she was eager to find out just what my "emergency" was. "Can you tell him Susan's stencil is on the light table?" I turned back to Susan. "Do you mind? Joel's fantastic." It wasn't like it was her first time. She had four other tattoos.

She smiled. "Sure, do what you have to do."

I leaned toward Bitsy and whispered, "It's Charlotte. Kyle called. She's sick. I've got Bixby meeting us at Chez Tango."

Bitsy's eyes were as wide as dinner plates. "I hope she's okay."

"Me, too," I said as I walked out.

I'd forgotten that I'd valet parked. I had to wait too long for my car to show up, and when it did, the valet got out of the car and stood by the door as I walked around to get in.

"Miss, I hate to tell you, but I think something's wrong with your trunk latch. It keeps popping open. Whenever it hits a bump." He cocked his head toward the back of the Bullitt, and I could see that the trunk was slightly open.

I went around the back and saw the lock had been punched out. My heart dropped, and I swallowed hard before I felt the anger rise. I looked up at the valet, who was shaking his head.

"I don't know what happened," he said, but he knew a complaint would be filed. I certainly wasn't going to pay to fix my trunk lock when the car had supposedly been safe in the parking garage under the eye of resort security.

He handed me a card with the name of the manager I needed to contact, and I stuffed it in my back pocket.

I lifted up the trunk lid farther, because something inside had caught my eye. Something that I hadn't put there.

It was Trevor McKay's makeup case.

Chapter 50

Immediately I thought about Rusty Abbott. Had he left this for me before showing up at Lester Fine's photo op? If he did, he must have followed me from Trevor's, then waited to see where the valet would park the car. Creepy. I thought about Jeff Coleman's stalker comment. And why put the case in my trunk at all?

I took the case out and balanced it on the edge of the trunk, opening the top. Trevor's makeup was strewn about, sort of in the same way things were strewn around his apartment. I tugged on the bottom drawer, and it slid out.

I shifted the hand that was holding the case, but I miscalculated. The case toppled to the pavement, lipsticks and mascaras rolling across the driveway. The valet gave me a dirty look.

"I'm sorry," I said, leaning down to gather them up.

The drawer had come out completely, and papers skittered along the pavement, a bunch of receipts from Wal-Mart and Terrible's—our local convenience store and gas station rolled into one—and what looked like a couple of pictures. As I picked up the drawer, I scooped everything up. I tossed the receipts into the trunk but held on to the photographs.

One of them was that picture I'd seen on Trevor's Facebook page of the drag queen, the one who'd been across the street at Chez Tango when Jeff's tires got slashed. I wondered again who she was as I turned over the other photo.

This one was the same picture of Lester Fine that I'd seen on Trevor's laptop.

I held the two photographs side by side, wondering whether Lester Fine was the drag queen in the first picture. I couldn't tell. These guys were so good at changing themselves into women that it was hard to pick out their male features under all the makeup and the glitter.

There was something, though, about the photo of Lester Fine that was tugging at my brain now. Not the intimate details, but something else. Finally I focused on it. Lester Fine had a tattoo on his arm. On his inner right forearm. I couldn't make out exactly what it was because of the angle, but considering the other tattoos I'd seen in that same spot lately, I wondered if it could be the same one.

It also would clear up who the third mysterious person was at Murder Ink that night of the Queen of Hearts Ball. If the drag queen in the other picture was Lester Fine, this all made perfect sense. And since Lester knew Colin Bixby, it might make a little twisted sense to use the doctor's name rather than his own. It's not as if he would have been recognized, since Jeff said he was in drag.

Granted, I had seen pictures of Lester and his wife at the ball, and Lester was wearing a tux. But maybe he'd dressed up to get the ink.

"Miss?"

The valet was staring at me. I tucked the pictures back in the makeup case drawer and left it in the trunk. I slammed the lid shut and hoped it would stay until I could at least get some string or something.

As I leaned down to get into the car, I felt the brooch in my pocket, where I'd stuck it when Bixby had given it to me. I'd practically forgotten it was there, I'd gotten so used to the way it felt. But I figured I shouldn't drive with it like that—what if the pin came unclasped and stuck me?

I took the brooch out of my pocket and stuck it in one of

the cupholders in the center console as my brain ran faster than a hamster on a wheel.

It seemed pretty clear that Rusty Abbott wanted me to find those pictures. He couldn't have known I'd already seen them on the laptop. And even if he did, I'd needed that little nudge to make the connection between them.

I wondered what his angle was. He worked for Lester Fine. Maybe Fine was a lousy boss.

I pulled out of the Venetian driveway and onto the Strip heading north. I hit a bump and the trunk opened. This was going to be a pain in the butt; however, I didn't really have time to stop and fiddle with it now. It bounced up and down as I drove, and a couple of people pulled up next to me to tell me my trunk was open.

No kidding. Like I hadn't noticed.

I ignored them and thought about Lester Fine. And that ink.

Something Bixby had said came back to me. I punched in his number.

"I'm on my way," he said without saying hello. "There's an accident, though. Traffic's stopped."

Great. "I have a question. The procedure that Lester Fine had? Did he have a tattoo removed?"

The silence told me my suspicions must be right.

"How did you find out?" Bixby asked after a few seconds.

"No time now. I'll explain when I see you. It doesn't seem like there's any traffic this way."

I wasn't sure which direction Bixby was coming from. I had no idea where he lived, and again I wondered whether he lived with his mother. I made a mental note to find out.

The sun had gone a little lower in the sky, and it beat down on the windshield. I squinted as I drove with one hand and found my sunglasses in my bag with the other. I slipped them on. Better. The palm trees in the median cast sporadic shadows. I hit another bump and the trunk opened even wider. I couldn't see out the back window now.

I needed to tie down the trunk lid. I didn't want to get stopped and end up with a traffic ticket. Granted, I needed to get to Chez Tango and find out about Charlotte, but Bixby was on his way, too, which made me feel better about a short detour. I turned right into a parking lot. It wasn't until I pulled in that I realized it was the lot for Cash & Carry, that first pawnshop I'd visited. I drove as far away from the pawnshop as I could, easing the Bullitt into a spot in front of Tip Toe Nail Salon.

I got out of the car and approached the salon. I didn't know whether they'd have any string, but it was worth a shot to ask. I pushed the door open.

The smell of acetate hit my nose, and I tried not to breathe too deeply. A short Asian woman scurried up to me, a big smile on her face.

"Hello, hello, welcome!"

She was so exuberant and the salon was so empty that I wondered if I was the first person to wander in there in a while.

"Hello," I said, trying to be friendly, but my anxiety was growing. "I'm having—"

"Pick a color. Any color," she interrupted, her fingers now wound around my forearm as she pointed to a wall filled with nail polish of all colors. She twisted my arm and began inspecting my fingernails. She began tsk-tsking as she explored my cuticles.

"I'm just here for some string," I tried lamely. I was starting to get a little anxious about the amount of time I was wasting here.

She had no clue what I was talking about.

I pointed out at my car, the trunk gaping open like Moby Dick's mouth. "I was wondering if you have some string. My trunk is broken. I need to fix it." I did a little pantomime, since I was pretty sure by now that English was not her first language. "Tie it closed."

She dropped my arm and nodded. "Yes, yes." She shuffled past me, behind me. A bunch of balloons that had seen better days sagged from a hook near the door. She took one of the balloons and brought it to me. "Here," she said.

It had lost enough of its helium that it hovered about three feet off the ground. It was a Bitsy balloon. I had no idea what to do. Should I accept it and be on my way?

The woman saw I was confused, and a huge grin took over her face. She took a pair of scissors and snipped off the balloon, handing me the ribbon.

"This will do?" she asked.

Okay, so sometimes I can be a little slow. She meant I should tie my trunk with the ribbon. I smiled. "Thank you," I said, and took a step toward the door.

But she wasn't going to let me off that easy. She pointed again at the nail polish. "What color?"

I didn't have time for a manicure. But she did help me.

I made an appointment for the next morning. I hadn't had my nails done in years. Since I was in high school and I would paint them black and draw little white skulls on them. I didn't like the way my nails felt when they were painted and I wore the latex gloves.

I'd have to suck it up for a day.

The ribbon worked perfectly, and now my Bullitt looked like it was all dressed up for a party. Considering where I was headed, it was probably appropriate.

I was walking around the car, about to get back in and on my way, when tires screeched behind me. The truck careened so close to me that I felt the heat from its engine.

It slammed to a halt just inches from the hood of my car.

I'd seen that pickup before.

I didn't have time to get into the Mustang before the pickup's door opened and Rusty Abbott charged right for me.

Chapter 51

I slammed myself flat against my car as he approached, my heart pounding so hard, I was sure it would jump out of my chest like that thing in *Alien*. I opened my mouth to say something, but my throat was so dry, no sound came out.

He'd stopped just about a foot away from me. Too close for comfort.

On impulse, I jerked my leg up and out and watched him crumble as my foot connected with his groin. He grunted with pain, and as I got into the Bullitt, I could see it etched across his face.

I started the car, shifted it into reverse, and stepped on the gas. I left him on the pavement, breathing in my exhaust.

About a block away, I wondered if I shouldn't have tried to talk to him. Ask him just what was going on.

Nah. Probably wouldn't have gotten a straight answer anyway. And I might have found myself in the middle of an "accident."

It was nice to know that in the moment, I could defend myself.

My hands were still shaking, though. I tightened my grip on the steering wheel and carefully made my way up Las Vegas Boulevard.

Kyle's CRV was the only vehicle in the parking lot. I wondered where Bixby was. Must be a pretty bad accident.

I gathered up my bag, slung it over my shoulder, and locked my car. Not that it would do much good, since the trunk was held closed only by a red balloon ribbon.

I walked across the lot and pushed on the back door, where Kyle and I had gone in yesterday.

Locked. I banged on it a couple of times, but no one came.

I went around the front of the building to the more formal entrance. The awning stretched over the walkway; the Christmas lights weren't on, but they sparkled anyway in the sunlight.

The front door was locked, too.

I took a deep breath, irritated. I took out my phone and dialed the number Kyle had called me from. The phone rang twice before I got a recording saying that it was Chez Tango and I should press one for hours, two for directions, or three for that night's show lineup. I didn't press anything; I just put the phone back into my bag.

Being a little OCD, I double-checked the parking lot, walking all around the building, careful not to step on the broken glass in the back by the Dumpster. My Mustang still sat next to the CRV.

But something was wrong. The trunk was open again.

There was no sign of the ribbon. It was gone.

Panic started to rise in my chest as I stopped looking down and started looking up, across the lot, out to the street. Had Rusty Abbott recovered enough to follow me?

I didn't want to stick around long enough to find out. I'd have to call Bixby and tell him I was standing him up. Considering Charlotte's behavior the last few days, I was starting to think she might be perfectly fine and this was some sort of trick.

I opened my car door and took another look around. Out of the corner of my eye, I saw something that made my heart leap into my throat. But when I turned to look, it was merely a skinny stray cat scurrying past, the red ribbon trailing from its mouth. I let out a long breath. I'd had enough of this place.

I scooted into the car as quickly as I could and slammed the door shut. I started the engine and shifted into first, ready to make my getaway.

Then a gold Pontiac pulled into the lot, heading straight for me.

What was Jeff Coleman doing here?

Because it *was* Jeff; he was getting out of his car and coming toward me with a little bit of a jog, a cigarette dangling from his lips.

I lowered the window but didn't turn off the engine.

"What are you doing here?" I asked as he stopped next to the car.

"Rusty Abbott said you might be here."

I frowned. "Excuse me?"

"Abbott called me, said something about you and a nail salon and you attacking him." A small smile tugged at the corner of his mouth, and the cigarette bobbed up and down.

"So, did you decide to just jump in your car and find me to make a citizen's arrest?"

"I was already in my car. About a block away. What did you do to Abbott?"

"I kicked him in the balls," I said matter-of-factly. "He was coming after me."

"Kavanaugh, you might want to ask a man what he wants before doing that," Jeff said. "Because he just wanted to talk to you."

"About what?"

Jeff glanced at his watch and then up at Chez Tango. "We've got to get out of here." He tossed the cigarette to the ground. "We don't have much time."

We didn't have any time.

Just at that moment, an explosion rocked the air.

Chapter 52

On impulse, I dropped down across the passenger seat, tucking one arm underneath me and covering my head with the other. Debris slammed against the windshield, and it shattered, cracking into a million pieces. It looked like an intricate spiral mosaic. Smoke so thick you could slice it settled on top of me. And while the windshield hadn't collapsed, it had spit tiny shards like mist across the interior of the car. I wanted to cough, but I was afraid to move.

Then I remembered Jeff.

I tried not to lean on any glass, but it was impossible. Shards that were practically invisible slit my skin like thin paper cuts as I rose and looked out the window.

The force of the explosion had thrown Jeff several feet. He lay still, faceup on the pavement between his car and mine.

I forgot about the glass and pushed the door open, finding purchase on the soot that covered the ground. Jeff's eyes were closed, and I stooped down and touched his cheek.

"Jeff?" I asked softly. "Jeff?"

His eyelids flipped open, and it took a second for him to focus. Then, "Kavanaugh? That wasn't supposed to happen for another ten minutes."

A siren pierced the air.

Jeff tried to raise himself on his elbows, but I touched his shoulder. "You might just want to lie there for a few minutes." The siren was getting closer. "You need to get checked out before you get up. Make sure everything's okay."

He snorted and sat up, cocking his head at the building behind me. The whole back had been blown away. I shuddered as I thought about how I'd wandered around the building, trying to get in. If I'd been a few minutes later . . . I didn't want to think about it.

"How did Rusty Abbott know about this?" I asked.

"Beats me. But he sounded frantic enough, so I believed him."

"Where is he now?"

Jeff rolled his eyes at me. "How am I supposed to know?"

"We have to tell the police."

"No kidding, Nancy Drew."

It seemed Jeff was perfectly fine, despite getting thrown. I thought about his time in the Gulf War. Maybe he had some experience with this sort of thing. Wasn't that what they taught the Marines? How to survive explosions? In between how to kill someone. Right.

Jeff got to his feet just as three police cruisers, two fire trucks, and an ambulance careened into the parking lot. He studied me for a second, his expression worried.

"You're covered in blood, Kavanaugh. What happened?"

I hadn't felt it at all until he mentioned it, and it wasn't the same as when Mickey inked my sleeve. Then, it was concentrated in one place at a time. This was all over, and there were no endorphins kicking in. I just felt the pain.

Jeff pulled his T-shirt over his head to reveal elaborate tattoos covering his arms and chest. He caught me staring and grinned.

"Want a tour, Kavanaugh?"

I felt my face flush, and I stammered, "No," although I couldn't tear my eyes away from the skeleton with the oversized skull stuck in a sombrero. It was curled around his abdomen, a Mexican blanket draped over one bony shoulder, a guitar clutched in bony fingers, flames licking skin. Even though it had faded somewhat with time, the colors were spectacular. "That's not flash," I said, more to myself than to Jeff.

"I designed it. Day of the Dead."

I raised my eyebrows. "Really?"

"When I got home from the Gulf. Surprised, aren't you, Kavanaugh?" He didn't wait for me to respond, since he already knew the answer, and held out his shirt to me. I wasn't quite sure what he wanted me to do with it, so he moved closer and began to wipe my arm carefully, and when he stopped, it was covered with blood.

It was the arm that didn't have any ink.

"You might have some scars," he said so softly I almost didn't hear him because of the truck engines and the fire-fighters yelling back and forth to one another and the cops. Flames were leaping out of the hole in the building.

An unmarked police car parked behind one of the fire trucks, and when the door opened, I saw a flash of red.

Tim.

He saw me as soon as he got out of the car and ran to-ward me. But before he could pull me into a hug, Jeff held out his arm to stop him.

"She's hurt," he said, showing him the bloodstained shirt.

Tim's eyes were wide with worry.

"I'm not that hurt," I said, shooting Jeff a dirty look. "I'm just a little cut up." I told Tim how I'd been in the car when Chez Tango exploded and the windshield spit all over me.

"Why are you here?" he asked.

I explained how Kyle had called me about Charlotte. "He said she was sick, that she was here and wanted to see me."

"Why didn't you call me?" He was trying to be angry, but he was too concerned about me to be successful.

Tears filled my eyes. "I'm sorry. I should have. But I wanted to see if she was really sick, and then I was going to call." I didn't know why I was still trying to protect the girl, considering, but I wanted to think that my initial instincts about her weren't totally wrong.

"Was she in there?" Tim stared at the building.

"I don't know," I said. "I tried to get in, but all the doors were locked. I called, but just got a recording." I indicated the CRV. "That's Kyle's car."

I didn't want to think that Kyle and Charlotte were in the building.

Tim was calling over the paramedics.

Oh, no, not again.

And an even stronger "oh, no" when I saw Frank De-Burra coming toward us. A firefighter stopped him just a couple feet away, and I heard DeBurra shout over the din, "Look for two bodies. A man and a woman."

The firefighter's face fell slightly; then he regained his composure and headed back to his crew.

Frank DeBurra wore no such compassion in his expression. It made me like him even less, if that were possible.

"I need you to tell me everything," he demanded of me, not even looking at Tim or Jeff. As if I were responsible for the explosion.

"She needs help," Tim said, indicating my arm, which was still bleeding.

DeBurra shot him a nasty look. "Last time she was in the emergency room, she disappeared and didn't tell anyone where she was going. I'm not falling for that again."

His words reminded me that Colin Bixby was still nowhere to be seen. What had happened to him?

Fingers were snapping in front of my face. I swatted at them and frowned at DeBurra, who didn't seem to realize that he was socially inept.

"I need to get your statement," he ordered.

"What about him?" I asked, indicating Jeff Coleman, who had wadded up his shirt and was standing with his feet slightly apart, his arms stiffly at his sides, like a cat about to pounce.

DeBurra gave a wave of his hand. "You're the one I need to talk to."

"But—"

He grabbed my arm, the one that had all the cuts on it, and I winced.

He didn't seem to notice and didn't let go.

Tim, however, shot out his hand, and it landed on De-Burra's shoulder. "She needs to go to the hospital, Frank," he said in a low voice, a voice that meant business.

"She can go after I'm finished with her," DeBurra said gruffly, shaking off Tim's hand.

Something in Tim snapped. Like when I was a kid and Robby Murphy grabbed me way too hard while we were playing Red Rover. Robby had wrestled me to the ground and kicked me in the side. Just once. Tim was hanging with his friends on the back porch and saw it. Robby didn't see what hit him.

Neither did DeBurra.

Chapter 53

Tim's fist shot out like a bullet and slammed into DeBurra's jaw, throwing DeBurra's whole head back, his body following. He landed on the ground with a thud that sounded almost as loud as that explosion, even with the cacophony of noise around us.

But unlike Robby Murphy, DeBurra had a lot more pent-up anger against Tim—and he was bigger. He squatted on the balls of his feet and pushed off, crashing against Tim's knees, which buckled, and Tim was now on the ground.

They rolled over each other, pummeling with both arms. Tim's jacket ripped right up the middle of his back. They were both covered in debris and soot from the explosion. I couldn't tell that Tim's hair was red anymore. It was like watching a movie, but there were no cameras.

Uh-oh. Spoke too soon. The TV crews had arrived, and one of the reporters—yes, Leigh Holmes, my brother's one-night stand—came jogging over with her camera guy.

Tim was straddling DeBurra now, but DeBurra had one other trick up his sleeve. He raised both arms and grabbed Tim's neck.

I looked to Jeff for help. "Do something," I hissed. "They're going to kill each other."

Their guns were still secure in their holsters, but I wasn't sure for how long—or whether one of them would just go off because it hit the ground at the wrong angle.

Jeff held up his hands and shook his head. "Not getting in between that."

I didn't really blame him, but someone had to stop them from beating the crap out of each other. They were rolling around again, arms and fists flying. I flagged down a couple of uniforms, who jogged over, their expressions grim, but I could tell they didn't want to get involved, either.

Domestic disputes are the worst.

Because this wasn't about me or Chez Tango. This was about Shawna. This was unfinished business.

One of the uniforms decided it was enough, and he tried to get between them.

He fell back after getting slugged. I have no idea whether Tim or DeBurra hit him.

I looked again at Jeff, pleading with him.

He sighed. "The things I do for you, Kavanaugh."

Jeff went over to the two men and managed somehow to wedge himself between them.

I turned around, didn't want to watch. I had a feeling Jeff would suffer the same fate as the uniform. But somehow he managed to get them to stand, a few feet apart, and while they glared at each other with fists clenched, both wearing red bruises that would turn to black and blue, they kept their anger at bay while Jeff shouted that this wasn't the time.

No kidding.

They were a mess; both their noses were bleeding, but they didn't seem to notice. I didn't want to see the damage. I started to turn away but then sensed someone watching me.

It was DeBurra. Not good. I knew he was going to try to rope me into another hours-long interrogation. Been there, done that. I wasn't in the mood.

One of the firefighters tapped him on the shoulder.

With just a quick glance at Tim, Jeff, me, and Leigh Holmes and her camera guy, who was still shooting, the firefighter told DeBurra, "There's no one in that building. No one at all."

I looked over at Chez Tango and saw that while my brother and DeBurra were beating the crap out of each other, the firefighters had done their job and it seemed the fire was out.

DeBurra's face scrunched up with anger. "What do you mean?" he asked.

"We didn't find anyone. No bodies, and no survivors, either."

Despite the rising irritation with Charlotte and the games she was playing, I breathed a sigh of relief. However, it certainly seemed as if DeBurra wasn't happy that no one was in the building. He was such a jerk. He glared at me and Tim and stormed off toward the fire captain in charge at the scene.

I took Jeff's shirt out of his hands and handed it to Tim. "Your nose," I said, and Tim touched the cloth to his face, grimacing with pain.

"I think you need the ambulance," I said.

He shook his head. The paramedics, however, agreed with me. Now that there were no bodies to attend to in the building, they seemed to need something to do. They fussed over Tim and escorted him to the ambulance, scoffing at my scratches when Tim tried to tell them that I was hurt.

DeBurra was several yards away, but I could tell he was still keeping an eye on me, even when one of the paramedics approached him as well.

"I think it's time to blow this Popsicle stand," Jeff Coleman said in a low voice.

I turned to him. "Why does he hate me so much?"

"You do know how to get under someone's skin, Kavanaugh." He said it matter-of-factly, with a touch of a smile at the corner of his mouth.

I wasn't quite sure how to respond; nothing clever was coming to mind, and while I was waiting for inspiration, Jeff just walked away toward my car. It couldn't have been something I said.

He leaned in through the window that was still open and came out waving my cell phone. "It's for you." I hadn't even heard Springsteen. Come to think of it, everything was sounding a little like it was in a tunnel. Probably because of the explosion.

I took the phone and said, "Hello?"

"Brett, I can't get anywhere near there. There are police cars and ambulances and fire trucks everywhere." It was Bixby.

"Where are you?"

"About a block down."

DeBurra had managed to get away from the paramedic and was coming toward me. I felt panic rise in my chest when I saw his expression—dark, cold, definitely out for blood, mine this time rather than Tim's.

Jeff saw it, too, and cocked his head at my phone. "Where is he?"

"Just down the street."

"Get going."

I leaned into my car and grabbed my bag, shaking the glass off it. As I did, the queen-of-hearts brooch winked at me from the center console. I took it out and stuck it in my pocket again. I must have been moving too slowly for him, because Jeff gave me a nudge and repeated, "Get going."

DeBurra was getting closer.

"Kavanaugh," Jeff hissed, "I don't know what you did, but you pissed him off, and he's not going to let you out after a few hours this time."

Jeff was right. I started walking backward, watching DeBurra. Jeff got between us. When I reached the sidewalk, I turned and sprinted. A black Audi sat idling by the side of the road, and as I approached, the headlights flashed twice. Bixby.

I opened the door and barely got seated when he spun the car around so we were going in the opposite direction. "I'm happy to see you," I said, letting myself breathe again and tossing my bag on the floor before latching my seat belt. "You might want to step on it."

Bixby heard the edge in my voice.

He glanced at my arm.

"What happened?"

I told him about the explosion, the fight between my brother and DeBurra. "I'm glad you came along when you did, or I'd be looking at another all-nighter," I said, keeping my eye on the sideview mirror for any sign of DeBurra. "Where are we going?"

"My place."

Somehow this wasn't the atmosphere in which I'd hoped to end up at Bixby's place. That fantasy included dinner, a nice bottle of wine, maybe some music. Not me all cut up and running from the cops—again. But going to his place was smart. No one would know to look for me there, and I could make some calls, try to see if anyone had seen or heard from Charlotte. I didn't know where else to start, so that seemed like a plan.

I leaned back in my seat and closed my eyes, trying to sort out everything that had happened. Music filtered in through the tunnels in my ears, something jazzy with a lot of piano and saxophone. I don't know a lot of jazz, and I don't normally listen to it—I'm more of a rock 'n' roll kind of girl—but there were times, like this, that it was soothing. Almost like a massage. Well, not exactly. I let my thoughts wander even further, wondering whether I could get a spa appointment tomorrow. I so needed one. Bitsy could rearrange my schedule.

"Penny for your thoughts," Bixby said, his voice interrupting my plans.

I didn't really want to tell him I was thinking about a massage—he might get the wrong idea—and I didn't want to get into all the stuff about Charlotte with him right now, so I asked, "How's the ink?" indicating his new Celtic knot.

He grinned. "It's fine, but it's starting to itch."

"Did you take off the plastic? Use some antibiotic gel?"

"I did."

"Good. You won't regret it."

"I know that." He glanced in the rearview mirror. "Do you know anyone who drives a gold Pontiac?"

I twisted around in my seat and looked out the back window. Jeff Coleman was following us. He was a couple cars behind, but I couldn't miss that car anywhere. His front windshield was still intact, thanks to the fact that while I was parked facing Chez Tango, he'd pulled in beside my Mustang facing the other way. It was his back window that was shattered, instead.

I settled back into my seat. "Don't worry about him. He's a friend."

"A friend?" Bixby's eyebrows rose with the question.

"Just a friend," I said. "He's looking out for me."

Bixby turned right.

Into the entrance of the Windsor Palms condominiums.

Now it was my turn to tense up. "Your place?" I asked Bixby, a sick feeling growing in my stomach.

He nodded. "Been here a little over a year."

"Did you know Wesley Lambert?"

His eyelids fluttered; then he smiled. "Bought the place because of him."

Chapter 54

I swung around to look out the back window. The gold Pontiac was nowhere to be seen.

"He turned off," Bixby said as he steered the Audi around the building to the parking garage. I did not want to go into that garage, because I wasn't sure exactly what was going on with Dr. Colin Bixby at the moment. It seemed way too much of a coincidence that he lived in the same building as Wesley Lambert.

"Kyle introduced us," he was saying, talking about Lambert. "Nice guy."

"He was making ricin in his condo," I said. "Not sure if that could be called nice. And he was poking around Chez Tango threatening Trevor, and then Trevor dies, mysteriously, from flu symptoms that could really have been ricin poisoning."

Bixby snorted. It was the first thing about him that I did not find attractive. "Are you a doctor now, Brett?"

I shrugged.

"Why don't you stick with your tattoos and I'll stick with medicine, okay?" The condescending tone was also bothersome.

He got out of the Audi, but I continued to sit there, until he came over to my door and opened it for me. He bowed low and swung his arm to indicate I was to get out. It was chivalrous; I had to give him that.

Or maybe he was just luring me into his condo so he could kill me. He knew I'd been heading over to Chez Tango, and he conveniently got stuck in traffic during the explosion.

My thoughts were all over the place. I had no proof of anything. I was being paranoid. After all I had been through, I felt it was justified.

Bixby shut the door behind me and put his hand on my lower back. My whole body stiffened.

He noticed.

"Are you okay?" he asked softly, leaning toward me and brushing my cheek with his lips.

If we weren't at the Windsor Palms, if he hadn't bought his place because of Wesley Lambert, I might actually encourage a little more romance, maybe even that massage, but instead I pulled back and said, "Stressed out. Explosions do that to me." I gave a sort of high-pitched laugh and crossed my arms, immediately regretting it because my arm was sore from being sliced up by glass shards.

He noticed.

"When we get upstairs, I'll take care of that," he said, his voice all husky and sexy, and for a second I dipped my toe in the water, but then got out of the pool.

I nodded, though, to keep up appearances.

He pushed the button for the elevator, and the doors slid open like they were waiting for us. Bixby put his arm around me and let me go in first. I shimmied around as he punched in seven, which I assumed was his floor, and then, just as the doors began to close, scooted out and watched him disappear. I think he was so surprised that he didn't realize he could've just opened the door again. I saw the little numbers above the elevator door climb.

With my messenger bag slapping against my hip, I hightailed it between cars and down the pavement, skipping down the open stairwell that led to the ground floor and outside. In the distance I heard the *ding* of the elevator. He was coming back down for me.

I came out onto the circular drive, the fountain spouting

all that water, but I didn't have time to lament it. I ran along the roadway and out to the Strip. I thought I heard someone shout my name, but I couldn't stop to turn around. It would slow me down.

When I hit the sidewalk, I almost crashed into two Hispanic guys who tried to hand me those little cards advertising the ladies who would do anything for a price. Like I'd be interested. I waved them off as I picked up speed and dashed between the tourists who were gazing at the Venetian, which was just across the street.

I wanted to go to the shop in the worst way. I wanted to sit in my room and close my eyes and smell the ink and feel the machine in my hand.

But I couldn't. DeBurra would track me down and cart me off to police headquarters again. Or worse, Bixby would show up. I had no idea what his agenda was, and I didn't want to find out.

The light had turned, and the walk signal indicated I could cross the street. Glancing left and right as I did so, wondering where Jeff Coleman had gone—I could have used a ride— my legs feeling more leaden with each step, I dug into my bag and pulled out my phone, hitting speed dial.

Three rings, then, "Brett, where are you?"

I sighed with relief. "Joel, I need a car."

"Where's yours?"

"No time for that now," I said, knowing if I told him what had happened at Chez Tango it would take way too long to answer his questions. "Can I borrow the Prius?" Not exactly a getaway car, but it would have to do in a pinch.

"Sure, but—"

"I'm going to the parking garage now. I'll meet you at the elevator, okay?"

"Sure, but—"

I hung up and went through the hotel doors into the Venetian lobby, this time not even paying attention to the décor. I was on a mission. I had no idea where I would go once I had Joel's car, but I'd figure it out. I still needed to track Charlotte down.

I rode up in the elevator. I eyed the passageway that led to the Venetian Grand Canal Shoppes, waiting for Joel. I paced a little, making a woman loaded down with shopping bags a bit nervous; I could tell from the way she kept hitting the elevator button.

Finally, Joel came through the glass doors. Instantly he enveloped me in a hug. Now, as I've said before, I'm not a hugger, but it did feel good.

I pulled away, and Joel was smiling at me.

"Can you give it to me in a nutshell?" he asked, holding the keys out.

I took them. "Okay, Charlotte wasn't at Chez Tango, but half the building exploded while I was there, Frank De-Burra showed up and wanted to take me in for another marathon interrogation, and then Bixby picked me up and took me to his place. Which so happens to be at the Windsor Palms, where Wesley Lambert had his little ricin-making lab. So I took off. I need to find out how Tim is, because he and DeBurra beat the crap out of each other over Shawna. And I need to find Charlotte." I clutched the keys, hoping he'd be okay with me taking the car now. It all sounded a little crazy, and I'm not sure I would have offered my car for the cause.

But Joel just nodded. "You don't have to go far for that."

"For what?"

"To find Charlotte."

"What do you mean?"

"She's inside. At the shop."

Chapter 55

Still holding the keys to the Prius, I said, "Let's go," and went through the doors and into the walkway that led to the Venetian Grand Canal Shoppes. Joel lumbered alongside me, every few steps patting my back. If I hadn't needed it, it might have been annoying.

"Has she said anything?" I asked.

"She looks like hell. That drag queen is with her."

"Kyle?"

He nodded.

"He's the one who called me. Told me she was sick."

"He says he didn't."

We'd reached the small kiosk at the entrance to the Shoppes, and I stopped. "What?"

Joel shrugged. "I told him you said you talked to him, but he's denying it."

If I hadn't spoken to Kyle, then who had called me?

I started walking again, not even looking in the window at Kenneth Cole, which meant I was really distracted. I always look in the window at Kenneth Cole.

Ace was sitting at Breathe, the oxygen bar, a tube in his nose, his eyes closed as he leaned back in the tall chair, a look of absolute serenity on his face.

"Look at that," I said, cocking my head toward him.

"He didn't want to be in the shop with Charlotte," Joel said. "She broke up with him."

Bitsy had said that earlier. This wasn't good. I couldn't have two of my tattooists not speaking to each other, or not able to be in the same room together. But that would mean I'd want to keep Charlotte around after all this. And the jury was definitely out on that one.

"This is why you never sleep with someone you work with," I muttered.

Ace didn't even open his eyes as we passed.

Bitsy was at the front desk, and her eyes widened when she saw me. "Are you okay?"

I nodded, indicating my arm. "Just a few scratches."

She jumped up to get a closer look, and she and Joel shook their heads over my injury.

"It could've been worse," I said.

They nodded in unison.

"Where's Charlotte?" I asked.

"In your room," Bitsy said.

"Kyle with her?"

She nodded.

I didn't say anything else, just walked back and opened the door. Charlotte was in the middle of inking something on Kyle's hand. As I took another step toward them, I saw it was a Chinese character. The character for strength. They both looked up, and the machine stopped whirring but Charlotte still held it over Kyle's hand.

"Are you back to work?" I asked Charlotte, aware of a sharp edge in my voice. I tried to tell myself that I needed an explanation before judging her, but I was having a hard time convincing myself.

She shrugged.

I waved my hand. "Might as well finish. You're almost done anyway."

She gave me a funny look, then went back to the tattoo.

"I didn't call you," Kyle said without any prompting.

"So who did? And how did Rusty Abbott know that building was going to explode?"

Charlotte glanced up at Kyle and they exchanged a look.

The machine stopped again; Charlotte sighed. "We were in the club. But we decided to go for something to eat. We were about two blocks away when it blew."

I looked at Kyle. "Your SUV was still in the parking lot."

"We had my car," Charlotte said.

I took a long look at her. Her face was paler than usual, but it could've been the lighting in here. The overhead light was off, and she had the desk lamp aimed right at Kyle's hand, its beam illuminating her work.

She had already gone back to finishing the ink. I watched as she filled in the last part, wondering what to ask first.

Charlotte turned the machine off again and put it down, pulling off her gloves. But before I could even speak, she gave a little sigh, and said, "It all started that night at the Queen of Hearts Ball."

She exchanged a look with Kyle, who nodded, encouraging her to continue.

"That's the night Trevor and Lester met each other."

Charlotte put some ointment on Kyle's tattoo, which was pink around the edges. He was admiring it.

"Nice work," I said absently.

"Thanks," Charlotte said. She patted Kyle's arm. "Why don't you go out and see what Bitsy's up to, okay?"

Kyle looked from her to me and back to her again. "Sure, honey," he said, standing. He knew she was trying to get rid of him.

When he was gone and the door shut, I said, "So tell me what happened that night."

"What *didn't* happen that night?" she said. "You've never seen such a party. Lots of champagne, dancing, gorgeous queens. Anyway, fast-forward to a few months later."

"What happened then?"

"That's when DeBurra showed up. Even though I'd already figured out there was something funny going on."

"Funny like what?"

She took a deep breath and smiled sadly. "I was pretty sure Trevor was blackmailing someone."

Chapter 56

"**B**lackmail?"

"I found some of that money in his apartment. He said boots were better than a bank. But he did have a spreadsheet for it. I saw it when I was doing his taxes, but he said it wasn't going to be reported. I should ignore it. He wouldn't tell me any more than that."

"But if he had all that money, and the money from Lester Fine, why would he need to pawn that brooch?"

"Lester gave him the brooch, and whenever they had a fight, Trevor would pawn it but then he'd regret it and buy it back. It's real, you know. Diamonds and rubies. It was Lester's; his wife had it made for him before the ball," Charlotte said, then frowned. "How do you know about the money from Lester?"

I admitted to having Trevor's laptop and looking at his documents.

"So that's where it is. That day you saw me on the balcony? I dropped off the makeup case and figured I'd grab the laptop while I was there. But I couldn't find it anywhere."

The mention of the makeup case reminded me ... "So the pin really belonged to Trevor? Then what was the mistake Wesley Lambert told Eduardo about that day?"

"Trevor and Lester had another falling out, but this time, Lester wanted the pin back. Trevor told him he'd pawned it, which he had, but then he went and bought it back."

"So Lester Fine sicced Lambert on him? He went to the club to find out where the pin was?"

Charlotte nodded. "Trevor got a message from the pawnbroker that they'd had a complaint that the brooch was stolen, and he wanted me to go see if I could find out what was going on."

"Why you? Why didn't he go?"

Charlotte took a deep breath. "He was afraid they'd arrest him on the spot."

It was likely, especially if it was Lester Fine filing the complaint.

"So Lambert *was* part of this, right?" I asked. "When he showed up at the pawnshop and knocked you around?"

Charlotte looked puzzled. "Lambert? At the pawnshop? No, Brett. That wasn't Lambert. It was Frank DeBurra."

A few days after the Queen of Hearts Ball, DeBurra showed up at Charlotte's door. He said he knew about Trevor and his "freelance work" for Lester Fine. It wasn't Trevor he was after, but Lester Fine. He knew she'd done Trevor's taxes and wanted to look at Trevor's finances, which verified Trevor's "work" for Lester. She handed over everything. Except Trevor's spreadsheet with the fifty thousand dollars noted on it.

"The 1099s from Lester were legit, but this wasn't," Charlotte said. "There was no proof that it was tied to Lester, and I didn't want to get Trevor into trouble."

"I heard, too, that you were giving DeBurra information about Lambert and that militia in the desert."

She gave me a funny look, then said, "That's right. I ran into Lambert at a club one night, and we were catching up. He was wasted and started telling me about making poison. I didn't believe him, but I told DeBurra anyway." She paused. "Who knew it was true?"

"So how did you end up in Lambert's condo?"

Charlotte took a deep breath. "I had a message on my voice mail from him asking me to come. He said he knew something about Trevor and that champagne cork. But he was dead when I got there. I couldn't risk calling the cops and having DeBurra find me there."

"Why has DeBurra been after you? Why did he show up at the pawnshop?" I asked.

"He said he knew I was holding something back and if I didn't tell him, he'd have *me* arrested for stealing that brooch. He's a cop. Who'd believe *me*?" Her eyes filled with tears.

"Why would you agree to do this at all?" I asked Charlotte. "Work for DeBurra, I mean?"

A band of flush moved up Charlotte's neck and into her face.

"What did DeBurra have on you?" I asked, suspicious.

She shrugged, but her face got redder.

"Charlotte, it's okay," I said, although I was remembering Tim's advice about background checks on all employees.

When she spoke, her voice was so low, I had to lean forward to hear her.

"I got caught tattooing a fifteen-year-old girl. She was the sister of a friend. Her parents weren't supposed to come home that early. They called the police."

I took a deep breath. I totally was going to be changing my hiring policies.

I wanted to be able to tell her it was all right, but I couldn't. Because it wasn't.

She could tell. Tears sprang into her eyes, and she blinked a few times. "I'm fired, aren't I?"

I nodded without thinking.

She jumped out of her chair and swung the door open, dashing out. I took a deep breath as I got up. I kept forgetting that she was ten years younger than me, that I might have reacted the exact same way if Mickey had threatened to fire me when I was just a trainee.

The front glass door was already closing when I emerged, and I saw a flash of her as she ran, Bitsy and Joel staring.

"What happened?" I heard Joel ask. I shook my head and sped past him after Charlotte.

She was fast. She was running along the canal, dodging shoppers and tourists. I had about five inches on her, but I'd had a slow start and wasn't gaining much. I kept my eye on her, bumping into a few people because I wasn't watching where I was going, and when I finally thought I'd catch up, someone stepped out from around a turn up ahead that made me stop short and caused my heart to beat even faster, but not for the right reason.

Colin Bixby.

He took two steps toward Charlotte, who was careening toward him.

She grabbed onto the top of the small railing that ran along the length of the canal and stopped short. She looked first at Bixby, then back at me. An expression of terror crossed her face, and before I had a chance to even shout out her name, she catapulted over the railing and splashed into the water.

A gondola sailed under the footbridge at just that moment and slammed into her.

I held my breath, considering my options. Should I jump in after her? I did have my lifesaving certificate from when I was fourteen.

But Bixby was seconds ahead of me. He was already in the water. Just as I was about to pull myself up over the railing to join him, a hand clamped down on my shoulder.

"Don't even think about it."

Chapter 57

As I stared into Frank DeBurra's eyes, which were black with hate, something popped into my head that was sort of a non sequitur, considering.

How had he known there should've been two bodies inside Chez Tango after the explosion?

No one had told him this. I knew only because "Kyle" had called me. Bixby knew, but he had been somewhere in traffic, supposedly. Jeff Coleman and Tim knew because I'd told them.

No one had gotten around to telling DeBurra, yet even before he'd spoken to any of us, he was telling the firemen to look for two bodies. A man and a woman, he'd said.

Why hadn't this occurred to me before? When I might have been in a better position to actually raise that red flag with Tim. Because at this moment, the prospects of talking to my brother seemed a bit bleak.

A crowd had formed around the canal, everyone angling to see the girl who'd jumped in and gotten hit by the gondola. The gondolier was in the water now, too; Bixby was cradling Charlotte's head in his arms and shouting that someone should call 911.

No one was paying attention to me, or the fact that I was being herded out of the mall by a scruffy cop who was taking advantage of the situation. He had my right arm twisted up behind my back, and to hide that, he was walking so close we might be mistaken for lovers.

So didn't want to go there.

Blood still caked DeBurra's nose where my brother had hit him, and one of his eyes was swollen shut. "You shouldn't run from the cops, Miss Kavanaugh." His voice was low and menacing, his breath hot against my neck.

My throat and mouth were so dry, I could barely swallow. I licked my lips, but it was like licking the desert sand.

"Where are you taking me?" I managed to croak.

"Where we won't be bothered."

"Why?"

"You and I have some things to settle."

"Like what?"

He snorted, his one good eye shifting back and forth as he pushed me forward toward the exit.

So he was no Chatty Kathy. Normally that would've suited me just fine, but I didn't like it that he was taking me to an undisclosed location.

We'd reached the end of the canal and entered the circular area that was the entrance to the Venetian Grand Canal Shoppes. The ceiling was painted with elaborate Renaissance frescoes, gold accenting everything. In a way, I preferred this area to the one where the ceiling was painted as if we were supposed to be outside. The illusion was less theme park–like.

The vestibule was remarkably free of people, most likely because they'd heard the splash and the screams and had gone to see what the fuss was all about. Maybe they thought it was another one of those little plays or dances performed periodically for entertainment.

My hand, the one twisted around, had fallen asleep. I tried to wiggle my fingers to wake it up, but he only gripped harder, like a vise on my wrist.

His other hand, the one not holding on to me, swung jauntily by his side.

He probably didn't expect me to try to wrench free, so that's exactly what I did.

I twirled around and yanked my arm down, pulling it from his grasp. I was free. Who knew those self-defense classes in high school would pay off someday?

But that's when I noticed that his sleeve had gotten pushed halfway up to his elbow. I hesitated.

He had ink.

Familiar-looking ink.

It was the bottom half of a queen-of-hearts playing card.

He saw me staring at it, and an ugly smirk tugged at his lips.

"Do you think you could've done better?" he asked, sliding the sleeve up farther so I could see the whole thing, as if we were just comparing tattoos like at Chez Tango the first night I met him.

I cleared my throat, trying to force the saliva into my mouth so I could speak. "It's flash," I said flatly.

"Yeah, it's flash," DeBurra said. "That's all Jeff Coleman does, isn't it?"

"Jeff did that?"

"His mother started it, but she's a whack job. I asked him to finish it after he finished up with Rusty's. It was a full house that night."

"The Queen of Hearts Ball," I whispered, unable to tear my eyes away from the ink. It wasn't Lester Fine after all. It was Frank DeBurra. "You were in drag."

He coughed. "For the job," he said.

But the band of flush that crawled up his neck said that could be a cover.

"Why did you say your name was Colin Bixby? I mean, did you know him?"

"Lambert and Abbott did. He was at that ball. I met him."

Of all the pictures I'd seen of the Queen of Hearts Ball, I hadn't seen one of Bixby. I hadn't even considered that he might have been there. "And you just decided to use his name that night?"

"Couldn't exactly use my own, could I?" he hissed.

Suddenly I thought about that picture on Trevor's Facebook page. The one of the drag queen whom I'd seen across the street from Chez Tango after discovering the slashed tires on Jeff's car.

As I looked at Frank DeBurra, it was all coming together.

He was that drag queen.

And if Trevor knew, maybe that money that he had coming in under the table *was* blackmail money, like Charlotte suspected. From Frank DeBurra.

It was possible Trevor had put that picture on Facebook to taunt him. And as I'd suspected before, but hadn't known the true reason why until now, DeBurra made those Facebook pictures disappear. So no one could identify him. Like me.

"How much did you pay Trevor?" I asked. "Was it just that fifty thousand?" As I spoke, I remembered something else. How quickly DeBurra had shown up at Trevor's apartment the day Jeff and I got shot at. "You were in Trevor's apartment," I said, not able to stop myself. "You were the one who shot at us. You took that money. You put it in Ace's bank account to set him and Charlotte up. You probably have lots of ways of getting into bank accounts, being in Homeland Security."

He stared at me, not admitting anything but not denying it, either.

Tim had been surprised that DeBurra was at Chez Tango the night Trevor got hit with the champagne cork. He said he thought DeBurra was racking up some overtime. But I was beginning to think there was another reason he was at the club that night.

The guy with the champagne. How tall was he? I'd been concentrating so much on the tattoo and the bottle and the sweatshirt that I hadn't thought too much about his height. DeBurra was about my height. I was about as tall as the guy in the club. I'd subconsciously registered that.

I also flashed back to a comment DeBurra had made when Wesley Lambert's body was found. About how this made "that queen's death" suspicious. At that point, I hadn't thought anyone suspected Trevor's death of being from anything other than natural causes. Tim and I had discussed the possibility of poison, but that was later.

"You killed Trevor to get him to stop blackmailing you. Did you pay Wesley Lambert for that ricin on the champagne cork?" I paused a second. "You were after Charlotte because you knew she might have something in Trevor's documents that could incriminate you. And what about the investigation into Lester Fine? Was that for real?" When I was on a roll, I couldn't be stopped. But then I made a mistake.

"Does Shawna know?" I asked.

I didn't even see his hand until it made contact with my cheek. My head whipped back with the impact, and it felt as though my neck snapped.

He laughed as I instinctively put my hand to my face, which was hot.

"It's the job," he said again.

"What? You dressed up like a woman for the job but then decided you liked it too much to stop?"

I touched a nerve, because he stepped closer, reaching out for me.

He underestimated my instincts. Just as I'd automatically kicked Rusty Abbott in the groin, my foot shot out and nailed him right in the shin. His knee buckled, and I took off past him, back toward St. Mark's Square, to the canal where the crowd had formed. I needed people around me. He couldn't touch me if there were that many witnesses.

I had to get back to the shop to call Tim. My gut told me if I tried to tell the uniforms who'd responded to Charlotte's accident, they might not believe me over the word of a detective.

And that said detective was gaining ground on me and holding out his badge as he shouted, "Stop her!"

I looked around like I didn't know he was talking about me, even though I was the only one running. I glanced at the scene in the canal as I passed: Charlotte being taken

out of the water by a couple of paramedics, Bixby helping, a gurney waiting on the walkway, two uniforms. Uh-oh.
DeBurra got the attention of the two cops, directing it toward me. They were young and eager to help. Now we had
a conga line, but no one was dancing.

I spotted Joel on the footbridge ahead, among a throng
of people. I needed to get over there.

"Joel!" I shouted. "Joel!"

He looked over at me and waved. I pushed my way to
him.

"I'm so glad you're here," I panted, clutching his arm.
"We have to call Tim." I started to nudge him down the
bridge the other way.

"Do you know if Charlotte's okay?" he asked, indicating the gurney, where she now lay. She was lying flat,
but her eyes were open and she was smiling at one of the
paramedics.

"Looks okay to me," I said, nudging a little more force-
fully now.

"Hey!" He frowned. "What's your problem?"

I felt my problem in the small of my back. I twisted
around slightly to see Frank DeBurra and the gleam of his
service revolver.

Chapter 58

I guess he figured I'd gotten away from him too many times, so he felt he had to resort to holding me at gunpoint. Still, it was risky to do it in a crowd. Even if I ran, I doubted he'd actually fire at me. Cops are trained not to do that. But then again, this particular cop was a bad guy, so all bets were off.

Joel was talking to me.

"What's going on?"

I sort of cocked my head back, hoping he'd notice DeBurra behind me, and because Joel and I have that kind of karma, he did. His eyes narrowed just slightly, and he blinked twice.

"You're not getting away from me again," DeBurra hissed from behind, throwing me off any psychic connection I had going on with Joel. He pulled my left arm around, and his hand encircled my wrist.

The pressure was off my lower back now, and I twisted a little to see him putting his gun back in his hip holster. He reached around behind his back, and I guessed what he was going for.

Handcuffs.

Crap.

I had to do something.

My right hand brushed the front of my jeans, and I felt it. The brooch. It was still in my pocket.

I had an idea.

Joel was staring at me; it had been only a couple of seconds, and he was still waiting for some sort of sign. I pulled the brooch out of my pocket and undid the clasp with one hand. I raised my eyebrows at Joel, then turned fast so I was facing DeBurra. At the same moment that he slapped the bracelet around my wrist, I shoved the pin into the top of his hand as hard as I could.

The queen of hearts winked at me as she stuck to DeBurra.

DeBurra yowled, pawing at his hand to try to pull the pin out.

With the handcuffs dangling from my wrist, I took advantage of the moment and ran, grabbing Joel's arm as I went, shouting, "Come on!"

The throng of people on the footbridge, without really knowing what was going on, parted like the Red Sea. I wondered whether Sister Mary Eucharista wasn't doing some sort of hocus-pocus from her seat in Heaven.

Joel lumbered more slowly than I liked, and he stopped suddenly, right in front of me, causing me to take a misstep and slip. My feet flew out in front of me and I landed on my butt, sliding down the stairs like a toddler and landing with a *bump* at the bottom.

It knocked the wind out of me for a second.

Joel didn't even notice I'd fallen. He just kept going. I put my hand down to push myself up, but then I felt someone's hand under my armpit, pulling me up.

"Kavanaugh, you certainly know how to make a statement."

I whirled around to see Jeff Coleman, a small smile at the corner of his lips. I opened my mouth to say something, but I was distracted by what was going on behind him.

Tim was handcuffing Frank DeBurra.

I looked back at Jeff.

"What's going on?"

"The detective here stole my car."

"Huh?"

"You have such a way with words."

I rolled my eyes at him. "What about him stealing your car?" I held my hands up as I spoke, and the handcuff swung around and almost hit me in the face.

Jeff grinned. "I had no idea you were so kinky, Kavanaugh."

My eyes should be on automatic roll when I'm around Jeff Coleman.

"They're DeBurra's. He was going to take—" But I didn't get to finish, because Jeff took my arm and led me back up the footbridge.

Tim looked annoyed when Jeff tapped him on the back, but then he saw the handcuff and Jeff said something so softly, I couldn't hear.

Within seconds, Tim was unlocking the cuff and my hand was free. I rubbed my wrist. "Thanks," I said, glaring at DeBurra, who was glaring back. "What are you charging him with?"

"He stole my car," Jeff said again. "Right after you took off. I hadn't taken the keys out; he just jumped in and drove off after you. I got your brother away from the paramedics and we've been looking for him." He chuckled. "Criminals are stupid. He left the car out front, told the valet he'd just be a few minutes, to leave the engine running."

A gold Pontiac had followed Bixby and me back to the Windsor Palms. I'd assumed it was Jeff. But it was DeBurra.

"He's done a lot worse things than that," I said.

Tim looked at me grimly. "No kidding. How do you think he knew there should have been two bodies in that building?"

So I wasn't the only one who'd picked up on that.

Bixby wasn't talking to me. I guess I couldn't blame him; I'd suspected him of . . . well . . . I wasn't quite sure of what, but I'd suspected him of something, and he wasn't stupid.

Made it a little awkward, however, when I tried to see Charlotte in the emergency room.

Bixby sent out some other doctor, who was about a hundred and fifty years old and who had about as much charm as a desert cactus. He told us we had to wait; Charlotte was still being evaluated.

"Boy, you really screwed that one up," Bitsy said, ever blunt, as we sat in the corner of the waiting room. Joel was with us, shifting on the uncomfortable plastic chair. The armrests were too close together and he had to sit at an angle, shoving his girth between them. I was uncomfortable for another reason—who knew what was on these seats? But I'd been standing for an hour now, and I finally had to give my feet a rest despite my reservations.

"How was I to know Bixby didn't know anything about Lambert's science experiments?" I asked. "He said he knew the guy, and I freaked. I admit it."

Kyle patted my hand. "Honey, if it's any consolation, his mother lives down the hall from him. You wouldn't want to be involved with a guy who's tied to mama's apron strings."

My cell phone warbled Springsteen, and the receptionist gave me a glare. I got up as I flipped the phone open, and went outside to talk to Tim.

"We found quite a few withdrawals from DeBurra's bank account that match the spreadsheet Trevor had," Tim said.

I'd given Tim the laptop before he took DeBurra to the station for questioning.

"We also found some correspondence via e-mail with Wesley Lambert." He paused. "DeBurra paid Lambert to lace that champagne cork with ricin. And the day before he died, Lambert sent him a threatening e-mail, saying he was going to rat him out."

"Do you think DeBurra killed Lambert?" I asked.

"There's no evidence of that. Lambert died of ricin poisoning."

I asked him the same question I'd asked DeBurra: "Was he ever investigating Lester Fine, or was that just a story he told Charlotte?"

Tim was quiet a second. "He didn't lie about that. But there's nothing that links Fine to the ricin lab. At least not that I know of." And since Tim wasn't with Metro Homeland Security, he might not be privy to that information.

"What about Rusty Abbott? Where is he? What's his story?" I'd told him everything about Abbott, from the roulette game to his sudden appearances all over the place.

"He made the bomb DeBurra set off at the club. We found his fingerprints."

"How did you tie DeBurra to it?"

"Abbott did. He left us DeBurra's fingerprints, too, on a second device that didn't detonate. It wasn't ever live." Tim paused. "DeBurra thought Charlotte had seen him at the apartment. He also thought she had Trevor's laptop."

"And she would put two and two together, which was why he wanted to get rid of her. And he thought I would figure it out, too," I said. "He's the one who called me pretending to be Kyle, right?"

Tim's silence verified it.

I had another thought. "The call came from Chez Tango."

"There's such a thing as call forwarding. He thought you might try to call back."

We were quiet a couple of seconds; then he said, "We can't find Abbott."

"What do you mean, you can't find him?"

"Just what I said. We can't find him. It's like he disappeared or something. He's gone."

"People don't just disappear."

Tim chuckled. "People like Rusty Abbott do. You know that's not his real name? He was using a dead guy's social security number to get paid. Someone else is living in his apartment, claims she's been there for five years, no one by the name of Rusty Abbott ever lived there. Lester Fine's not talking, either, if he knows where Abbott went. He says he's as surprised about all this as we are. All he asked about was that brooch. He wants it back."

No kidding.

I remembered how I hadn't been able to find Rusty Abbott when I Googled him, except listed on Lester Fine's site.

"How did you get his fingerprints, then?"

"He was working for Lester Fine. All his employees are fingerprinted."

"So he can't really disappear then, can he?"

"As long as he stays out of trouble."

I pondered that a few seconds; then Tim spoke again.

"The money in Ace's account that disappeared? DeBurra did put it there, but before he could move it to his own account, it disappeared on him. We managed to trace it to another account with Abbott's name on it. But it wasn't there for long. Maybe a few minutes. Now it's in the wind, just like Abbott."

I mulled this over. I'd suspected Abbott of a lot of things, but being a ghost—a comfortably well-off ghost, thanks to Trevor's money—was not one of them. Somehow I found it suitable justice that Abbott had taken DeBurra's money after DeBurra had gone to all that trouble to retrieve it.

And even though Rusty Abbott did know how to make accidents happen, as Jeff Coleman so aptly put it, he'd actually tried to help me. He'd given me a clue by leaving that picture of DeBurra in drag for me in the makeup case. It was too bad he hadn't taken out that picture of Lester Fine, because it threw me off completely. Abbott also warned me about the explosion, and he gave me that casino chip and I won all that money.

"What about Charlotte? Are you going to charge her with anything?"

"As soon as the doctor gives us the all clear on her, we're going to be questioning her extensively. As far as I know, she didn't do anything criminal except run, and that was to get away from DeBurra."

"What's going to happen to Shawna now?" I couldn't help but ask.

"Who knows?" Tim was still indifferent to her. He'd moved on. I just wish DeBurra had realized that and let his one-sided feud go.

We hung up, and I went back inside. Bitsy and Joel and Kyle were still in the same spot, only now Joel's head was bobbing against Kyle's shoulder as he slept. Kyle didn't seem to mind.

I heard a swish as the frosted doors slid open across the room, and Bixby stood there, looking at me.

My Tevas felt like concrete weights. I wanted to go apologize while I had the chance, but I was uncertain how to do it.

I waited too long. He gave me a sad smile and touched his chest. Where his new Celtic knot was inked.

Then the doors were swishing closed again, with him behind them.

Chapter 59

Jeff Coleman carefully pulled the stencil off my arm. I studied it, and even though I was looking at it upside down, it was spectacular.

Who knew?

The Japanese koi swam in a curve around my biceps; ocean waves and lotus flowers danced around it. I'd told Jeff I wanted the fish to be gold and white, the flowers yellow, red, and pink, and the waves different shades of blue and purple.

It was half a sleeve, enough to cover up the tiny scars from the windshield glass. Jeff had tried to talk me into a full sleeve, but I needed more time to think about what I wanted.

"It's okay?"

Jeff's hesitation made me pause. He was nervous about this. He hadn't cracked a joke since he came to the shop, didn't call me "Kavanaugh" once.

I made him come to The Painted Lady because, honestly, I wasn't quite sure just how clean his shop was. I knew how clean mine was. He acted all put out at first when I said he could do my ink, only on *my* turf. But he was strangely quiet when he arrived with his case, explaining that he needed his own machine.

"It's great," I said, meaning it.

It wasn't flash, either. He'd designed it. He hadn't wanted

to, but when I pointed out the brilliance of his Day of the Dead tattoo, he finally acquiesced.

"You know," I said, "you could start doing custom designs."

He snorted, then rolled his eyes. "I'm going to leave that to you, Kavanaugh. The drunks need a place to go at two a.m. I'm happy to provide that."

The machine started whirring, and just before he touched it to my skin, he added, "And don't tell anybody about this, all right? I don't need that kind of reputation."

I grinned. "Your secret is safe with me, Coleman." Then I closed my eyes, feeling the first sting of the needle before it mellowed into the familiar and welcome pain.

The envelope arrived two days later. Bitsy handed it to me when I got in. I shoved it under my armpit as I went into the staff room. Dropping my messenger bag on a chair and taking a sip of my to-go coffee, I plucked it out from under my arm and saw there wasn't a return address and the postmark was smudged so I couldn't see where it had been mailed from.

It was one of those big yellow envelopes with the Bubble Wrap inside. I ripped it open and took out a sheet of paper.

"Luck didn't have anything to do with it," it read.

It was signed "Rusty."

I peered into the darkness of the envelope, wondering what the note meant. Something was stuck in the bottom of the envelope, so I turned it upside down and shook it once.

A fifty-dollar casino chip dropped onto the table.

Read on for an excerpt
from Karen E. Olson's next
Tattoo Shop Mystery,

Driven to Ink

Coming from Obsidian in Fall 2010.

When Sylvia and Bernie came back from That's Amore Drive-Through Wedding Chapel with my car, it would've been nice if they'd taken the body out of the trunk.

As it was, I didn't discover it until a day later when I hit a bump and heard a thump that made me curious about what I'd forgotten to unload on my last trip to the grocery store. By that time, Sylvia Coleman and Bernie Applebaum—Sylvia said at her age she wasn't about to take on any new names—were at the Grand Canyon on their honeymoon, and I was in my driveway staring at the corpse of a man in a tuxedo, as if he'd expected death would be a black-tie affair.

Being both the daughter and sister of police officers, I did the first thing that came to mind: I called Sylvia's son, Jeff Coleman, to find out whether he knew anything about this.

"Murder Ink," Jeff's voice bellowed through my ear. Murder Ink was his business, a tattoo shop near Fremont Street, next door to Goodfellas Bail Bonds. He specialized in flash, the stock tattoos that lined the walls of his shop, even though I knew firsthand that he was an amazing artist when he put his mind to it.

Despite the flash, Jeff was one of my main competitors in Vegas. I own The Painted Lady, where we do only custom designs. We cater to a classier clientele, and my shop is in the Venetian Grand Canal Shoppes on the Strip, a high-end themed mall that would never have allowed a tattoo shop to sully its image without a little blackmail by the shop's former owner.

"It's Brett."

"Kavanaugh?"

"Your mother seems to have left me a little something for the use of my car yesterday." Sylvia had asked me nicely whether she and Bernie could use my red Mustang Bullitt convertible for their drive-through wedding. She said it was preferable to Bernie's 1989 blue Buick and her thirty-five-year-old purple Gremlin, which looked like a lizard with its tail cut off.

"What about Jeff's Pontiac?" I'd asked her.

"It's bright yellow. It looks like a pimp's car."

I couldn't argue with that. It did look like a pimp's car. I told Sylvia that she was welcome to use my Mustang, but she had to drive. Bernie's cataract surgery wasn't scheduled for another six weeks, and even though Sylvia said she "watched the road" for him, it didn't inspire much confidence.

"What are you talking about, Kavanaugh?" Jeff asked.

"There's a man in my trunk."

A low chuckle told me that perhaps I hadn't described it properly.

"A dead man. In a tuxedo."

"And you're sure my mother left it there for you?"

"I certainly don't remember it being there before she borrowed my car."

"So, let me play devil's advocate for a minute. Maybe he climbed into your trunk and died *after* my mother and Bernie returned the car."

Hmm. I hadn't thought of that. I recounted where the car had been since they dropped it off for me at the Venetian, and it had been only there and here, in my driveway overnight, and then at Red Rock Canyon this morning when I went for a hike. I leaned farther in toward the body. On the right breast pocket I could see something embroidered with red thread: "That's Amore."

"He's from the wedding chapel, Jeff. His tux is an advertisement. It's got the name sewn on it."

"Is your brother home? Has he seen the body?"

My brother, Detective Tim Kavanaugh, hadn't been home all night. I could only surmise that either he was catching bad guys or he had a late date that spilled over into morning.

"No."

"Have you called the cops, then?"

"Doing it now." I punched END on my cell and sent Jeff Coleman into oblivion as I now entered 911. But just as I was about to hit SEND, I knew I should try to reach Tim first. Before he came home to a driveway full of police cruisers and the coroner's van.

He answered on the first ring.

"What do you want, Brett?"

His tone was cold, but the fact that he'd actually answered his phone meant that he was probably doing police stuff and not with a woman. A good thing for me, but perhaps not for him.

"You remember how I let Sylvia and Bernie borrow my car for their wedding the other day?"

A heavy sigh told me he wasn't into tripping down memory lane and I should get on with it.

"Well, they left me a body. In the trunk."

A second of silence, then, "What are you talking about?"

I told him about Mr. That's Amore. "He's from the chapel. The drive-through." I explained about the stitching on his pocket.

A heavy sigh. "Brett, how do you get yourself into these messes?" He was referring to a couple of other incidents in the past six months, incidents that were completely out of my control, thank you very much.

"I told you not to let that wacko borrow your car," he said.

"She's not a wacko," I said, although not with much confidence. Sylvia had her moments. I didn't know exactly how old Sylvia was, but I guessed she was in her seventies or early eighties. She and her former husband had owned Murder Ink before he died and she retired, handing over the business to Jeff. She spent a lot of time at the tattoo shop and had actually inked my calf—Napoleon going up the Alps. It was one of my favorite Jacques Louis David paintings, and I did the stencil. Sylvia, as far as I knew, didn't do any original designs—and sometimes I wondered whether she didn't have a touch of dementia. But I was happy she and Bernie had hooked up. They had started swimming together at the Henderson pool a few months back and it developed into a late-in-life romance.

"So you don't recognize this man?" Tim asked, completely reversing the conversation and throwing me off balance for a second.

"You mean the guy in the trunk?"

"Yes, Brett, the guy in the trunk." Exasperation had seeped into Tim's tone, and I totally did not need that right now.

But I counted to ten as I leaned forward again and peered at Mr. That's Amore. His face was whiter than that zinc stuff you put on your nose so you won't get sunburn. His eyes were closed, but his mouth hung open slackly, as if he didn't have the energy to close it. The tux was remarkably neat, considering he was stuffed in my trunk—just a few spots of dust and dirt.

He looked uncannily like Dean Martin.

But I didn't have time to ponder that, because I could also see the side of his neck, just below his ear.

He had a tattoo of a spiderweb.

I told Tim, who made a sort of *mmm* sound. I knew what he was thinking: Spiderweb tattoos were popular in prison. And from the looks of this ink, it could've been a prison tat; it was sort of blue-black with rough edges that bled into the skin.

And what was that? I leaned in even farther, my finger precariously close to pulling back the white shirt collar.

Tim was warning me not to touch anything.

I yanked my hand back.

"No kidding," I said, eager not to give myself away. "Although I did open the trunk, so my fingerprints are on that."

"I should be there shortly," he said, then added, "The forensics team and a cruiser are on their way. Just stay where you are and wait for them."

Where I was was in the driveway. I was just back from Red Rock. I wanted to change out of my grubby jeans, long-sleeved T-shirt, and hiking boots, and, most of all, I wanted something to eat. I'd had some toast before I left at seven, but that was four hours ago. I also needed to get to the shop by noon, because I had a client scheduled.

"Do I have time for a shower?" I asked hopefully.

"No." Tim hung up.

Without thinking, I leaned against the back of the car. Immediately I felt it bounce a little—not that I'm heavy; I'm actually pretty skinny—and Mr. That's Amore shifted slightly with the movement. I jumped away from the Mustang as I stared at the body, which rocked for a second.

There it was again. It was poking out slightly through the collar of his shirt.

I couldn't help myself. I reached in and moved the fabric so I could see it better.

It was the end of a cord.

A clip cord.

I'd recognize it anywhere.

A clip cord is used to attach a tattoo machine to its power source.

Also Available from

Karen E. Olson

The Missing Ink

A Tattoo Shop Mystery

Brett Kavanaugh is a tattoo artist and owner
of an elite tattoo parlor in Las Vegas. When
someone calls to make an appointment to
get a tattoo of her fiancé's name embedded
in a heart, Brett takes the job but the girl
never shows. The next thing Brett knows,
the police are looking for her client, and
the name she wanted on the tattoo isn't
her fiancé's...

**Available wherever books are sold or at
penguin.com**

Also Available from

Karen E. Olson

DEAD OF THE DAY

An Annie Seymour Mystery

A soggy April has hit New Haven, Connecticut—along with an unidentified body in the harbor. The strange fact that there were bee stings on the body gives *New Haven Herald* police reporter Annie Seymour an intriguing excuse to put off her profile of the new police chief—a piece that becomes a lot more interesting when the subject is gunned down.

But this is only the beginning of a killer exposé—because as she connects the dots between the John Doe, the police chief, and the city's struggling immigrant population, Annie's drawing a line between herself and someone who doesn't want her to learn the truth— or live to report it...

Available wherever books are sold or at penguin.com

Also Available from

Karen E. Olson

SHOT GIRL

An Annie Seymour Mystery

New Haven police reporter Annie Seymour
has a talent for running into trouble. So it
should come as no surprise when her
co-worker's bachelorette party at a local
club quickly turns into a crime scene.
What is surprising is that the dead club
manager in the parking lot happens to be
Annie's ex-husband—and the bullet shells
around his body match the gun she has
in her car...

**Available wherever books are sold or at
penguin.com**